3 25

"LET'S GO TO BED," HE WHISPERED

She moved up close and the moment their lips touched, everything stopped—her breath, the rain on the canvas, the world around them. It was the sweetest sensation she'd ever known—just pure happiness. It floated from where they touched, through her body, and out into the air. She gazed into his eyes and realized that she wanted to stop everything this instant. Never take another breath. Never move from this spot. Never risk losing this feeling.

As if watching him in a dream, she saw him take her by the hand into the tent. He stood outside in the rain while she took off her damp clothes and pulled on her dry shimmy. She spread out the blankets to make a bed. Then she crawled beneath the covers and pulled them up to her chin.

"You can come in now," she said.

"First-rate novel, full of humor and heart."
—Janet Evanovich, author of *Three to Get Deadly*, on *Lucky Stars*

PRAISE FOR PATRICIA ROY AND HER DEBUT NOVEL, *LUCKY STARS!*

"Filled with humor . . . easy-going and smooth. . . . Ms. Roy's story is filled with emotions and inner thoughts of the protagonists that make them human and likable. As in the "Lucky Star" quilt that adorns their bed, their love will endure."

—Rendezvous

Please turn this page fo

"Four stars! Patricia Roy's debut novel is an Americana romance with a touch of grit and mystery that make it a standout."

—Kathe Robin, *Romantic Times*

"Roy is a talent to watch for. With her superb skill at storytelling, laced with a rare wit, and wonderful characters—another great addition to the Western romance genre."

—Suzanne Barr, *Cape Coral Daily Breeze*

"4 1/2 bells! Ms. Roy shows an ingenious skill for historical romance; her humor shows through always. Wonderful!"

—Donita Lawrence, *Bell, Book & Candle*

"Sparkles with charm and warmth that cheers like a certain lucky star blazing across the horizon. A writer to watch ascend."

—*Book Page*

"Full of warm characters, humor, and a wonderful sensual tension. . . . I'll be looking forward to this talented newcomer's next book."

—*Heart to Heart*

"Refreshing . . . fun to read. . . . A very humorous look at a by-gone era. . . . With more novels like this one, Ms. Roy will rightfully move to the celestial levels of the historical romance sub-genre."

—Harriet Klausner, *Painted Rock Reviews*

THE WEDDING KNOT

Also by Patricia Roy

Lucky Stars

PATRICIA ROY

THE WEDDING KNOT

WARNER BOOKS

A Time Warner Company

WARNER BOOKS EDITION

Cover design by Diane Luger
Cover illustration by Mike Racz
Handlettering by David Gatti

Warner Books, Inc.
1271 Avenue of the Americas
New York, NY 10020

Visit our Web site at
www.warnerbooks.com

A Time Warner Company

Printed in the United States of America

First Printing: April, 1999

10 9 8 7 6 5 4 3 2 1

For Tom, who has always been my hero.

Her blue eyes sought the west afar,
For lovers love the western star.

—Sir Walter Scott

Chapter One

Duluth, Minnesota, Spring of 1875

Goblins followed her everywhere she went. What else would explain why her life was nothing but one disaster after the next? There was only so much a body could blame on chance or coincidence.

No matter what Meg Reilly tried or where she traveled, they always seemed to find her. Though she never actually saw the gangly creatures, she knew they were there, snickering, spying on her, scheming up her next misfortune. Undoubtedly, they were flashing their crooked smiles in glee over the latest setback in her circumstances.

Up until now, Meg had always found comfort in knowing that at least she hadn't sunk to selling herself by the hour. There was always that.

But from here on out, she'd have to come up with some other thought to lift her spirits.

"So it's come to this," Meg muttered, discouragement wrapped around her like a ratty shawl. She stared out the second-story window of Bouncing Bess's and wondered which of the fellas shuffling along the street below would be her first customer.

She'd had such high hopes on the train ride out to Duluth. With the boom in mining and timbering going on and this being the shipping center for the Great North, she'd thought that surely she'd make the acquaintance of some well-situated gentleman who would take her under his protection.

Not that she expected marriage anymore. At twenty-nine, Meg had given up on that. Oh, she'd had her share of proposals over the years. Sadly, none of the proposed arrangements had ever included marriage. Either the fella wasn't ready to take on the responsibilities of a wife and family, or she was too independent, or he already was married. There was always some piddling excuse.

Probably just as well. Though the word "love" was usually bandied about in the beginning, that talk generally ended when she insisted on a wedding ring before things got out of hand. Not a one had wanted her enough to marry her, and she hadn't wanted them badly enough to give in to their sweet talk. Though she tried to look on the sunny side, disappointment and despair seemed to be her lot in life.

Meg slumped against the edge of the open window, and her mood fell a notch each time she thought about spending nearly every last penny she had on that stupid train ticket only to end up working in a bawdy house. She could have done that back in Boston.

A flash of red caught her eye and she watched a square-jawed, broad-shouldered young man in a crimson coat come striding toward Bess's. Meg wondered what in the world a British soldier was doing in Duluth. He stood out like a bright poppy in a field of dry, brown weeds.

She leaned out the window and watched him make his way across the front porch. He walked with the bold, easy movements of a young man still confident about the world and his place in it.

But upon reaching the front door, he appeared to lose a great deal of that boldness. He pulled off his odd white helmet of a hat and tucked it under his arm. Then he ran his fingers through his black hair. One strand kept falling back over his forehead despite his repeated attempts to get it out of his eyes.

He finally quit fooling with his hair and raised his hand as if to knock. But for some reason, he couldn't seem to work up the daring to pound on the door. Finally, he dropped his arm and turned around.

Meg looked out across the street to see what had caught his attention. As far as she could tell, there were only the usual early-evening activities—shopkeepers locking their doors, saloonkeepers opening theirs.

He stood staring out for the longest time. Then he turned around and faced the door again, still holding his hand just inches away from making any sound.

"God above," Meg muttered. "Just get on with it." Surely, he wasn't confused abut this being Bess's Buffet, the words that were painted on the sign. Everyone for miles around knew that the only thing Bess served, besides booze and pickled eggs, was willing women. Or, as in Meg's case, resigned-to-their-fate women.

If only that poker scam on the *Mississippi Princess* had turned out better. The money had been good, the hours appealing, and the work interesting. She sighed, thinking of how she'd probably still be gaily gambling her life away if it hadn't been for that unfortunate cheating incident.

Goose bumps shivered down her arms at recalling that cold plunge into the river. She'd been terrified that those sopping-wet petticoats would pull her under. It was only by the grace of God that she lived to tell about it.

But that was yesterday, water under the bridge, so to speak. This was today, and after weeks of postponing the inevitable, Meg Reilly found herself wishing that young man below would stop dithering about and come on in.

Just hours ago, Bess had made it clear that she was tired of Meg's dawdling, that she'd given Meg enough time to get used to the idea of being a lady of the evening. She'd understood her hesitancy and she'd waited out her week of being indisposed. Bess said she wouldn't push her into anything she didn't want to do, but neither could she allow Meg to continue living here if she wasn't willing to work. She needed the room for someone who *was* willing to entertain customers.

Since Meg had already thoroughly explored every other employment possibility available to her in Duluth, she'd gone ahead and agreed to accept her first gentleman caller that night.

But she dreaded the thought of intimacies with Bess's steady customers—the grimy miners and dusty loggers who snapped their suspenders off their shoulders as they stepped through the door. Perhaps with this fella it wouldn't be such an awful experience.

To tell the truth, she didn't find the soldier all that objectionable. He appeared freshly shaven and, she hoped, freshly bathed. He seemed handsome enough, and she'd always held a special admiration for shoulders as broad as his. She told herself that she was in no rush to get on with it, it was only that it was aggravating to watch him start to knock, then drop his hand time and again. What in the world was he waiting for? Did he expect a butler to come out and escort him in?

Apparently, Bess had also tired of watching him dither about. She stepped out on the porch. Meg could see her ample bosoms bobbling around, nearly spilling out the top of her too-tight dress. Bess put her fleshy hand on his arm and escorted him inside.

So, this is it, Meg thought as she pushed herself off from the window ledge. She walked over to check her appearance in the cracked mirror above the dresser. Tucking in a few stray strands, she wondered if Bess was really envious of her wild red hair or if she'd only said that to boost Meg's confidence.

Humiliation burned across Meg's face at overhearing Bess describe what an hour or an evening would cost the young man. *There's nothing to be ashamed of,* Meg reminded herself. This was honest work, which was more than she could say for some of the jobs she'd held over the years.

It was easy to hear what Bess was saying. Since her foghorn voice could've kept sailors safe from the shoals.

But the soldier was softer spoken. Try as she might, Meg couldn't hear what they'd settled on. She hoped it was for all night as she had quite a bit planned.

"No rough stuff and no refunds," Bess said.

Rough stuff? Meg's hand covered the sudden flutter of panic in her chest. "I hope to shout there's no rough stuff," she muttered.

Before she had a chance to calm herself down, she heard Bess calling out, "Lorena, come here, dear."

Meg hesitated a moment, then stepped out onto the landing and leaned over the railing as she'd been instructed.

"Hello," she said, wishing her voice sounded more sultry and less shaky. She tried lowering her tone. "And have you been waiting long?" Now she sounded like she had a sore throat.

He looked sharp enough to pose for a painting in his brand-new uniform, with the white hat tucked under his arm. He also looked as nervous as she felt. His Adam's apple was bobbing up and down like the needle on a sewing machine. She swallowed a time or two herself before leaning over the banister and carefully letting her green wrapper fall open just a wee bit.

His eyes popped wide, and he seemed shocked by what he saw. *Whatever had he imagined he was in for?*

What was she in for? That was the big question.

The more she leaned, the better he looked. It was too bad she couldn't get close enough to see the color of his eyes, but her feet were barely touching the floor as it was. She hoped the railing held.

On second thought, falling into those strong arms

might not be all that bad. She shivered at the thought of it, but couldn't tell if it was from fear or fascination.

"Go on," Bess said, giving him a gentle shove in the direction of the stairs.

Meg turned and walked slowly into her room, exaggerating the swing in her hips and leaving the door open behind her just as Bess had told her. She drew the curtains together, hoping that less light would make the room more romantic. *Might as well keep a positive attitude about this,* she told herself.

Waiting by the window, she heard him stumble coming up the stairs and hoped this was due to excitement and not to natural clumsiness. She also hoped he had some experience in this matter. It wouldn't do for both of them to be beginners.

He stood at the doorway as if uncertain whether he was welcome inside. *Just where does he think he is?* Surely, he realized that once he'd paid his money he didn't need any further invitation.

Meg stepped forward to take his coat and get a closer look at him. She was surprised to see that his eyes were that pure shade of blue that babies are born with but that always changes over time. Only on this man, it hadn't changed.

The baby blue eyes were the only things that weren't all man about him. Between his strong nose and his square jaw was a set of the most kissable lips she'd seen in a while, full with just a hint of a frown as if he disapproved of the place, or perhaps of her.

Forgetting the coat, she stepped back and tried to smile. But her lips refused to move. No matter how fine he looked, she just couldn't summon friendliness out of the mixture of dread, embarrassment, and nervous excitement that bubbled inside of her.

"Make yourself comfortable," she suggested, indicating the bed with a quick wave of her hand, "while I change."

Meg ducked behind the dressing screen and peered through the gap between the hinges. He was still standing in the doorway, staring at the shabby room. Even in the dim light, the place wasn't much to look at. The fancy red flocked wallpaper was water-stained and peeling off in places. The dresser was so scratched and nicked it looked like someone had taken a chain to it. The chipped water pitcher didn't match the basin beneath it, and the mirror had a huge crack running right down the middle.

On the other hand, the iron bedstead seemed sturdy enough, and she thought her green, appliqued quilt brightened the room up quite a bit. Her mother had made that quilt for Meg's trousseau, and she'd have been just sick to see where it was now. Mam had always wanted life to work out better for her only child than it had for her. But since her dear mother was in the ground and had been for close to a dozen years, there was little chance of her ever finding out where that quilt was spread these days.

Aye, and it's just as well.

All of a sudden, Meg felt the urge for a good cry. Why hadn't she stuck with teaching?

Stop that, she told herself. *You know perfectly well why you quit that job.* As far as Meg was concerned, teaching was a job for the damned. All those misbehaving youngsters crowded into one hot, smelly room, taunting one another and refusing to follow even the simplest of directions. She cringed at the memory of how she'd scrimped by on tea and toast for two and a half years to get that teaching certificate. Then she'd only taught for eight months.

Now that was enough to make a strong woman weep. Spending a pleasant evening with a nice young man and getting paid for it was hardly worth a single tear, let alone a bucket of them.

"My name's Lorena," she called out, trying to sound carefree and happy. It wasn't easy. "And what might you be called?"

"Robert." He stopped to clear his throat before continuing. "Robert Eugene Hamilton."

"That's a fine name, it is."

He sounded like a gentleman by birth and blood. She, on the other hand, sounded like a ninny. Surely, she could think of something to say besides what a nice name he had. Usually, she could talk up a storm, but tonight it seemed she had a sandpaper tongue.

She wasn't the only one having trouble talking. Robert looked to be at least twenty, so it couldn't be that his voice was changing, but it sure sounded like it was. He kept clearing his throat. Not in a disgusting way, more like he was getting set to say something, then couldn't get the words out. Either he was a lot younger than he looked or he was every bit as uneasy as she was over all of this.

"Robert, why don't you take off that grand red coat of yours and hang it on the hook?" Meg tossed a chemise over the edge of the screen. She didn't plan to wear the chemise, but she thought just the sight of it might get his mind working in the right direction.

Hearing the click of heels on the floorboards, Meg peered through the crack between the folding screens again. She was surprised to see Bess push herself past Robert with a bottle of whiskey in one hand and two glasses in the other.

For a moment, Meg pictured Bess remaining in the room with them, instructing them on every step of the procedure like a governess teaching two children how to play a duet on the piano. The thought of Bess showing them each where to put their hands and how to entwine their legs brought Meg her first honest smile of the day.

She watched Bess pour them each a half glass of whiskey, setting one glass and the bottle on the dresser and holding the other glass out to Robert.

"I'll trade you for your coat, handsome," she offered in a voice so throaty a person would've thought she was the one who was going to hop in that bed with him.

Robert's fingers fairly flew down that row of buttons. He couldn't have gotten his coat off any faster if Bess'd been holding a gun on him.

My, this young man doesn't need any shoulder padding, that's for certain. He was built like a bull.

Then Bess took him by the arm, guided him over to the bed, and tugged on him until he sat down. *Maybe she really does intend to stay. Oh, surely not!*

"You two have a good time now," Bess said as she hung his coat on the hook. "Call if you need anything," she said, and pulled the door closed behind her.

Robert perched on the edge of the mattress like a

schoolboy on a detention bench waiting for a reprieve. Meg would've liked a reprieve herself, but she doubted one was coming.

So this is it. No more pretending life is going to hold more for me than it held for my mother or her mother before her.

Overwhelmed by the unfairness of it all, she leaned back against the wall, looked up at the water-stained ceiling, and willed away the stinging in her eyes. *How can I go through with this?*

She'd go through with it like she'd gone through every day at that cursed linen mill. That had been no picnic in the park either. At least here she wasn't at risk of losing a finger or having her hair jerked right off and her scalp along with it. *Why be ashamed of something you have no choice about?* It wasn't her fault that opportunities for women were so few and far between. Lord knows she'd tried every possibility she could come up with.

She peered through the gap again and noticed that he'd finished his drink and was gazing around the room.

"Be right out," she said, forcing a gaiety she certainly didn't feel. "Why don't you have another drink while you're waiting?"

"I doubt that would be a good idea, ma'am," he said. This time, he had a wonderful deep, rich voice, like someone who should be singing in a church choir. Well, maybe he would be singing before the night was over. Maybe she would too. Who knows?

"Go ahead," she urged. "And hand me one. It'll calm us both down."

It didn't take much to convince him because he stood

right up and walked over to the dresser. He poured his glass clear full this time. When he handed hers over the top of the screen, he turned his head aside so that it was clear he wasn't trying to sneak a peek at her.

Now if that wasn't something else. Here he was going to see her in the altogether before this night was done, yet he was too much of a gentleman to take a quick look now.

She watched him walk over to the window and pull the curtains aside far enough to see what was going on down in the street. He seemed like such a sweet man, so polite and all.

Might as well get on with it, she told herself. She finished buttoning up the filmy blue dress she'd made in anticipation of attracting a banker or perhaps a business tycoon. Reaching out around the edge of the screen, her hands found the music box sitting on top of the dresser. She cranked the key until it wouldn't turn any more and lifted the lid. Then, to the tinkling sounds of "Pop Goes the Weasel," she leaped out from behind the screen and threw her arms in the air.

Now that caught his attention. He blinked twice and pulled his head back as if he couldn't quite believe what was right before his eyes.

Meg twirled about the room, waving a tasseled scarf this way and that as she sang, "A penny for a spool of thread. A penny for a needle." It was too bad it was such a silly song, but it was the only music box in the house, and she imagined it was the dancing and not the tune that was important anyway. Every time she got to the "Pop goes the weasel" part, she'd toss her head back and kick a leg out in front of her. Sometimes she kicked higher than her head, she was that good.

Judging from his saucer-eyed stare, she figured that he was impressed by her performance. Well, why shouldn't he be? The Irish had invented dancing, hadn't they? And wasn't she Irish from tip to toe?

She flipped the scarf over his head and pulled it off, inch by inch. Then she winked at him and whirled around the room, slowing gradually as the music box wound down.

"You're quite a dancer," he said as he gulped down the last of his drink.

"Thank you," she said, accepting his compliment like the lady she was. His frown was gone, and she was gaining confidence in her ability as a seductress.

None of the other girls danced for their customers, but Meg felt that given her age, she had to do a little something extra to attract attention. Dancing was going to be her specialty. Though Bess had repeatedly assured her that men rarely needed much in the way of enticement, she told Meg that as long as she didn't spend all evening parading around the room, she didn't see any harm in the idea.

When the music tinkled to a stop, Meg dropped the scarf over his head and disappeared behind the screen to wiggle into another outfit. This one was covered with fake snakes. It was her own original design. She'd sewn and stuffed tubes of material, painted them to look like snakes, then stitched them to a tea-dyed union suit. In the right light, she looked like she was dancing with nothing but snakes covering her body. Meg thought it was rather eye-catching and hoped Robert didn't have a thing against snakes.

"Would you care for another drink, Mr. Hamilton?" she asked as she finished hers off. She was already feeling a little woozy, but this evening would probably go a whole lot better if they were both good and tipsy.

"I think I'll pass," he answered. "Drinking always makes me sleepy."

"Oh, don't be such a spoilsport," she called out. "Live a little. Life is short, it doesn't have to be dull." That was her motto at least.

She noticed he was just a wee bit unsteady on his feet as he made his way over to the dresser. However, he did manage to pour them both another drink without any mishaps.

Once he was settled back on the bed, she pushed up her sleeve so she could reach around and crank up the music box without revealing any part of her costume. She wanted him to be surprised.

When the "All around the mulberry bush" part came, she leaped out from behind the screen and proceeded to writhe in a circle in front of him. Meg felt that this was by far the most sensuous part of her performance.

Obviously, so did he. His mouth fell open like a cheap valise, and he reached down for his drink without ever taking his eyes off her. She'd just bet he'd never seen anything quite like this before.

When the music finally ground to a halt, she blew him a kiss as she slithered behind the screen. While changing into her next costume, she called out, "There's a mental as well as a physical aspect to all of this, you know."

"When do we get to the physical part?" he asked, his voice croaking like a bullfrog.

"Hold your horses, handsome," she called back.

"Just keep your pants on, fella," had nearly slipped out, but she didn't think that would be appropriate, given the circumstances.

This time it was the Dance of the Seven Veils, and it was taking her forever to get each of the scarves pinned on where it was supposed to be. Nonetheless, she was glad she'd gone to all the effort of costumes and dancing. Not only had it calmed her nerves, but it had given her more confidence. She needed that tonight.

"What brings you to Duluth?" she asked as she tucked the corner of a green paisley scarf in her hair, then draped the rest across the lower half of her face.

Her hair was a mess. It was thick and curly and with all the jumping about and costume changes, it was starting to come loose every which way. She pushed in a couple of pins here and there but didn't bother doing it up again. It would all be down before long anyway.

"Just passing through," he replied. "I'm heading north in the morning, then out west."

He certainly wasn't very revealing about his business. She liked that in a man. Most men would talk your ear off whether you were the least bit interested or not.

"What's a British soldier doing heading out west?" Given the history of the country, a person would think he'd do well to stay clear of the United States, especially the trigger-happy end of it.

"I'm a Canadian Northwest Mounted Police, ma'am," he said. There was no mistaking the pride in his voice.

She didn't have to peer out to know that he'd pulled his shoulders back when he said that.

"Never heard of them," she said, immediately wishing she hadn't sounded so brash. There was no sense in being rude to the man.

"The Mounties just started up last year," he explained. There was a long silence before he added. "It's my first assignment."

Meg bet this was his first time for a lot of things. Since this was her first time, too, perhaps Bess should've stayed after all.

"How'd a beautiful woman like yourself come to be working here?" he asked.

She'd been dreading this question and had hoped he wouldn't ask.

"I didn't come to work here," she said, tucking the tail end of a scarf into her waistband so it wouldn't come loose, at least not before she was ready for it. "But my other plans fell through, and, well, a girl's got to support herself."

"I guess so," he said. His "s's" were melting into "sh's." "But I'm surprised a woman like yourself isn't already married."

"I find it shocking myself at times," she told him.

"Your hair is a wonder."

"You don't say," she answered, pinning the last scarf in place.

"Quite striking, really."

"Why, thank you." The way they were chatting, you'd have thought they were sitting in a parlor somewhere, sipping tea.

"I don't believe I've ever seen hair quite that color before."

"It's my own color if that's what you're hinting at." Bess used henna, but Meg had no need of it. Her hair was as red as it comes. It had been the source of endless fascination for the children she'd taught, and, eventually, she'd resorted to using a tea rinse to put an end to the continual comments.

"Didn't mean to offend you, ma'am. I do believe you've got the most beautiful hair I've ever seen."

She'd better get on with it. The man was close to corked. If she waited any longer, this evening might end up a disaster.

This is it. She was down to her last costume. *Time to get serious. Fish or cut bait.*

While Robert mumbled on about what a gorgeous women she was, Meg reminded herself that she was *always* uneasy the first day on a job. She recalled how nervous she'd been starting out as a lady's maid. Had she known that along with fixing Mrs. Worthington's hair came the disagreeable task of fending off Mr. Worthington's advances, she'd have never taken that job to begin with.

Imagine thinking that anyone would put up with those clammy hands grabbing you every time you turned a corner just so you wouldn't lose a job that paid a pittance and involved listening to a cranky old woman gripe about how no one ever did an honest day's work anymore. For the love of Pete!

The only good job she'd ever had was keeping the accounts and handling the ordering at that dry goods store in Chicago. Then that stupid cow had to go and set the town on fire. It was always something.

She was cursed, no doubt about it.

But this was no time for dwelling on the past. Robert had stopped talking, and she peered through the crack again to see if he was getting restless. She was relieved to see that he'd stretched out on the bed. From the looks of things, she doubted any more dancing would be needed to get him in the mood. But she'd practiced this dance and she was going to do it.

"While you're waiting, why don't you take off your things and slip under the covers," she said. This was another one of Bess's suggestions. According to her, the evening would go a whole lot smoother if he got his own self in bed.

She watched as he pulled off his polished black boots and lined them up at the foot of the bed. Then he shucked off his shirt and carefully folded it in a square before placing it on the dresser. Meg was impressed. From what she'd seen, most men just dropped their things every which way.

He turned toward the wall, but there was little doubt about what he was doing now. The sound of buttons popping on his britches brought a flush to her cheeks.

Stop it, she scolded herself. *You might as well get used to that sound.*

He dropped his drawers along with his pants and draped them together across the bedstead before sliding under her quilt. She stared in awe at the brief sight of his well-muscled back and behind. *Oh, my.*

This time Meg only cranked the music box up halfway.

The end part would be slower and better suited for the dance she had in mind. She lifted the lid and began weaving around the room, her arms stretched out, scarves waving back and forth and dropping off as she danced.

But it was all for naught. For when she looked over to see what effect this was having on Robert, she was dismayed to see that it was having none at all. His mouth was hanging open all right, but his eyes were shut, and he was making soft snoring noises.

Now what? Things weren't working out quite the way she'd planned. Should she wake him up and proceed with the evening or let sleeping dogs lie?

As Meg stood there trying to figure out where to go from here, she heard Bess arguing with someone down below.

Strangely enough, that someone sounded like Black Jack McCain.

Surely, not!

Fear prickled down her legs and arms. The last time she'd seen Black Jack, he'd been stepping lively across the deck of that riverboat with half a dozen armed and angry poker players after him. Meg had jumped over the side, and that's the last she'd seen of him. How had he ever tracked her to Duluth? She was a long way from St. Louis.

"I'll be right back," she whispered, although the state this Mountie was in, it was unlikely he'd be missing her anytime soon.

She slipped out into the hallway, dropped to the floor, and wiggled over to the edge of the landing.

Sure enough, it was Black Jack McCain, in the flesh—

string tie, swallowtail coat, and handlebar mustache. There was no mistaking his drawl and no misunderstanding who he was searching for.

"Don't give me that she-ain't-here business," he shouted out. "I have it on good authority that Meg Reilly's working one of the upstairs rooms, and I'm going to find her, come hell or high water."

Merciful Mary. Who would've thought he'd still be so upset by their little scheme falling through? It wasn't her fault that old codger from Memphis had figured out that Black Jack was slipping aces from her garter while everyone else's attention was focused on her bosoms. Just her luck, that old fool had turned out to be a leg man.

But she had no idea Black Jack would still be so upset about it. As far as she was concerned, it was over and done with. But maybe he believed she'd set him up, or perhaps he thought she still had their bankroll.

That was nothing but ridiculous. Money had been the last thing on her mind when she'd taken that flying leap into the murky Mississippi. All she was able to salvage was her quilt, and if it hadn't been for her friendship with one of the maids, that would've disappeared as well.

But Black Jack didn't appear to be in a mood to listen to reason. There was fire in his eyes, and Meg doubted that Bess would be able to hold him back forever. Charlie, the handyman, was doing what he could to block the stairway, but even he couldn't hang on much longer, not against a man as determined as Black Jack.

Meg didn't even want to know what her former gambling partner had in mind for her. When they first teamed up, he'd warned her to expect the worst if she ever double-crossed him. She believed him.

With her heart pounding a mile a minute, Meg ducked back into her room and jerked the quilt off the bed. *My, but he's good-looking.* For a moment she was frozen in place at the sight of her sleeping customer. Too bad things were turning out this way. But tempting as he was, sticking around here would be courting disaster. She'd seen Black Jack in a rage once, and once was enough for her.

Meg felt more than a twinge of regret at leaving Robert stretched out on the sheet without a stitch on. It was certain to be an embarrassment to him. But she'd had no end of trouble getting her quilt back the last time she'd left someplace in a hurry. She didn't intend to repeat that mistake again.

One thing Meg could say about herself, though she made new mistakes all the time, she rarely repeated the same mistake twice. "Sorry about this," she said as she scurried out of the room, leaving a trail of scarves behind her.

Staying as low as possible, she raced to the back stairs, where she tossed caution to the winds in her haste to reach the bottom floor. As she ducked into the handyman's room, she hoped that the shouting and scuffling going on in the parlor covered up the terrible racket she'd made on the stairs.

Meg tore off the rest of the scarves and grabbed a pair of pants and a shirt off the wall pegs. Her hands were shaking so, she couldn't get the buttons done up right and finally settled for covering herself up with an old coat. Then she stepped into Charlie's worn-down boots and stuffed her hair up under his battered hat. Nothing fit right, but at least it wouldn't be immediately obvious that she was a woman.

"Thanks, Charlie," she whispered to the room. "I'll pay you back the first chance I get."

She rolled the quilt up, tucked it under her arm, and jumped out the back window. Her heart pounding like a paddle wheel, she ran to the outhouse and ducked behind it to catch her breath.

Even from that distance, she could hear Black Jack swearing and slamming doors all over the place. Bess and Charlie were yelling, "Get out of here before we call the law." That was clearly an empty threat. They should have sent someone in the direction of the police station long before now. As he burst in on one woman after the next, their shrieks and screams mixed in with his shouting and swearing. The whole place was in an uproar.

In the midst of the commotion, Black Jack kept yelling, "Meg Reilly, come out here. I just want to talk," as if she might actually be fool enough to do it! She had no intention of being around anyone with a temper like his, especially when *she* was the cause of his foul mood.

It was a relief to hear Robert's voice stoutly insist, "I tell you, there's no Meg Reilly in here." Thank goodness she'd decided to call herself Lorena. She'd always loved that name.

Meg felt bad about leaving him like she had, and hoped Bess would refund his money. But there was absolutely no way she was going back in there, not as long as Black Jack McCain was in town.

And he'd be in town as long as he thought she was.

Though she'd only known him a few weeks, he'd proven himself a dangerous and persistent man in that time. She doubted he'd be leaving Duluth until he found her.

So now what?

Since she was safe, at least for the moment, Meg slid down to the ground and began to plan her next move.

She could shuffle around pretending to be a man for a day or two, but then what? Getting out of Duluth wasn't going to be easy. She'd already used up the money she'd sewn into the corner of her quilt, so a train ticket was out.

Walking was ridiculous. It had to be better than a hundred miles to St. Paul, and, as far as she could recall, there wasn't much of anything between here and there.

Darkness and discouragement were settling in as she sat behind the privy, dreaming up and discarding one unworkable idea after another.

Then it hit her. She'd head out west. Black Jack would never think to look for her in that direction. There were all sorts of opportunities out west, but Black Jack had laughed at her whenever she suggested they try their luck in that direction.

"You're a city girl," he'd say, "not a pioneer woman. You wouldn't last a week out in that rough-and-tumble."

When she'd point out that there were cities out west, he'd tell her, "just barely," and that she might as well forget about it because the West was too uncivilized for a woman like her.

The truth of the matter was that the West was too uncivilized for a man like Black Jack. He preferred traveling by train and riverboat, not by stagecoach and horseback. Even if he found out where she'd gone, she doubted he'd follow her.

It was as if the clouds had parted to reveal the answer written across the sky. Meg was pleased to know that she wasn't merely choosing between the lesser of two evils but actually had a plan with a chance of success.

The weight of desperation lifted from her shoulders, and a smile pulled at her face. Her excitement over coming up with a plan dwindled when she realized that she had no idea how to actually get west. She slumped back against the outhouse to reconsider matters.

Somehow, she didn't think Robert would be willing to take her with him. It was just a hunch, but she doubted that tomorrow morning he would be regarding her with the same enthusiasm he had tonight.

Without the train fare or a horse, she was in somewhat of a bind. She could hardly set out alone. She'd have to travel along with somebody going that way. Surely, someone in Duluth was heading west and would let her tag along. No one came to mind.

Then she remembered Hank, an older guy she'd met when she first came to town. He wore fringed leather britches and talked about being a mountain man. Maybe he was heading back into the mountains or at least knew someone who was.

By this time, the uproar inside had died down to Black Jack loudly insisting that he meant Meg no harm.

Right.

With his very next words, he swore that if he ever found out they were hiding Meg Reilly here, there would be hell to pay, and that wasn't a threat, that was a promise.

Meg decided it was time to get going. Keeping to shadows along the back of buildings, she made her way down to the lake.

There were all sorts of tents on the beach, and she wandered around for some time before finding Hank. He was sitting by a campfire, answering questions about what would be useful to have if you were planning on wintering out in the woods.

There was a space open next to a fat man who smelled distinctly of skunk. She sat down. No one paid her any mind, and she didn't call attention to herself, just sat and nodded and listened to Hank. He seemed to relish being the expert, and she wondered how far he was stretching the truth in all this advice he was handing out.

Not that she personally had any objections to adding details to make a story more interesting, but some of this seemed pretty far-fetched to her. He started telling the men about how when the temperature dropped to where you could hear the sap snap in the trees, they were to rub snot all over their faces or risk losing a nose or part of a cheek to frostbite.

Now that was carrying it a bit far. How was snot going to protect your face? As far as she was concerned, a person would be better off to forget about the snot and go for a wool scarf or a warm fire!

As darkness settled around them, one by one the men drifted off to their tents or in the direction of the saloons. Soon it was just Hank and her staring into the coals.

"Well, Meggie," he said, "what brings you out tonight?"

"How did you know it was me?" she asked, startled that he'd recognized her. None of the other men had known who she was or even acknowledged she was a woman.

"Well, my memory may be fading with the years, but I can still remember a good-looking woman when I run across one. Especially out here. What can I do for you?"

Meg smiled at his compliment. "Maybe I just wanted to sit around a fire and listen to some stories."

"Maybe," he said, then sent a stream of tobacco juice sizzling into the fire. "I heard you'd found a job over at Bess's."

"That didn't work out," she said, without offering any details. "Thought I'd head out west."

"You don't say." He reached over, picked up a chunk of driftwood, and dropped it on top of the dying fire. After a time, it caught, and they both watched the orange-and-yellow flames dance around as if this were the most fascinating thing in the world.

"You don't happen to know anyone heading that way, do you?" she asked after a while.

"I'll be heading up that way myself in a month or so."

"I need to leave sooner than that," she said.

"Well, I know a fella who's planning to leave tomorrow morning."

"Do you think he'd take me along?" she asked. Her luck was changing. She could feel it.

"He might. He seems like the chivalrous type."

A chivalrous type? Things were working out better

than she'd imagined. There were a lot of men she wouldn't care to be stuck with out in the middle of nowhere. But a chivalrous type, now that would be the answer to her prayers.

"Let's go meet him. See what he says," she said, making no effort to contain her enthusiasm.

"Well, he's all tied up now. This being his last night in town, he's out having himself a good time. You might have already run across him. He was heading over to Bess's the last time I saw him."

Meg's hopes sank. "Was it a young man in a red coat?" she asked, knowing what the answer would be before he said it.

"That'd be the one. I take it you met up with the kid. Did you ask about going with him?"

"We didn't get to that," she said. They hadn't gotten to a lot of things. "Somehow, I doubt he's going to be too keen on the idea of me as a traveling companion." He probably wouldn't even speak to her after leaving him there stark naked for all sorts of folks to bust in and stare at.

"Didn't get along, eh?" said Hank. "That happens. But there'll be others going that way. It's just a matter of time."

"I'm a little short on time," she said, trying not to sound too anxious.

"This wouldn't have anything to do with that gambler fella asking around about you, now would it?" he asked.

"It would." She sure didn't want to tell the whole tawdry tale but didn't see any way out of it, not if she wanted his help tonight. "You see, we had a falling-out some months ago, and I have a hunch he thinks I made off with money that belongs to him."

"Did you?" Hank asked plainly.

"No. We both got out of there by the skin of our teeth. I didn't have any more time to grab that money than he did. But try explaining that to a man who believes he's been played for a fool."

"That can be tricky all right." Hank nodded in agreement.

"So, you see, I don't think it's such a grand idea for me to hang around town waiting for just the right situation. I'd be better off to get going and work things out along the way."

"I can see your point there," he agreed, rubbing his hand along his chin. "What would you think about traveling by canoe?"

She'd never really thought about it before. "I've never tried it, but it doesn't seem like paddling could be all that difficult."

"You wouldn't be paddling," he said. "More like lying low for a while while someone else did the paddling."

"I imagine I could do that." She imagined herself doing all sorts of things. Lying in the bottom of a canoe seemed simple enough.

"Let's give her a go then," he said. "You want to go back and get your things."

"I got my things with me," she said, pointing to the rolled quilt in her lap.

"Don't you have any better-fitting clothes?" he asked.

"These are heading-west kind of clothes," she pointed

out. She had no intention of going back to that cathouse. Not now. Not ever.

"All right," he reluctantly agreed. "But you need to get a pair of moccasins at least. You do any walking at all, and those boots will rub blisters all over your feet and up your legs."

She followed him to a dry goods store. It was closed, but they went around back and found the owner unpacking a wagonload of goods. After she and Hank gave him a hand bringing things inside, he found her a pair of moccasins and a hat, some pants, a wool shirt, and a coat that fit her well enough. She was glad to be shed of Charlie's worn-out clothes. These were sturdy, going-west clothes, and as long as she kept her hair up under the hat, she was certain she still looked like a man.

"I'll pay you back," she promised Hank as they headed back toward the beach.

He just shrugged. "Whatever."

"Will you get these clothes back to Charlie?" she asked, holding up the string-wrapped parcel.

He nodded like it was no big deal.

It was to Meg. She might stretch the truth from time to time, and she wasn't totally against cheating at cards or bending the law a bit, but a thief she was not. It was a relief to know Charlie wouldn't be thinking of her as such.

They walked down the beach a ways. A slight breeze was blowing in off Lake Superior, and the water shimmered in the moonlight. The sounds of town faded behind them as they made their way along the rocky shoreline. It was so fresh-smelling and peaceful.

Every once in a while they'd pass a collection of tents

and men sitting around a campfire. Occasionally, Hank would call out a greeting and someone would reply. But for the most part they stayed far enough away that it wasn't necessary to exchange pleasantries.

There was only one campfire ahead of them when Hank stopped and told Meg to sit down and wait for a few minutes. Then he walked over and started talking to the man hunched over the fire.

After a time, the man got up and walked away. Either he didn't see her or was just unsociable by nature, because he didn't say a word.

As soon as he disappeared into the darkness, Hank called for Meg to come over. He was standing near a canoe packed clear to the top.

"Here's the plan. Just before dawn, you'll crawl under that canvas tent back here. Then you'll have to be still as a stone until he pulls in for the night. Think you can do that?"

"I don't see why not." Staying still didn't seem too difficult.

"You sure you wouldn't rather just get a train ticket?"

"Positive," she said, leaving no room for any doubt. "Even if I had the money, which I don't, that's the first place Black Jack would look."

"Well, I just hope you're not going from the frying pan into the fire."

"It wouldn't be the first time," she said grimly.

As they sat drinking coffee, Hank explained how he'd helped Robert get outfitted for the trip. According to him, the young Mountie wouldn't think a thing of it when he got back and found Hank had sent the guard off to get some sleep.

He offered Meg another cup of coffee, but given that she was going to be stuck in a canoe all day tomorrow, she thought it best that she not spend the night filling up on coffee. Besides, she didn't have a strong liking for the bitter brew. Now tea, that was another matter altogether.

They talked about one thing and another, and she dozed off from time to time. Finally, he said she'd better get in that canoe and did she have any business she wanted to take care of first.

She did. When she returned from her trip to the bushes, he had a spot cleared out for her in the canoe bottom. Using her rolled-up quilt for a pillow, she curled up in the spot he'd made for her and tried to get comfortable. It wasn't too bad. She'd slept in worse places. Then he handed her a hardtack cracker and a canteen of water before pulling a length of canvas over her.

It was weird being all covered up. Hank was arranging things to leave space around her head, so she didn't feel suffocated at all. It was rather warm and cozy, actually.

"Thank you," she said, settling in.

She must have drifted off to sleep because she woke with a start at the sound of Robert's voice. He was telling Hank that he didn't want to know how his night had gone. It'd been a bit thick, and he was looking forward to some time to sort it all out.

He didn't sound in the best of moods. Meg held herself stiff so she wouldn't make any noise. She expected he would sit and have breakfast with Hank. But it seemed he was ready to go, because the next thing she knew the bottom was scraping across the sand.

"Seems to be riding rather low in the water," Robert said.

"She'll hold," Hank assured him.

Meg felt the canoe rock back and forth as Robert stepped in and got situated. All of the sudden, the frightful possibility of sinking entered her mind. She'd been so concerned about getting out of town, she hadn't given any thought to how safe this was. Black Jack would definitely have knocked her around some, but he probably wouldn't have killed her. Probably. Whereas this adventure . . .

She stopped herself right there. No sense dwelling on the unpleasant. There were risks to every course of action. At least this would get her heading west, a direction she'd been dying to go for years now. Well, maybe not dying, but aching to go. She was headed west, and she was only going to think of pleasant things from now on.

Within a short time, the steady slapping of the water against the canoe and the rhythmic splashing of the paddles lulled her back to sleep. Later, she woke up with cramps in both legs and the desperate urge to pee. Carefully changing positions helped the first situation. There was nothing to be done about the second but endure.

It was hot and hard to breathe. Wasn't he ever going to pull ashore for a break?

He continued on hour after hour. What had she gotten herself into?

CHAPTER TWO

IT WAS GOOD TO BE BACK ON THE WATER. ROBERT FELT AT peace there. The rising sun was painting coral clouds across the sky and reflecting off the lake in silver ripples as far as the eye could see. The air smelled pure and fresh, like the taste of water from a hidden spring. As he glided through the water at a steady, sure pace, he worked the kinks out of his back and shoulders as well as his mind.

Out here it was easy to see the sense of things. He didn't know how men stood being cooped up in buildings all their lives. Ever since he was a kid growing up on Lake Ontario, he'd gone off canoeing and sailing whenever he could. There was a rightness about being out on a lake with just the water and the wind for company. When Hank had tried to convince him to take the overland route, Robert had known better. He stuck with his plan to canoe the lake up to Port Arthur's Landing, then follow the rivers and lakes across. This should give him a good idea of whether it was feasible to bring men and equipment over this Dawson Route on a regular basis. How could he possibly report on a route he'd not experienced firsthand? In a month, Hank would meet him with the horses in Winnipeg, and they could continue from there.

Gazing out across the water always had a calming effect on his mind. The endless jumble of thoughts, ideas, and memories slowed down to where he could consider them one at a time. So much had happened the last few weeks that he imagined it would take him all the way to the Rockies to get them sorted out, let alone made sense of.

Last night had certainly been a disappointment. He was so tired of all the jokes about how he hadn't "dipped his wick," so to speak. It wasn't as if he was saving himself for marriage. It was just that all the girls he knew were.

And he didn't know any other kind of girls. Robert had never felt right about asking his uncle for money to accompany school chums on their randy excursions on the town. His uncle Walter had always been generous in covering Robert's college expenses, but one could hardly expect him to foot the bill for bouts of drunken debauchery.

But since he was making his own money now. If he wanted to spend it on loose women, that was his own business.

Robert was still a little groggy from last night, but the steady paddling was clearing the cobwebs. He felt like kicking himself over how he'd bungled his big chance by going asleep. Who knew how long it'd be before he'd have another opportunity with a willing woman?

It'd probably be a long time before he came across another woman like that Lorena. She was something else. She had spirit and fire and legs that went on forever.

And that red hair! What he regretted most was falling asleep before he had a chance to see her take it down. On second thought, he probably should move that down a place or two on his regret list.

There was nothing to be done about it now. This expedition had more than its fair share of setbacks.

"It'll make a man out of you," his uncle Walter had said when he'd encouraged him to undertake this adventure. He hoped so. At almost twenty-one, Robert was ready.

Oddly enough, Hank had used those very words—"It'll make a man out of you,"—in encouraging him to go to Bouncing Bess's. Well, it hadn't made a man out of him. It'd made a fool out of him.

He winced at recalling how that gambler had stormed into his room, followed by all those prostitutes peering around him. There he was, stretched out without so much as a sheet to cover his nakedness—too drunk and confused to come up with any way out of the situation. What a humiliation that had been.

Hope you learned your lesson, he thought to himself, and not for the first time.

The next month was going to be different. He was in his element. There was something magical and mysterious about gliding through the world on your own power. It wasn't such a bad deal getting paid to paddle around and enjoy life in the wilderness.

A distant "honk-honk" pulled his gaze skyward. There, among the stray, puffy clouds were close to twenty great gray geese making their way north in their distinctive V pattern.

A yearning to be up in their midst flooded over Robert. It wasn't that he wanted to fly, it was that he wanted to be part of a group that looked out for one another. As an only child, it seemed as if he'd been by himself forever. The notion of "all for one and one for all" had been part of the appeal of becoming a Mountie. He hoped that what had happened so far wasn't an indication of what was to come.

By midmorning, his back hurt and his shoulders ached, but it was a muscle-building, soul-refreshing, exhilarating feeling. He'd sleep well tonight.

By noon, the breeze had shifted until it was coming directly from behind. Things were finally working out for him. He rigged up a makeshift mast sail, and, for hours and hours, the canoe practically flew across the water.

Does life get any better than this?

He would've sailed on into the dark, but he could see storm clouds starting to stack up in the sky and thought it best to make camp before the weather blew in.

Since a good deal of the shoreline was covered with granite boulders and rocky cliffs, it was some time before he found a sheltered bay. Shadowed white pines surrounded the sandy beach like guardian angels, and he headed toward it.

He paddled until the bottom settled on the sand, then hopped out to push the canoe the rest of the way up on shore. The cold water chilled his cramped legs and sapped their strength, making it difficult to push the canoe all the way out of the water. He knew he shouldn't have brought so many supplies.

That bedroll will sure feel good tonight, he thought as he tossed it up on a dry, sandy spot.

Then he pulled up the tent to throw it out as well and his easy peace came to an abrupt halt. There was a hand lying there—a soft-skinned, long-fingered hand with an arm attached to it.

Stunned didn't begin to describe his reaction. Here he hadn't even been a Mountie for a month yet and already his second death to deal with. He dreaded pulling back the rest of the tent to get a better look, but what else was there to do?

Robert took a deep breath to steady himself. He should've taken two.

It was that Lorena from last night! He'd recognize her wild red hair anywhere. No wonder she hadn't been around this morning. It made him sick to his stomach to think of her being murdered. But why would the killer dump her body in *his* canoe?

He pulled the canvas clear off, and had another surprise waiting for him—she was dressed as a man. While he was attempting to make sense of the situation, he thought he saw a slight movement of her hand, a mere flutter of a hello-there wave. Then she smiled at him. It was a weak smile, but it was more than he was able to manage at the moment.

Robert was dumbfounded. "What on earth are you doing here?"

"Could we talk about that in just a moment?" she asked, pushing herself up and stepping out of the canoe.

Relief that she wasn't dead was quickly replaced by resentment over her trickery. How dare she stow away on his canoe while he was passed out on her bed! Now he'd have to take her all the way back to Duluth. *Damn.* He hated thinking of the time involved in taking her back to Duluth. He was already way behind schedule, and there was no way of predicting what delays lay ahead. At this rate, he never would get to the Rockies.

She hobbled away toward a patch of shrubs. Funny, he didn't recall her having a limp last night. In fact, she'd seemed fairly lively last night. The image of her whirling around the room, flinging that fringed scarf over his head, added an amorous dimension to the emotions running through him.

Forget last night, he told himself. What was she doing in his canoe?

When she disappeared into a clump of trees, it occurred to him that she might be taking off.

"Stop right there," he shouted after her.

"Be with you in a minute," she yelled back.

Then he realized what she was up to. He'd been able to relieve himself all day. She'd been unable to do that. Well, she should have thought of that before she stowed away in his canoe!

Questions like "What in the world were you thinking of?" and "Lady, have you any idea how much trouble you've caused?" sprang to mind. He immediately discarded them. Righteous indignation was not going to solve anything; nor was there any reason to start a quarrel with her. Regardless of why she'd hidden herself in his canoe, he'd return her to Duluth the next day.

The wind was whipping up a storm, and there he was, standing around like he had cotton for wits. He decided he'd best get the tent erected and save the detective work for later.

While he worked at getting the tent set up, possibilities for the evening began crowding into his mind. Maybe they'd get to finish what they barely began last night. He could hardly wait until they were settled in for the night.

The tent pegs were in the ground, and he was putting the poles up by the time she got back. Her arms were piled with wood, and within a few minutes she'd dug a fire pit and had a stack of twigs and branches all arranged and ready for a match. He pulled one out of his tin pocket canister, struck it across a rock, and lit the pile of curled birch-bark strips at the center of the pile. They caught, and the flames licked up through the center of the stacked branches.

"You're a woman of many talents," he said, in an attempt to be pleasant.

"You don't know the half of it," she said.

"But I'm sure looking forward to learning," he said, smiling in her direction. He was glad he hadn't winked as well because she didn't smile back. In fact, she seemed offended by the remark.

"I wouldn't count my chickens just yet if I were you," she advised him before leaning over to blow on the fire.

"Raising chickens wasn't what I had in mind," he said.

"I don't care what you have in mind, you can just forget about it," she said.

"You're awfully unfriendly all of a sudden," he pointed out.

"Well, what did you expect?" she asked. "That I'd just hop out of the canoe, flop down in the sand, and we'd take up where we left off last night?"

"No, but I will admit I was hoping for more than a few churlish remarks. After all, you're the one who hid away in my canoe."

"What do you mean by that?"

"You sneak away into the wilderness with a man you danced in front of half-naked not twenty-four hours ago. What did *you* expect?" he asked.

She shrugged.

"Surely, you didn't think that we'd be spending the evening playing cards?"

"Well, I certainly didn't think I'd be spending the evening fending off unwanted advances." She made it sound as if he were a lecher of some sort.

"It didn't appear they were unwanted last night," he said in his own defense.

"Oh, bring that up." She said it like he'd broken some rule on fairness. "And here I was believing you were the chivalrous type."

"I *am* the chivalrous type," he said.

"So prove it," she challenged him.

"How?"

"Be chivalrous. I'm a damsel in distress. Rescue me."

"I've already done that," he pointed out.

"So now I suppose you're waiting for your reward?"

"I wouldn't put it that way." But that was indeed what he was hoping for.

"What way would you put it?"

"I was thinking more along the lines of how we didn't

get a chance to finish what we started last night and, fortunately, now we can."

"Think again, bucko."

He felt his spirits sag.

"Things are different now."

"What's different?" he said, dismayed at her stance on the matter. "You're a desirable woman, I'm a healthy man . . ."

"For one thing," she said, making it sound as if there were a whole list of things, "we hardly know each other."

"We hardly knew each other last night," he said, frustrated. This conversation was headed in the wrong direction, and he didn't know how to go about turning it around.

"I don't see the point in discussing this any further," she said.

He did.

"Do you mean to say that last night you would sleep with me but tonight you won't?" he asked, reluctant to believe what he was hearing.

"I didn't say that."

"What are you saying then?"

"I want to get to know you a little. Is that too much to ask?"

That seemed like a reasonable enough request. "What do you want to know?" She wouldn't have to interrogate him. At this point he was willing to divulge anything he knew and make up whatever he didn't.

"Nothing in particular," she said. "I'd just like to know a little about you, where you grew up, what you're doing out here, what your plans for the future are."

"I grew up in Ottawa. I have one more year left to complete at Upper Canada College, but my uncle encouraged me to take a year off and join this expedition. He said this would be a once-in-a-lifetime adventure and that the experience would be invaluable for me in my future career."

"And what career might that be?"

"I plan to work in the family shipping business for a time, then join my uncle in politics. It's what he's done, and it seems to have worked out well for him."

"Well, hallelujah for him," she said, obviously not impressed.

This conversation wasn't going anywhere, at least not anywhere productive. Perhaps she was hungry. After a good meal, maybe she'd be in better spirits.

Robert walked over to the canoe and returned with a kettle of water and the food box. He put both on the ground next to her.

"And I guess I'm supposed to fix dinner." She sounded testy, and he wondered why. If anyone had a right to be irritable, it should be him. He was the one who'd have to paddle all the way back to Duluth now because of her irresponsible behavior.

Rather than get involved in an exchange of snide remarks, he ignored her for a moment and put his attention to pushing the canoe up on shore and covering the rest of the supplies to keep them dry through the coming storm. He watched her rummage through the food box and take out a few things. But his mind wasn't on food. It was on wondering what she felt like under that green-wool shirt and what it would be like lying with her tonight. He could feel himself flush just imagining the pleasure awaiting him if everything worked out well.

The water was boiling, and she was mixing up biscuit dough when he sat down on a rock across from her.

"I've always been fascinated by the way flames suddenly appear, meld together, then change colors and form before melting away," he said. Perhaps if he stayed on neutral topics, things would go better between them.

She didn't add a comment of her own, so he plunged on. "My nanny told me that the first word I ever spoke was 'hot.'"

"You don't say," she muttered.

It didn't sound as if she was interested in him or his attempts at conversation, so he kept his thoughts to himself. But how did she expect they'd get to know each other if she didn't want to talk?

He didn't bother to tell her that it wasn't just the patterns of light and color that attracted him to fire. By focusing on the flames, he was able to think things through a step at a time. That often came in useful.

For example, now that he thought it over, it seemed that in his desire to get things on a pleasant basis between them, he'd somehow missed a step. Perhaps before they could relax with one another, they needed to get a few things settled first. Like, for example, what she was doing here in the first place.

"I'd like to know what's going on," he said. Even as the words left his mouth, he wished he had asked in a gentler manner.

"I'm making us a wee bite to eat," she said, acting as

if he was asking a silly question but she'd humor him anyway. "That's what you wanted wasn't it?"

"Well, yes," he admitted. He'd never seen a woman in pants before. Try as he might to keep his eyes off her as she moved about, he couldn't, and it was having a disturbing effect on him.

"Oh, I know what you want, bucko." She stared him right in the eyes. "The question is, will you give me what I want?"

"Which is?" he asked.

"Take me west with you." She spoke as if it was a reasonable request, like "please pass the sugar" or "hand me the front page of the newspaper, if you will."

He had to take her back to Duluth. There was no question about that. It wasn't as if he was looking forward to the return trip, but a woman had no business out here in the wilderness.

He felt like cursing. First that fiasco in St. Paul, where his commander had been shot, and now this.

"I have to take you back," he told her. They might as well get that straight right from the start.

"No, you don't." She said this as if he was the one being unreasonable. "You can take me with you."

"I most certainly cannot take you with me," Robert said, leaving no room for argument.

"And why not?" Now she seemed offended.

"Well, for one, there are hardships ahead," he said.

"I've dealt with hardships before," Meg said. "I think I can handle them."

"And for another, I think it's highly suspicious the way

you disappeared from that brothel and reappeared in my canoe." There, he'd said it.

"Chance and coincidence," she said, with a wave of her hand, as if brushing aside a matter of little importance. But he wasn't fooled, not for a second. He'd seen the startled expression on her face a moment ago. What did she take him for, a simpleton?

"I'd say your hasty exit was connected to that gambler showing up." He watched her face. Though this time she was careful to hide her emotions, Robert could almost see the gears grinding away behind her eyes. He wished she would just tell him the truth, but that appeared unlikely.

"Would you be believing me if I told you he was my long-lost brother?" she asked.

"No, I would not."

"You've got a grand mind on you, Robert Hamilton," she said, her voice softening into an obvious attempt at flattery. "And I don't mind telling you that isn't the only grand thing I've noticed about you," she said with a knowing look toward his nether regions.

Robert was taken aback by this turn in the conversation. He glanced down to see if by chance he needed to readjust his trousers. He did.

"Excuse me," he said, blushing. Getting to his feet, he headed off into the trees. He knew there was no reason to be embarrassed, not after last night. Still, he'd been raised to be a gentleman, and sitting around with your whiskers showing hardly seemed like gentlemanly behavior.

He wished he could remember more about last night. Oh, he could recall her dancing well enough. That'd been unforgettable. On his deathbed, he would probably be thinking of her writhing around in that odd long underwear outfit. But apparently, the liquor had erased all the memories of what had occurred after that. If anything had occurred at all, which he had his doubts about.

After that gambler had left his room, he must have fallen asleep again. When he'd wakened this morning, he'd been disappointed to find himself alone. On his way out, the hefty woman who ran the place had nudged him repeatedly and made no end of ribald remarks about how the two of them had frolicked the night away, leaving Lorena so exhausted she'd gone off to sleep in another room. All he could recall was her dancing, then, later, that gambler bursting in.

This was the second experience with liquor he'd had in less than a week. The first had been a disaster and this one merely a disappointment. Regardless of what Bess had tried to make him believe, he doubted that anything other than dancing went on in that shabby room last night.

He failed to see the appeal of being intoxicated and made a pact with himself to abstain, at least for the remainder of his year's tour of duty. As addled as alcohol made him, he had no business consuming it.

The wind was packing in the dark clouds above them. Robert decided that he'd best get back and eat before the storm broke.

"He's not my long-lost brother," she admitted when he returned to the campfire.

Robert was pleased that though she appeared unable to reveal the truth, she was at least able to recognize it.

"And my name's not Lorena," she added sadly.

Somehow he'd guessed as much. He watched her eyes turn upward and flash back and forth, just like his mother's used to when she was trying to decide how many facts to weave into one of her fabricated tales in order for it to seem believable or at least plausible.

"Would I be safe in assuming that your name is Meg Reilly?" he asked. He wasn't exactly sure where that came from, then recalled that was the name the gambler had been shouting last night.

She closed her eyes and nodded. He could barely hear the yes she whispered.

"And would this gambler be the reason you're reluctant to return to Duluth?"

Though she nodded yes, she didn't make a sound and didn't look up this time.

He couldn't help but feel sorry for her. Despite his misgivings over how she conducted her affairs, he knew how difficult it was for a woman to make her way in the world without the protection of a man. He wished he could offer her that protection, but it was simply not possible, not in his present situation.

He didn't know what to say. It was easy to see why she didn't want to go back to Duluth, but taking her with him was out of the question. He was an officer of the law. There were responsibilities and obligations that went along with that. He couldn't just take up with a woman of easy virtue.

If his uncle ever heard of it, he would be appalled. Robert was certain that consorting with a light-skirted woman wasn't what his uncle Walter had in mind when he arranged for him to be on this expedition. His uncle had made it quite clear that he was grooming him for a position of political leadership in this grand new Dominion of Canada. No doubt he would overlook an occasional visit with a prostitute, but taking up with one would be another matter altogether. Robert was certain of it.

Besides, once he knew the whole story about her and that gambler and who knows what else, he probably should arrest her, not invite her along as a traveling companion.

But neither could he just abandon the woman to her fate. That seemed needlessly cruel.

"Couldn't you seek protection with the police?" he asked.

She looked up at him as if he'd asked her to put her trust in the wildflowers to protect her. "What good would that do? It's my word against his. Just who do you think they're going to believe?"

The woman had a point. He didn't believe her, and Black Jack wasn't even here presenting his side of the story.

"Besides," she continued, "there are parts of the story I'd just as soon the police didn't find out about."

He hoped the parts she was referring to did not involve a murder. Strictly speaking, he didn't have jurisdiction until he crossed the border. But still, he'd have to do something. A Mountie couldn't just ignore a crime like that.

"Perhaps you could leave town," he suggested, in an attempt to be helpful.

"That's what I did, bucko." she said, disgust plain in her voice and on her face. "You think hiding in the bottom of a canoe all day is my idea of a good time?"

Though it put him in a bind, he had to admit, given the circumstances, she might have chosen the most appropriate course of action.

"Regardless," he said, "I cannot allow you to accompany me on the rest of my journey. You'll simply have to think of something else."

"Like what? Turn into a fairy princess and slip away with the wee folk?" she asked, with more sarcasm than he thought necessary.

Robert ignored her last comment. He did not intend to be bullied about by her and her snide remarks.

"You must go back and straighten things out," he said.

"Must I?" she said, lifting her eyebrows, her head, and one shoulder as arrogantly as any society matron.

"Running away from your problems isn't the way to handle them. You face them square on. That's the best way." He knew he sounded like an earnest headmaster, but he couldn't help it. Facing your problems truly was the best way.

But arguing with her about it was not a great idea, not if he wanted to fulfill even his tamest fantasies for tonight.

They ate in silence. But before they'd finished their biscuits and jam, lightning sparked across the sky, and the expected rain arrived. Almost immediately, the raindrops gave way to a deluge that threatened to douse the fire and sent them both scrambling into the tent.

Since there were two of them in a one-person tent, it

was impossible not to touch, not if they wished to avoid contact with the canvas sides and thereby encourage the water to seep in on them. He tried to ignore the way their legs and arms were pressing up against one another, but it wasn't easy. The thought was more disconcerting than the actual touching as their damp clothes formed a cold barrier to each other's warmth.

He turned his mind on other matters, such as hoping the trench he'd dug around the tent was sufficient to keep them from being carried out into the lake. But it was impossible to smell her rose-and-lemon scent and not wonder what it would taste like on his tongue. He wondered what it would feel like to have her chest against his, her legs wrapped around his, her . . .

Rein yourself in, he told himself. He wondered if she thought they knew enough about one another to consider having relations. Should he wait for her to give some indication that she would welcome his advances, or was she waiting for him to make the first move? It struck him that school had been a total waste of time. For all the tedious lectures on literature and economics and how a gentleman behaves at a ball, not once had anyone mentioned what to do if you were stranded in the wilderness with a warm, spitfire of a woman. He'd have remembered that.

Perhaps he should wait for her to suggest something. After all, she was the one with the experience.

"So, how come you want to be a Mountie?" she asked in the darkness.

What? The question caught him off-balance. He didn't want to talk about being a Mountie. He wanted to talk about taking his clothes off and crawling under the blankets with her.

But it seemed crass to suggest it, so he said, "When I signed up, it seemed like a grand adventure." He didn't mention that according to his uncle it was supposed to make a man out of him. Robert was hoping she'd do that.

"So you thought going off to fight Indians would be a grand adventure?" It was obvious that she didn't think much of the idea.

"Not fight them, protect them," Robert explained. "We're a police force, not an army. The Canadian government would go bankrupt trying to tame our western lands the way America is attempting to. We simply don't have the resources."

Or the stomach for it. He didn't think he needed to go into how abhorrent the Canadians found the massacres that the Americans seemed to take for granted. "Our mission is to establish the rule of law and ensure peaceful settlement of the prairie land."

"Well that seems noble enough," she said. "How many Mounties are there?"

"Three hundred," he said.

"Three hundred? Is that all?" She didn't sound the least bit impressed.

"Three hundred handpicked men," he pointed out, proud that he'd passed muster to be part of the Force.

"Each of you are out on your own then, are you?" She made it sound as if this was an amusing, foolish adventure he was on.

He'd about had it with her sarcastic remarks. He could

say a thing or two about how it beat working in a whorehouse, but he decided against it.

"No, the Force operates with troops. My situation is the result of an unusual set of circumstances." Circumstances he would just as soon not go into. A great many things had changed since he'd first set out. He hoped he was making the right decision about going forward with the expedition.

I've got to get out pen and paper and write an account of my journey thus far, he reminded himself. He wondered how to summarize that fateful night and in what order he should list the reasons the rest of the men gave for abandoning the mission. "This whole mess was a crock of shit from the beginning," hardly sounded like the appropriate terms in which to describe the underlying disillusionment.

He felt her shiver against him and decided that putting his arm around her would help move the conversation away from that dreadful experience in St. Paul and on to something more enjoyable. He shifted around until he was able to drape his arm across her shoulder. She didn't shrug it off, but neither did she acknowledge it by relaxing against him. It felt awkward, but it would have been even more awkward to remove it.

To ease the situation, he decided to explain how he came to be by himself.

"Originally, there were fourteen men in my troop. We had permission from the U.S. government to take the train to the end of the line at Fargo, North Dakota, and go up from there. Though we had a peacekeeping mission, our main responsibility was to gather accurate information on the condition of the trails and the native peoples and to evaluate how effective the Northwest Mounted Police could be in establishing the rule of law."

He realized he was prattling on like a tedious professor who'd given this lecture far too many times. But he couldn't just sit there with his arm dangling over her shoulder like a nincompoop. He wished he could think of something else to talk about. But nothing came to mind, so he plunged on.

"Six years ago, when the Dominion purchased the western lands from Hudson's Bay Company, there was strong support for establishing a police force. But the Prime Minister kept putting it off because of the heavy cost and the lack of settlers. That all changed with the Cypress Hill massacre. He was forced to take action. It was either that or hand the country over to the whiskey peddlers, murderers, and criminals."

"Oh," she said without much visible interest in what he was saying.

He supposed he could say something about the weather. But the phrase, "Cow pissing on a flat rock," was the only one that came to mind. Aside from the crudeness of it, it didn't seem to have much chance of leading anywhere.

They couldn't just sit there in silence, and she didn't seem willing to talk, so he plunged on. "Last summer, the Mounted Police were sent out to establish a presence in the western territory. The reports have been anything but encouraging. The loss in horseflesh alone is staggering, and the health of the men isn't much better. Morale is so low that desertions are a never-ending problem. The worst of it is that the reports submitted by Commissioner French seem at odds with those submitted by his subordinates."

He paused, waiting for her to say, "How dreadful," or give some indication that she was listening to him. The situation was becoming more uncomfortable by the moment, especially when he realized that he'd just run down the Force as well as hinted that his commanding officer was a liar.

"Of course, they were dealing with a harsh country and extreme weather," he quickly added. He thought it wise not to mention anything further about misguided leadership. "Hard to say what was what, so they sent Inspector Parker to make an unbiased assessment of the situation, and he picked me to be one of his men."

Robert decided it was best to stop on a high note.

"So, where is this Inspector Parker?" she asked.

Damn. She finally showed some interest, but in the one subject he'd just as soon not talk about.

"We became separated," he said vaguely. Then he squeezed her shoulder and pulled her in closer. Perhaps words weren't necessary between a man and a woman. She accepted this without any reciprocal move on her part but no resistance either. He bent his head with the intention of kissing her neck.

"What do you mean 'separated'?" she asked, turning toward him and bumping her cheek against his chin. "Where are the rest now?"

"It's a long story," he said, pulling away. Actually, it wasn't all that long, but it was gruesome in parts and depressing all the way through. He'd just as soon not go into it. What he'd rather do is roll around on the blankets with her, but he couldn't figure out how to get there from here.

"Do you plan to meet up with them before long?"

"No," he said, nuzzling his face into the side of her neck. The rose-lemon scent was intoxicating. He was set to make his next move when she scooted away from him.

"Are you a deserter?" she asked.

"Certainly not." He was appalled at the very idea of going back on his word and shirking his duty. Reluctant as he was to go into it all, he decided that since she wasn't going to forget about it, he might as well tell her what had happened.

"No," he said. "As a matter of fact, I was the only one who didn't desert. Our train trip worked out just the way we planned until our layover in St. Paul to exercise the horses and purchase a few supplies. Word spread about us. Our last night in town, we were approached in a saloon by a band of men who insisted on telling us what a rough deal a man got in the Mounties—poor leadership, meager provisions, scrawny mounts, few blankets, endless drills, long marches for no good reason. The list went on and on. Then they started in on how only fools would think that three hundred men could establish law and order over three hundred thousand square miles. Someone asked how they knew so much about the Mounties, and one of them admitted they'd deserted. The fight was on."

The memory of how that fight had turned out pushed a wave of nausea up his throat. He stopped talking and swallowed.

"What happened?" she asked after a time.

"Inspector Parker was shot in the forehead," he said, sounding as if he was filling out a report. The Inspector's death had shocked the fight out of everyone. "One moment we were defending our honor with our fists. The next moment, we were all standing around, bruised and bloodied, unable to grasp what had just happened."

"How dreadful," she said.

It was every bit of dreadful. "An officer of the law was called, but no one admitted to pulling the pistol or knowing who had. He left, and that was it for the investigation." Even now it left a sour taste on his tongue.

"What happened to the rest of the men you were with?"

"Some of them were injured and unable even to sit up without assistance, let alone travel across the continent. I tried to persuade the able-bodied ones to fulfill their obligations, but they weren't about to listen to a green kid, not when seasoned men were telling them what they were up against. They all quit that night."

Cowards, that's what they were. Imagine turning tail over a bit of bad news. "Since I was the only one who planned to continue, I took possession of the money the inspector was carrying, paid the funeral expenses and the doctor's fees, and wired headquarters that I was continuing with the mission and would send reports back as circumstances permitted."

"So how did you end up in Duluth?"

"I did what I'd agreed to do," he said simply. "I just changed the route somewhat." When he'd heard about an uprising among the French-Indian Métis up north of

Fargo, it seemed foolhardy to go that way. Four years ago, it'd taken an army of over a thousand men to put down a rebellion there. There was no need to go into all of that, though, so he just said, "It seemed wiser all the way around to take the Dawson Route from Port Arthur's Landing to Winnipeg. A guide named Hank Ryan will meet me there with the horses."

It was difficult to believe that he was yammering about all of this when one of the most desirable women he'd ever met was in his arms. Robert directed his thoughts to the best way to approach Meg about taking up where they'd left off last night.

"Well, guess we'd better get ready for bed," he suggested.

She didn't say anything.

"My shirt's wet. I think I'll take it off," he said, hoping she'd offer to do the same.

She didn't.

Robert pulled his arm off her shoulder and began unbuttoning. Strange how this should be so awkward in the dark when last night he'd disrobed completely in the lamplight and all he'd felt was a sense of excitement. He noticed the excitement was still there.

After he took his boots off, he stretched out on his bedroll.

"Would you care to lie down with me?" he asked. It seemed rather forward, but unless she planned on sitting there all night, there was really little else for her to do. She could hardly go out in the pouring rain.

Apparently, she realized that as well and followed his suggestion.

There they were, side by side, barely touching, staring up into the darkness. If only they'd been out under the stars, he could have shown her where to look up in the northern end of the sky to find the Little Dipper. Then they'd have followed across the faint dragon stars until they came to the four keystone stars of Hercules.

The story of Hercules and his twelve labors had been one of Robert's favorites while growing up. He feared he'd begun a journey every bit as arduous as Hercules' and only hoped he had the strength to see it through.

But at least Hercules had his labors all laid out for him, had known what he had to do. Whereas he had to keep figuring out for himself what the next move should be.

He considered commenting on what gorgeous eyes she had or how much he admired her hair. In fact, he admired quite a bit about her. But it seemed self-serving to start talking about how beautiful she was while they were in the dark. He should have said something when it was still light enough to see. It was a bit late for flattery now.

He thought about putting his arm around her. She'd gone along with it before, and it was probably as good a place to start as any. But it was one thing to casually drape an arm over her shoulder while they were huddled together, quite another to shove his arm underneath her back now. It was too much to hope that she might make the first move. Nonetheless, he wished she'd give some sign that she would at least welcome his advances.

Then it hit him. Why hadn't he thought of it before? She was probably waiting for him to settle the financial arrangements before they proceeded.

"Would four dollars be enough?" he asked. It was fifty

cents more than he had paid last night, but she was worth it.

"Enough for what?"

"Enough for, you know . . ." He couldn't think of a word for it, at least not one that wouldn't earn him a slap across the face. "What we were going to do last night," he finished lamely.

"You've got your nerve!" She sounded as if she might slap him after all.

"How much do you want?" He'd give her just about anything she asked for at this point. He'd been thinking about it on and off for the last twenty-four hours. Who was he kidding? He'd been turning it over in his mind for the last ten years.

"I want you to take me out west," she said in no uncertain terms.

Anything but that. As much as he wanted her, there was no way he was going to take her with him on this mission. Aside from the danger, he'd be the laughingstock of the Force.

Or the envy. She wasn't cheap-looking by any means. Why, if it wasn't for her profession, he'd be proud to escort her to a nearby destination.

"I'll take you to Port Arthur's Landing," he offered. "You can take a steamship to Chicago from there."

"I've been to Chicago, and once was plenty," she said. "I've no desire to go back."

"What's the matter with Chicago?"

"For one, the last time I was there, the whole place burned clear to the ground."

"I'm certain they've rebuilt by now."

"Who cares? I intend to go west, to the Montana Territory or maybe Seattle. I want to go where there are more opportunities."

"Just what do you plan to do in Seattle that you can't do in Chicago?" Surely, there were bawdy houses in both places.

"I believe I could make my way in the world as a dancer. Don't you think I'm unique enough to attract attention on stage?"

"Unique was the very word I was thinking of," he said, agreeably. "In fact, I'll bet you could join a dance company in Chicago," he continued in an attempt to direct her thoughts in that direction.

"Have you ever been to Chicago?" she asked. Her tone of voice clearly conveyed that if he had, he wouldn't be making such a ridiculous suggestion.

"I passed through it on the train," he said, wondering if that counted for anything.

"Well, I've lived there, and I can tell you for a fact that Chicago is full of desperate women who'd dance naked on your noggin for the price of a meal."

Robert instantly regretted not stopping over in Chicago to exercise the horses and purchase their supplies. The expedition might have gotten off to a better start all the way around.

"I won't do that," she said firmly. "So I have to go where there are fewer women and more men willing to pay for a look at them."

"That does make more sense," he had to admit.

What didn't make sense was why they were on top of

the blankets instead of underneath them. It was turning chilly; he could feel goose bumps forming on his arms.

"Why don't we get under these blankets?" he suggested.

"Oh, you'd like that all right," she said, sounding as if she thought he was trying to trick her into something.

"Yes, I would," he said. "But I give my word as a gentleman that I won't force myself on you."

"How do I know I can trust you?"

"You were quick enough to trust me when you hid in my canoe," he pointed out.

When she didn't say anything, he couldn't help adding the obvious. "Besides, you'll freeze tonight if you don't cover up."

"Don't you be worrying about me," she said. "I brought my quilt along."

Damn.

For the next few minutes, they squirmed around in the dark until they were two cocoons snuggled side by side. He sure wished he knew what he could do or say that would convince her to be more affectionate.

"Are you sure you won't change you mind?" he asked.

"Take me west, and I'm all yours."

"Good night, Miss Reilly," he said, trying not to let on how frustrated and disappointed he was.

"Good night, Mr. Hamilton."

Chapter Three

He was such a sweet young man, a babe in the woods, really. She wouldn't be surprised if he still had puppy breath. What had his uncle been thinking of to send him on such a journey? To take a young man who'd had such a sheltered upbringing and throw him in with such ruffians. Why, it was a shame that's what it was.

That killing in St. Paul had certainly knocked him back on his heels. He sounded so shocked about the lawman not taking more of an interest in the murder, like it was an unusual event or something. She'd lay odds that getting shot in a barroom brawl probably happened fairly often in St. Paul. Given the direction he was headed, Robert needed to get more used to it.

She needed to quit worrying about the direction Robert was headed and show some care for where she was going. One place she knew she wasn't going was back to Duluth. Even if she waited until Black Jack moved on, she had no desire to go back. There was nothing there for her.

She never went back, not to a place, not to a job, and definitely not to a man. As far as she was concerned, if it didn't work out the first time, give up and go on.

This fella would sure be hard to give up on though. He was what every woman dreamed about, a man who would protect and care for you, a man you could trust with your heart.

Not that she'd be trusting him with her heart. Not hardly.

Perhaps if she were lace-curtain Irish and not shanty Irish, she'd stand a chance. But it would be a slim one. No, Robert would marry a woman from his own kind, someone with the right social connections, someone who knew how to chat about the weather all afternoon. There was no sense setting her cap for this one. Even if she were younger, he was a heartache waiting to happen.

But it would be fun to travel with him. Maybe she could get him to loosen up a little. He was too serious for his own good.

She wondered if she should reach over and tickle him a little under his chin, just enough to get him to relax a wee bit.

Her hand was in the air when she decided against it. *No sense giving him ideas. He has plenty of his own already.*

She was disappointed in how last night had turned out, or rather how it had not turned out. It was a letdown, to be sure. Despite her misgivings, in a way she'd been looking forward to having relations with Robert. She'd waited so long. But there'd be other chances, she was certain of it.

In fact, it probably wouldn't take much more than a nudge tonight. But then what would she do? She'd been around long enough to know that once a man had his way with a woman, a good deal of his interest disappeared. She needed to play the cards she had. His lust was her ticket west.

It was a pity. He was such a grand young man. Not only the way he was built, although that was certainly nothing to sneeze at, but the way he acted—his refusing to peek over the dressing screen, his bumbling attempts to be affectionate without forcing himself on her, his continuing on with this Mountie business when most men would've thrown in the towel.

She felt a tingle of awakening deep within her and was surprised by it. Surely, she'd turned that off years ago.

The important thing was keeping *him* feeling those tingles. She'd be walking a tightwire, especially out here all alone. But she didn't see any other way, really. As long as he wanted her, she had a chance. Once he'd had her, he'd be sending her away, and that she could not endure.

The rain was letting up. In the lull she listened to his steady, slow breathing. If only she could drop off to sleep as easily as he did. But then, she'd been napping for most of the day.

It was grand to be beside him. For a time, she wondered what it would be like to have him coming through the door every day for dinner, to feel his legs against hers in the night, to grow old laughing over their adventures together. What she wouldn't give for a man like him to be hers.

Don't go wishing for the moon. Not only was she going to be growing older a lot sooner than he was, but there was no way such a fine English gentleman was going to marry a shanty Irish. Not in this lifetime or the next. *You might as well give that wish a rest.*

No. They'd have a pleasant enough time of it and then they'd part. He'd end up sleeping on featherbeds and she'd spend her nights on straw ticks. Cursing the fates that squelched her every attempt at happiness, her thoughts wandered until she drifted off.

Morning found her cuddled up against his side, her head nestled into his neck, his arms holding her close to him. What would it be like to be cherished and protected for real, not just pretend? It felt so fine, she dared not move for fear it would end.

An image wandered into her mind of herself as a little girl, sitting with her arms around her knees, holding herself tight together so she'd be invisible. She remembered the sharp points of the coal chunks poking through her flour-sack dress and the sound of her mam's boss calling for her to come out, saying he wasn't going to hurt her, that he just wanted to talk with her.

Sure. And pigs fly on Mondays. No, she'd be staying right where she was.

She'd not thought of that in years. It must be the safety of Robert's arms that let the frightful memory back in. Or maybe it was the memory of the safety she'd always found in the coal bin. Not only was she hidden away from searching eyes, but should they find her, she could always escape out the coal chute. Meg liked having an escape route handy.

She noticed that the rain had started up again. The separate thap-thap-thaps were now a constant drumming against the canvas above them. Gusts of wind were trying to shake the tent pegs loose. But inside they were dry and safe.

There was a glow inside the tent, not really morning light yet, but the beginning of it. It was that in-between time when dreams blend into day.

"Guess we won't be going anywhere soon," she heard him say against her ear.

There was a flash of regret that he'd not slept for just a wee while longer. Now she'd have to give up this warm, safe feeling. She pulled away, and he loosened his arms to let her go.

"You don't have to," he said. "I won't hurt you."

"I know that. But there's no sense leading you on." There was indeed sense in leading him on, but rubbing their bodies together seemed a bit much and likely to move things forward faster than she considered wise.

"I've been thinking. Could we just forget that business at Bess's?" he asked.

"I imagine so." She wondered what had brought this on. "But why?"

"I just think we got off on the wrong foot. It appears we'll be spending the next few days together, and I don't want you to be uncomfortable, that's all."

"It's forgotten," she said. Although now she was thumbing through the memories of that night, trying to figure out what part he wanted her to forget.

"Let's just start over," he suggested. "Hello, my name is Robert Eugene Hamilton."

"Pleased to make your acquaintance, Mr. Hamilton. My name is Margaret Teresa Reilly." She reached her hand over to shake his and was surprised when he pulled it to his lips and pressed a kiss against the back of it. *My, but that felt grand!*

"Please to make *your* acquaintance, Miss Reilly," he said in that deep, rich voice of his.

A shiver passed through her, and she realized she'd not turned those feelings as far off as she'd thought.

"Looks like this will be an inside day. It's too bad we don't have a deck of cards to pass the time with."

"It is unfortunate," she agreed. "I guess blindman's buff and hide-and-seek are out."

"I suspect so. We could always play twenty questions," he said.

"All right," she agreed, sitting up and rearranging her quilt around her. "What am I thinking of?"

"Does it have to do with me?" he asked. He sat up himself.

"In a way," she answered.

"No fair. It has to be either 'yes' or 'no.'"

"Yes, then."

"Does it have to do with what a fine and handsome gentleman I am?"

"No."

"No?" He sounded surprised, with just a hint of hurt hidden behind it.

"Yes, you are indeed a fine and handsome gentleman, but no, that's not what I'm thinking of," she said.

"Does that count as one of my twenty questions?"

"Yes."

"Does this one count as well?"

"Yes, it does," she said with a smile.

"What question am I on now?"

She held up six fingers.

"This isn't going very well, is it?"

"No." She put up another finger and did her best to keep from grinning.

"Does it have anything to do with you?" he asked.

"Yes," she said, eight fingers in the air now.

"Does it have anything to do with you traveling west?"

"Yes," she said.

"Are you thinking about a stage in Seattle where you're dancing and the audience is applauding and cheering?"

"How did you know?" She closed her hand into a fist and tapped his shoulder in mock anger.

"Easy. You seem determined to get to Seattle. No doubt you have an image in your mind as a goal. I just guessed what that image might be." He seemed quite satisfied with himself, smug even.

"All right. Your turn."

"Not so quick. You haven't paid your forfeit yet." His smile stretched so far across his face, it was a wonder his lips didn't crack.

"Don't get too carried away, bucko," she warned him.

"I guess I'm not getting a kiss?" He said this as if he really hadn't expected one.

"No, I guess not."

"Then I think you deserve a good tickling." With that

he reached over and began wiggling his fingers under her chin and down her side.

She just sat there, surprised at his sudden familiarity with her.

He stopped abruptly. "You're not ticklish," he said.

"I turned that off a long time ago," she explained.

"Why?"

"Everyone wants to tickle a cute, little red-haired girl. I just got tired of it and turned it off." She didn't mention that it was when her mam's fellas started in on the tickling that she turned it off. When she didn't respond, they quit. She'd just never bothered to turn it back on again. What was the use?

"Seems that isn't all you turned off," he said after a space of time.

"That too. It's easier this way. I don't yearn for what I can't have." That wasn't entirely true. But close enough.

The mood had gone from silly to serious, and she was grateful when he asked if she was hungry. She was.

He opened up the food box he'd hauled in from by the fire last night. They chewed on dried apple rings and agreed that a cup of tea would sure be nice. No chance of that until the rain let up, and it didn't show signs of doing so for some time.

She was heavyhearted now and wished she hadn't thought of those sad times.

"So, has anyone ever told you about Tir-nan-og, the Land of Promise?" she asked. The stories would take her away for a time. She needed that now, else she would sink into despair.

"Doesn't sound familiar," he said.

"Well, in the long time ago, the bard Oisen told about a country that neither age and death nor tears and sorrow had found. Many have gone in search of Tir-nan-og, but no one has caught more than a glimpse of it off in the horizon. Some say it's an island, some say an underwater land. But it's known to be the favorite of the fairies, so I'm certain the wee folk weave their magic around to keep it hidden and protected."

Without a word between them, Robert laid himself down and pulled her close beside him.

"It was there that Angus Og found the beautiful Caer Ormaith, who'd bewitched him by playing her harp for him in his dreams. And it was there that the wise and proud Emer sent her husband's mistress to lead him from his doom, for she knew he would listen to her and follow her to safety."

She went on, finding comfort in the old stories as she always had. Outside, the wind and rain snatched at the tent, making for a dismal day. Inside, they adventured through the lush green fields of Tir-nan-og with Cuchulain and Angus Og.

These stories were more than just a means to while the hours away. They brought back memories of being cuddled warm in bed with her dear mother. Mam would mix fanciful details of the day in with the ancient stories, and they'd laugh away the hurt and pain until there was nothing but wonder to go to sleep on. Many a night Meg'd dreamed of changelings and questioned whether she might be one herself. Those stories were her way of keeping that long ago time close. It gave her a measure of peace and comfort.

Sometimes she looked over to Robert to see if he was bored. He never seemed to be, so she kept on, using the stories to keep the drearies away.

By midmorning, the legends had worked their magic. The storm had passed over them, and Meg was ready to get out and stretch her legs. It was such a brilliant clear day that it hurt her eyes to look about. The sky was almost too blue, the trees too green. Raindrops dripped off the pine needles and splashed in the puddles below. The birds were singing for all they were worth. She felt like running barefoot down the beach.

So she did. At the far end was a rocky ledge. Without a care to how slippery it was, Meg climbed up to the top and threw her arms wide. *What a glorious day!*

Looking down, she saw Robert climbing up after her. He came and stood nearby, not touching or wanting anything more than just to enjoy the moment with her. They looked out over the lake that spread as far as a body could see.

"Isn't it something, Robert? The whole world stretched out before us, our whole lives just out there waiting. It's a pure wonder, it is."

Chapter Four

It was. But Robert didn't have the words to tell her. This woman stole his breath away, literally. One moment she held out the promise of introducing him to mysteries as ancient as time. The next, she was racing the wind with the wild exuberance of a child.

Looking over at her, he realized there was no way he could take her back to Duluth. It wasn't just that Black Jack was waiting for her. It was that Bess's was waiting as well. He couldn't stand the thought of that.

Maybe she'd never have much of a stage career. It was hard to say if that business with all the costumes and leaping about would have that wide an appeal. But she definitely didn't belong in a brothel.

The only choice was to take her with him and put her on a steamship to Chicago. It would mean dipping into company funds, and he hated to do that, but he would make arrangements for reimbursement out of his pay.

Once she realized how difficult the journey was, he

was certain she'd be more than willing to get on a steamship to civilization. It was one thing to imagine oneself on a daring adventure, quite another to live through it. As he was finding out.

"Let's get packed up," he said.

"I'm not going back to Duluth," she said firmly. "So you can just forget about that."

"We're not going back to Duluth. We're going on to Port Arthur's Landing."

She stared at him as if she wasn't certain whether he was fooling or not. "Really?"

"Really," he said.

She threw her arms around him and kissed him full on the mouth, just a quick one. It was over before the shock wore off. He sure wished he'd come to this decision last night.

"Let's go," she shouted, turning to scramble down the rocks.

Within the hour, they were back on the lake. They'd rearranged the packs so she could sit in front of him. Using the paddle he'd brought as a spare, he began teaching her how to dip it in and pull it through the water in the steady, efficient pattern that a person could keep doing all day.

He taught her to sing "Alouette," the song the voyageurs sang on their long trek across the Great Lakes. He enjoyed listening to what her Irish lilt did to the French phrases.

She told him about how the current president, Ulysses S. Grant, had a reputation for being a tippler and how when he was a general in the union Army, somebody told

President Lincoln that Grant was a drinking man. According to the story, Lincoln had told the tattler to go find out what Grant was drinking and give it to all his generals.

Robert said that liquor must have had a different effect on Grant than it did on him. It just put him to sleep.

"That's because you'd been having such a rough time of it," she assured him. "You were worn-out when you walked through Bess's door."

"It has been a dreadful couple of days," he admitted.

"Death is always a bit of a shock." She said this as if she'd had some experience with it herself.

Well, so had he. "I've dealt with death before," he said. "It was just that Inspector Parker's passing happened so unexpectedly. One minute, he was calling for order and demanding that the men, 'Cease this altercation immediately,' and the next minute, he'd toppled over with a stunned look on his face."

"What did you do?" she asked.

"I did the only thing that I could think of at the moment. I pulled the inspector's side arm and threatened to shoot the lot of them and the devil take the consequences if they didn't cease and desist."

"You were quite the hero," she said admiringly.

"Hardly," he said, although he did give himself some credit for thinking on his feet. "I'd like to think my quick action might have kept the situation under control but I think the gunshot itself had already stopped the fight."

"It's hard to say. But you did what you thought best at the time."

That was really all one could do.

"So, what other murders happened right in front of you?"

"None." *Thank God.*

"You said this wasn't the first time you'd had to deal with it." She turned and looked back over her shoulder at him as if she'd caught him making things up.

"I was referring to my mother's demise," he said.

"That wasn't a shock?"

"Hardly. She'd been threatening to kill herself on a regular basis for years."

"Whatever for?" Meg sounded shocked. But she wouldn't have been if she'd known his mother.

"Who knows? She threw herself down the stairs every time she imagined my father's attention was wandering. She cut both her wrists when she thought he'd flirted with an aunt of hers. She even tried to hang herself from a chandelier once when he stayed out all night gambling. Oddly enough, when he died, she hardly shed a tear."

"Not everyone grieves the same way," she said.

"I imagine you're right."

"My own mother lived through some discouraging times, but she never tried to kill herself. She fought for every breath, right up to the end."

He imagined Meg's mother had led a hard life. From what she'd told him earlier in the day, she'd died of consumption, and it probably wasn't in a sanitarium either. His own mother sounded like a lunatic by comparison. She had everything a woman could want or ask for, yet she still wasn't satisfied with her lot in life.

"What happened to your father?" she asked after they'd paddled in silence for a time.

"His heart gave out on him. At least that's what the physician said." He'd died in the arms of a woman half his age. In fact, two women half his age. But Robert didn't think that was worthy of mention. It was his father's dislike of business matters and fondness for merry times that'd left Robert dependent on his uncle for support. Not that his uncle Walter ever begrudged him a penny. Far from it.

"My uncle took me under his wing," he said. "As soon as I finish college, he has a position waiting for me in his shipping firm. Once I gain some experience, he intends to guide me in the direction of a political career." It sounded quite impressive, but in fact, most of the young men of his class had similar aspirations and family support.

"Well, that sounds rosy," she said. "It seems you know what your life will be twenty years from now, and I don't even know what tonight holds."

"I wish it was me holding you tonight," he said with a hopeful smile.

"All you have to do is say you'll take me west with you, and I'll make all your dreams come true." Meg looked back over her shoulder and winked at him. He nearly fell over the side.

"You're teasing me, aren't you?"

"I'll do that, too. In fact, I'll do things you've never even heard of, never even dreamed of. Haven't you ever heard about red-haired women?"

He had and it made him weak-kneed just to think about it. He was glad she'd turned back around and couldn't see the desire on him.

"What do I get for taking you as far as Port Arthur's Landing?" he asked, trying not to sound boyishly eager.

"You get me snuggled in against you every night, blowing softly in your ear, and," she turned around again, "sighing 'Take me west, Robert. Take me west.' "

Shoot. He was afraid of that.

"You're a cruel woman, Meg Reilly." And she was. Didn't she know how hard this would be for him?

"You have no idea how cruel I can be, Robert Hamilton." She spoke in a husky voice, as if being cruel was some sort of sensual experience. He wondered about that for the next few hours.

They finally pulled in at a beach and set up camp for the night. After cleaning up from their meal, Meg suggested they go for a little walk along the shore before settling in for the night. Perhaps this was what she meant by being cruel, this postponing the part of the day that he was so looking forward to.

When they returned, the water was boiling in the kettle. He poured some in the basin to shave and clean up, then took his shirt off to begin washing. When he'd finished shaving, he rolled his shoulders around in an attempt to loosen up the tightness that came from long hours at the paddle.

"Would you like a backrub?" she asked.

Robert's hope rose. "A backrub would be heavenly," he said.

Robert lay down on his bedroll. Meg straddled his back and dug her thumbs into his shoulder muscles. It was all he could do to keep from moaning. He wondered if she was the kind of woman he'd heard about, the kind that dug her fingers into a man's back in the throes of passion. He wondered if he'd ever get a chance to find out.

He could feel the muscles give way as she pushed in on the tight places with the heels of her hand, then used her fingers to knead them loose. While his back relaxed, the rest of him tightened up. In an odd way, it was rather erotic having her seated across his lower back. He wondered if it was going to lead somewhere.

"Where did you learn to give backrubs?" he asked right before she began pummeling up and down the sides of him with the flat of her hands.

"I used to rub my mam's back at night. It helped her go to sleep."

Robert knew what he felt like doing, and it wasn't sleeping. He just didn't know how to get there from here. Deciding he couldn't stand it much longer, he reached back to still her hands, then pulled her off onto the blankets and sat up next to her. Perhaps the sight of his masculine chest would excite her the same way everything about her excited him. When she didn't move, he put his arms around her to pull her to him.

"No," she said, pushing against his chest. "You promised."

"You're a cruel woman, Meg Reilly."

"I'll show you cruel, Robert," she said, then leaned over and whispered in his ear, "It's your turn."

She was right. While they were switching places, just the thought of running his fingers up and down her skin was enough to set his hands to shaking. When she inched up her shirt, revealing where her back flared out to her hips, it was all he could do to keep himself from covering every bare bit of skin with kisses. He held his breath, hoping against hope that she'd pull her shirt all the way off.

To his disappointment, she didn't. She left it bunched up around her neck, covering her arms and shielding the sides of her bosoms from his gaze. As much as he'd ached when she dug her fingers into his muscles, it was ten times worse when he ran his hands over her bare back, down the rippled indentations of her spine, across the bones of her shoulders. She allowed him to feel the sides of her breasts but not the front of them.

"Say yes, Meg," he pleaded.

"Say you'll take me west."

"I can't." Much as he wanted to at this moment, he knew it was wrong.

"Then neither can I."

"It would mean so much to me." She had no idea.

"It'd mean a lot to me, too."

"Please," he said, hating the sound of the word but not able to keep it from escaping his lips. "I want you so much."

"I can't, Robert. A deal's a deal."

He took what he could get, which was a half hour of intense pleasure caressing her back from one end to the other. He had a feeling that this was going to be the best part of the night.

It was. At the end of the backrubs, she rolled up in her quilt, and he rolled up in his bedroll.

He was so keyed up it took him hours and hours to get to sleep. It didn't seem to affect her the same way. From the sound of things, she'd dropped right off to sleep. It was a cruel world in which half the world had what the other half wanted.

Robert toyed briefly with the idea of just telling her he was going to take her west, then later going back on his word. But even the thought of doing that disgusted him. It was underhanded and dishonest. A man was known by his deeds, and that wasn't the kind of man he was.

The following days settled into a pattern. He watched her graceful back bend and turn as she paddled throughout the day. In the evening, he watched her across the fire and marveled at having his own personal Scheherazade to tell him tales in the night.

Meg was affectionate and teasing with him all day long. Every evening they rubbed each other's backs into relaxation and rolled up in their own blankets. She'd go to sleep while he lay awake wondering how much more of this he could stand before he went out of his mind. If there was a lunatic asylum in Port Arthur's Landing, he should probably sign himself in. He found he was grinding his teeth all the time now and worried that he'd flatten them out until he might never be able to eat meat again.

The tension between them didn't seem to bother Meg, or if it did, she didn't show it. She was happy and carefree as a fairy from one of her stories. He wondered if she worked charms on him at night while he slept, because every day she seemed more beautiful, more enchanting. He was being charmed, that's what it was. And he was helpless to resist.

He dreaded getting to Port Arthur's Landing and found himself pulling up earlier every evening and dawdling about getting packed up in the morning. He noticed she wasn't in any particular hurry either.

Then early one afternoon, there it was, a line of wooden buildings strung out behind a dock. Robert resisted the urge to turn the canoe around and spend just one more night out on their own.

But what would be the point? There was no sense in trying to avoid the unavoidable. Might as well face it square on.

Meg didn't say a word, not while he engaged a guard for their canoe, not while they attempted to find rooms at three different establishments, and not while they checked into the makeshift hotel that had only one remaining room to let. She stoically faced what was coming. It was unnerving. Silence was so unlike her.

"It's unfortunate that the steamship was through here just two days ago," he said over a dinner of some sort of stew.

"Isn't it though," she said, holding her mouth so tight it could almost have been sewn shut.

"The hotel proprietress assured me that this batch of adventure seekers will be geared up and gone within a few days. You'll be able to get more suitable accommodations then.

"The accommodations suit me fine," she said, not even looking up at him.

"I'll sleep on the floor tonight," he offered. Naturally, he'd be the one to sleep on the floor. The only room he'd been able to find had just one single bed in it. It would hardly be right for her to sleep on the floor.

"Suit yourself."

He ate his first bite of stew. It fell like a mouthful of mud down to the pit of his stomach.

"I don't like it any more than you do," he said finally.

"That's a comfort." But he could see it wasn't.

"Meg, you can't come with me. It's too dangerous." Why wouldn't she understand?

"Robert, you're not going to get me to agree that this is best because it isn't. You have no idea what's best for me. You've made up your mind, and that's that. You might as well stop talking about it."

She was looking straight at him now, defiance set on her face and tears pooling in her eyes. He hated the thought of sending her back to the life she'd known before, and, for a moment, his determination wavered. But the only alternative was to drag her along on a journey that was known to try the toughest of men. How could he make her understand?

"According to Hank," he said, "the Dawson Route isn't fit for man nor beast, not unless the beast has fins and flippers. It's nothing but mile after mile of swampy ground and creeks and rivers going the wrong way. The mosquitoes are so enormous that when you slap them, they slap back. They're so thick, you have to walk along waving willow branches in front of your face in order to catch a breath of air. And that doesn't even take into account the bears that are just now coming out of hibernation. It's a perilous journey, Meg."

"I tell you what a perilous journey is, Robert Hamilton. It's the one I'm making to the poor farm." Her voice was bitter, and he felt its sting.

"Why don't you look on the bright side. See this as making a fresh start?"

"Do you have any idea how many 'fresh starts' I've made?"

He shook his head. She'd told him of a few of her positions in the past, and hinted at others, but he really didn't know the total number.

"You're so naive about things, Robert. You with your nannies and your future in business and politics all arranged for you. How'd you like to be out on your own? With no Uncle Walter to bail you out of scrapes?" She was glaring at him as if all of this was his fault.

"How'd you like having to be pleasant to cranky old women who call you 'Biddy' and count the silverware whenever you leave the room? How'd you like to try to make an honest living always knowing that if your boss gets mad at you, you'll be back on the streets before you can explain your side of things? How'd you like knowing that your future depends on being healthy and young, that injury and old age are certain doom?"

"You make it all sound so bloody bleak," he said, dismayed at the venom in her voice.

"Get your head out of your arse, Robert," she said, standing up and leaning over the table at him. "It *is* bloody bleak."

Then she turned and took off, knocking chairs aside as she ran out of the restaurant. All eyes were on him, as if somehow he'd done something improper. He folded his napkin, placed it properly on the table, paid the bill, and followed her.

Naturally, she was not waiting outside the door for

him. He wandered about asking everyone if they had seen someone in a green-plaid shirt. He searched until way past dark and still hadn't found her.

At a loss over what else to do, he headed back to the hotel. It hardly seemed advisable to let her fend for herself in this outpost of ruffians and rascals. But he couldn't come up with anything to do about it. She knew where to find him if she wanted him.

Robert made his way reluctantly up the hotel stairs. His boots felt like they were lined with lead as they clumped from one step to the next. He'd grown use to Meg's teasing, laughing ways, and he did not relish spending the night alone. Even the mounting frustration of lying next to her each night like brother and sister was better than the loneliness he knew was his lot tonight. Opening the door was one of the more difficult things he'd ever done in his life.

He was surprised to see a candle flame flickering in the dark room. This rude establishment hardly seemed like the turn-down-the-covers, leave-a-chocolate-on-your-pillow sort of place.

But if he was surprised by the lit candle, he was downright shocked when he looked at what was waiting for him on the bed.

It was Meg in all her glory.

He stood there in openmouthed awe at the sight of her long slim legs, flat belly, and rounded breasts. Her glorious red hair was fanned out, framing her face. If he could have moved at all, he would've fallen to his knees in reverence before this Botticelli goddess of a woman.

"Well, it took you long enough."

"I was looking for you," he said, trying to take it all in. She was more beautiful than he'd ever imagined, and he'd imagined quite a bit.

"Well, you've found me," she said. "Are you just going to stand and stare or what?"

The "or what" appealed to Robert. He wanted to run his hands down the length of her, bury his face in her hair, feel her next to him without the barrier of clothes and quilts and covers. But where to start?

"Why don't you take off your boots," she suggested in answer to his unasked question.

He unlaced his boots and pulled off his clothes without ever taking his eyes off of her. She was magnificent. He was the luckiest man alive.

Then he stretched out next to her, knowing he wanted it all but not knowing where to start.

Chapter Five

He slid his arm underneath her and kissed the side of her neck. Tingles ran down Meg's spine. Then his lips moved to that hidden place behind her ear, and the tingling went all the way to her toes. He rubbed his cheek against hers. She felt just the softest bit of stubble and smiled, remembering that he hadn't yet had a chance for his nightly shaving ritual this evening. She turned in his arms and, drawing his face to hers, kissed him for all she was worth. A floating feeling carried her away.

She'd waited forever for this man, and she'd just realized it a few hours ago. Robert was honorable and goodhearted and honest as they come. If she lived to be a hundred, she'd always regret not loving with him. Her mother had always told her to hold out for a special one for that first time. Robert was special, there was no doubt about it. She knew she wouldn't be with him for the rest of her life, nor even the rest of the week, more than likely. But if she passed by the chance to have Robert for her first lover, she'd always regret it. She knew that as sure as she knew which way the sun came up in the morning.

He gently pulled her lower lip in between his, and she ran her hands down his chest and around to his back, where she dug her fingers into his bunched muscles. She arched back at the sheer wonder of it all. They ran their fingertips over one another as if they were both blind and had just found out there was someone else in the world after all.

For a time, they mirrored each other's movements. When she touched his spine, he touched hers. When she squeezed, so did he. And when she ran her fingers lightly up his sides, he did the same to hers.

They touched and teased and lost all track of time. At one point he announced that he was going to kiss every inch of her body, and she shivered in delicious anticipation. She wanted this to go on forever and couldn't wait to see what came next.

"Sweetheart, you're going to have to help me here," he whispered into her ear. "This is my first time."

"Mine too," she whispered back, pleased to hear that he had saved himself for her.

The kissing and fondling came to an immediate halt, and she felt him stiffen up next to her.

"What?" he asked. "What did you just say?"

"I said this is my first time, too," she said, and placed a kiss on the center of his chest.

"What do you mean this is your first time?" he said, putting his hands on either side of her face and pulling her head back so he could look down at her.

She looked up but, try as she might, couldn't make out his features in the shadows.

"Are you a virgin?" he asked, sounding a great deal more astonished than she thought the situation called for.

"Well, for a few more minutes," she said, adrift in the deliciousness of it all. "Maybe not even that long," she added in a flirty voice.

But he wasn't flirting back. "What were you doing at that bawdy house then?"

"Same thing you were doing, Robert. Only I was getting paid for it." *Why did he have to bring that up now? Talking about it made the fine feelings fade away.*

"You mean you were a maiden, yet you still took a job there?" He sounded both astonished and disapproving.

She tried to lighten the mood. "I still am a maiden, but I'm willing to make a change in my situation. Unless, of course," she said, tickling his sides, "you'd rather talk about all the other positions I've had in the past. But I have to warn you, it may take a while. I've had my share of jobs over the years, you know."

He reached down and stilled her hands between his.

"Do you mean to tell me that you've never done this with a man before?"

"And from the looks of things, I'm not going to be doing it with one now either," she said, frustrated as the mood between them took on a serious tone. "Come on, Robert." She wanted to recapture the passion and playfulness they'd had between them just a few moments ago. "You've known all along that I worked at Bess's, why are you making so much out of it now?"

"I didn't know all along that you were a maiden, Meg,"

he said, as solemn as if he was accusing her of murder. "That makes a big difference. Your first time should be special, not just rolling around on a musty mattress with anyone."

"And just when did you get appointed to be my guardian angel?" she said, struggling to remove her hands from beneath his.

"Meg, don't be angry," he said, hanging on to her fingers and pressing them together between them as if he was going to lead her in a prayer.

"It's your first time, too, and I notice the musty mattress isn't bothering you any."

"But it's different with a man. I'm not saving myself for marriage," he said. Then added, trying too hard to be funny, "It's just that all the girls I know are."

"I suppose you think I should be." She yanked her hands away from his and wiped the moisture from her eyes with the backs of her wrists. *Why did he have to go and spoil it?*

"Meg, please." He kissed her forehead, and she brushed it off.

"Just go to sleep if that's the way you feel about it, Robert." Her mind was filled with images of the young women he was probably used to—the ones with maids to pull their corset strings and pour their afternoon tea. Next to them, she probably looked like an old cat, and a mangy one at that.

She tried to summon up enough anger to keep the tears away. "Maybe I'll save myself for marriage, too."

But it was no use. Meg couldn't help herself. A sob burst forth, then another. She pressed her lips together and choked them back. If this wasn't pathetic, she surely wouldn't know what was. Here she finally offered her virtue to a man only to be turned down and humiliated in the process.

"Meg, don't take it like that." He tried to wrap his arms around her.

"Go sleep on the floor," she said bitterly, shrugging off his touch. She scooted as far away as she could without falling off the bed. "Your notions of what's proper and what's not are just a wee bit ridiculous."

"I hardly think it's ridiculous to sully a good woman for a moment's passing pleasure," he said, sounding all righteous. "I appreciate what you're offering to me, Meg, but I just can't accept it. It wouldn't be right."

She thrilled at knowing he thought she was a good woman. Then her spirits sank when she realized what a fragile notion his opinion of her was based on. Obviously, there were feelings between them. But should they act upon these feelings, he would regard her as a fallen woman, someone hardly worthy of his affections. *Damned if I do and damned if I don't. Why don't things ever work out for me?*

It was enough to make the angels weep.

"Go to sleep, Robert," she said as she struggled to wrap a blanket around her. "The sun'll be up before you know it."

"Meg, I wish you'd try to understand."

"Oh, I understand better than you know."

She gave him a good shove, and he tumbled off the bed. *Good riddance.* "Bastard," she hissed.

The whole situation was loony. Here she'd hung on to

her virtue when a lot of other women would've just said, "Who cares?" Now, when she'd found the one she'd been saving herself for, he wouldn't touch her because of some silly rules about virgins and gentlemanly behavior.

One of these days he'd regret treating her like this. But it would be too late then. Who did he think he was, anyway?

But it sounded hollow even as she said it. She knew that with a gentleman like Robert she didn't stand a chance of more than just a casual tumble. But she would've settled for that. Just once, she would've settled for that. But oh no, he was too high-and-mighty for her.

He shuffled around in the dark until he finally got settled on the floor.

"I'm sorry," he said. Which only made her heart ache worse.

But she couldn't go to sleep, not with him being this close. She'd have to learn to sleep without feeling his arms around her, without hearing his heart beat against her ear. But she didn't have to learn that tonight.

"Come up here," she said, resigning herself to the situation.

He stretched out beside her on top of the blankets. She burrowed her head in next to his chest and smoothed her cheek against his soft, downy hair. She loved his smell. Usually, she found the sweaty, sour smell of men repulsive, but Robert's scent was different. It reminded her of a puppy's breath, sweet and unspoiled.

Wanting the taste of him in her mouth again, she reached up for a kiss, but stopped when she realized that his cheeks were wet with tears, just as hers were.

"Promise me," she asked.

"Anything."

"Promise me that you'll wait until you find the one. Don't just take up with any floozy who'll agree to bed you. Wait for the right one. Promise?"

"I give you my word," he said softly.

They held on to each other for dear life. She didn't know why he was so sorrowful unless it was for his own precious honor, and he still had that. But then, she didn't know why she was crying either, unless it was for her independence, which she still had plenty of.

Maybe they were mourning all those things that might have been but rarely are.

Sunrise found them exhausted, drained by sadness as much as lack of sleep. They ate breakfast in silence, and she walked with him down to the steamship office and stood by while he purchased a ticket for her on the ship due in two weeks' time.

They went to a dry goods store, where he tried to buy her a dress, but she told him not to bother as she wasn't interested. She'd grown used to wearing pants and wasn't of a mind to switch back to those cumbersome skirts.

While buying supplies for the next leg of his journey, he met up with a group of men who were taking off for Winnipeg later in the day. He asked their advice on what to take, and, after a time, they asked if he would like to join them. They seemed to be a sturdy, honest bunch, and it was good that Robert wouldn't be traveling through the wilderness alone.

He was such a sweet man, but he labored under the notion that he could handle anything that came along. Time would teach him about human limitations. Knowing that brought her a sudden sadness. She hoped the lessons wouldn't be too hard.

His invincible attitude was endearing. But it was also a danger to him. So it was good that he was traveling with men who'd had more experience in the world.

The goblins must be having a grand time of it today. Here she was, mooning over a man who couldn't wait to get away from her.

She helped him carry his supplies to the canoe. Then they took everything out and repacked it. He was leaving a number of things behind. As much as he loved biscuits, he'd decided that the weight of the cast-iron Dutch oven would be a hindrance on the portages ahead. The canvas tent was traded for a much smaller and lighter one.

He left room for the supplies of the man who would be in the canoe with him. The lake crossings would be easy enough, but the rivers all ran against the direction they were going. It would be much easier with two paddling.

As Meg helped him rearrange things so they'd fit, she tried to keep from thinking about this being the end of it all. This was the last time she'd see him push back that one stubborn strand of hair that was forever flopping over his forehead, the last time her heart would race in response to his wide, innocent smile, the last time her soul would sing at the sound of his laughter.

How could she bear it? How could she go to sleep without his arms to hold away the night? How could she face tomorrow and all the tomorrows after it without him?

You're carrying things a wee bit too far, aren't you,

girl? You've lived for years without knowing he even existed.

It reminded her of when she'd found out about strawberries. Before she'd tasted one, she'd never given it so much as a moment's thought. But ever since she'd bit into her first strawberry, she'd always longed for another. In fact, each spring she made a point of eating her fill of strawberries at least once. And every one she bit into was part of that search for that perfect strawberry, the berry that would amaze her with its juicy sweet strawberry flavor.

There were lots of fine things in life. Robert was just one of them. Though the need for him flowed strong through her now, there would be others. Just like there were other strawberries.

It was just that he was such a fine one.

Her thoughts were interrupted when he pressed a flat packet into her hands.

"I've paid for the room until the steamship gets here," he said. "This is for food and whatever else you might need."

She looked down at what was obviously a stack of bills.

"I know it's not much, but it should see you through. I wish there was more I could do for you, Meg." He was shifting from one foot to the next, awkward and ill at ease with their parting.

She felt removed from it all, as if she was standing afar watching some other woman say good-bye to him. She wondered if he'd kiss her. Or if she'd kiss him back. He didn't.

In fact, he didn't seem to know what to do. He was obviously ready to go, so why didn't he?

"Just go," she said finally to ease the awkwardness between them.

"I'm sorry I can't take you with me," he said. "I've written my uncle's address down for you in case you're ever in dire straits."

Why would I be needing that? Surely, his rich uncle wouldn't be helping me out of a bind.

It felt like someone had planted a boot on her chest, and every word out of his mouth pushed the heel in harder. If only he would stop talking. She could hardly breathe as it was.

What is he waiting for?

"Go on," she said, surprised that she found enough air to get those two words out.

"I'll miss you, Meg."

Aye, but nothing like I'll miss you, Robert. I doubt I'll see the likes of you again.

He reached out to touch her, and she stepped back. There was no way she could keep the tears away if she let him put a hand on her.

"Well, they're waiting for me. I better get going."

"Aye."

"You're not making this easy, Meg."

"It's not an easy thing to do, Robert."

She could see the guilt on his face and wondered if the anguish showed on hers.

"Write and let me know how things turn out."

"Why bother with the writing? I can tell you right now. On my way back to the hotel, I'll be meeting up with a wealthy gentleman who's crazy about women who wear men's pants and can paddle their own canoe. He'll beg me to marry him and move with him to his grand home in New York, where I'll live out my days taking tea with the gentry."

"I bet you will at that." There was just a glimmer of a smile shining on his face.

"Go on. Your life is waiting for you, and mine for me."

Because she couldn't bear to stand there and watch him leave, she turned and walked away herself. But she hadn't gone far when the urge to see him just one more time overwhelmed her. She couldn't stop herself from turning around for one last look.

His red coat stood out against the cream-colored canvas and the blue-green water. His wide shoulders moved in that rhythm she'd grown so used to these many days. Every paddle splash tore at her heart, until she found herself waiting for that final tug that would rip it in two.

Warm, thick tears followed one another in a steady stream. She didn't bother to wipe them away, just let them fall off her cheek onto the ground. Fairy tears, her mam would've called them. If you let tears of sorrow fall to the ground, they would turn into fairies. Well, there would be enough for a merry time of it tonight.

Just before he glided around that point of land protecting the bay, Robert turned and their eyes found one another. Long after he'd disappeared, Meg stood watching where he'd been.

So this was it. Not only had she seen the last of the

finest man she'd ever met, she'd seen the last of her best chance west.

She felt like swearing but didn't know any strong enough words.

Chapter Six

Her spirits sagging, Meg made her way back to the hotel. She threw herself on the bed and cursed her fate until sunset, then cursed Robert way into the night.

Dawn was starting to steal away the dark when it hit her that Robert was not the only man heading west in this town. She sat straight up at the thought of it. Here she'd been so distraught over his leaving, she hadn't realized that the town was full of men heading west.

With her hair braided and tucked up under her hat, Meg was out on the street within minutes. On her way to the steamship station, she kept an eye out for groups of men who seemed to be gearing up for a trek. She decided that two bunches looked like they knew what they were doing.

The steamship clerk reluctantly refunded her ticket, and she walked over to the first group of men. Keeping her voice low so she sounded as well as looked like a man, she asked about going along with them. They were agreeable, but they weren't going all the way to Winnipeg. They planned to "follow the color" in looking for gold deposits and be back in Port Arthur's Landing by fall.

The second group was heading to Winnipeg, but there was some reluctance about taking another man along. Finally, they agreed that as long as she brought her own gear and provisions, she could go with them. She was back in an hour, ready to go.

She'd introduced herself as Matt and decided that she'd best keep to herself during the journey. A woman alone in the wilderness with a group of men was probably a poor idea. She'd bought a pistol and ammunition at the dry goods store and kept both in her jacket pockets. It wouldn't be much protection with five of them and one of her, but it was the best she could come up with. They should be in Winnipeg within a couple weeks at most. Surely, she could manage to hold her own until then.

She had misgivings about this venture, but then she'd had misgivings about a lot of things in her life. Some of the things she felt best about had turned out terrible, so there was no telling ahead of time.

Since they were paddling upstream, they were all exhausted at the end of the day. There was little energy or reason to do more than grab a bite to eat and go to sleep, for which Meg was grateful.

The portage across to the first lake was knee-buckling. Meg wasn't certain how many of these trips she could endure. But the trip across the lake was an easy day, and they camped early that night at a spot that had obviously been used by previous travelers. More than likely, Robert himself had been at this very spot a day or so ago.

That cheered her up. No doubt, she'd be seeing him in Winnipeg if not before. She whiled away long hours of paddling by imagining whether she'd spurn him and go on her merry way or throw her arms around him and promise him undying devotion. She knew he had feelings for her but was just too honorable to act on them. Surely, once she was already out west, there'd be no need to send her packing.

Meg sort of thought they might catch up with him, but they didn't. They never even caught sight of him camping across a lake.

She grew weary of the endless rounds of paddling and packing parcels between one spot and another. They settled into a routine. Except for some grumbling about how she wasn't big enough to carry the loads they could, for the most part the men paid little attention to her.

She avoided the pissing contests the men had by pretending to have diarrhea and needing to go off in the bushes at every stop. She always made a point of shaving every evening, ignoring the teasing about her having little more than peach fuzz to remove. They weren't the sharpest tacks in the box, but sooner or later they would start to wonder why she never sprouted any whiskers.

They were a day out of Lower Fort Garry and two days out of Winnipeg when they found her out.

Her downfall was deciding that she couldn't enter the fort smelling like she hadn't bathed in weeks, which she hadn't.

Meg took off up the river to a shallow pool they'd

passed a while earlier. Since none of the men ever seemed inclined to wash up, she wasn't worried about any of them suddenly deciding it was time to bathe. She was midway through sudsing herself when one of the men walked around the bend in the river.

"What the hell?" he shouted out, bringing the others running.

She raced for her clothes and had her jacket on and her pistol out before they got there. The jacket barely reached the top of her thighs, and she was keenly aware of the interest the men were taking in her bare legs. Since she'd not had time to button up, she held the jacket closed with her left hand and her pistol in her right. Her heart was pounding a mile a minute and her breath was racing even faster than that.

"She won't shoot," said one of them.

"Don't bet on it, bucko." She let loose of her jacket and used both hands to steady the pistol.

It was a standoff. They all stood there drooling and staring. Meg's stomach clutched in fear as if someone had tied a rope around her middle and was jerking at the knot. Bile rolled up into her mouth. She didn't bother to swallow it down, just spit it out on the ground as it came up. It left a nasty taste, but she couldn't be worried about that now.

"Just calm down, now. We ain't going to hurt you," said the thick-lipped man she'd been uneasy about all along.

"You're right about that," she said.

"Why didn't you tell us you were a woman?" another of them asked.

"We should've known when we saw that long red hair of hers," said a third one. "Why didn't one of us figure it out before now?"

Meg didn't answer. Her hands were freezing cold, and her mind was jumping from one idea to the next, trying to think of a way out of this predicament.

A rough-talking man who had been going on for days about how he hoped there would be enough whores to go around when they got to Winnipeg stepped forward.

"Now, missy . . ." he started in.

She pressed the trigger. His hat flew off and rolled on the ground.

"Damn," she said. "I missed."

She'd been aiming over his head, but this stopped him in his tracks which is what she wanted anyway. He reached up and felt his head to see if he'd been hit. The rest of them turned to look in his direction, then back to hers.

"I'll have to work on my aim. Now, all of you, start marching in a line back to camp," she ordered in the voice she'd worked on when she was a schoolmarm. It seemed to work better on this group. Perhaps it was the gun. She should've thought of that when she was teaching.

They all headed back without any further instructions. Meg grabbed her pants and her moccasins and followed at a distance. Either they had to leave or she did, and she couldn't decide which would be best.

If she left, they'd probably follow her and, being stronger paddlers and more of them, they'd probably catch her.

If she made them leave, they'd probably double back and she'd be in the same predicament again.

What she wouldn't give for a Mountie right about now.

"Throw my gear and my bedroll over in that first canoe," she told them once they'd reached their camp. She wasn't going anywhere without that quilt.

They looked back and forth, waiting for someone to make a move. She pulled the hammer back on her pistol. At the sound of the click, the rough-talker finally worked up the nerve to grab her things and pitch them into a canoe.

"Now, all of you stand back," she ordered as she walked over next to the canoe and dumped in her pants and moccasins.

"She won't be able to get us all," said the thick-lipped one.

"I'll get enough of you to make it worth my while," she told him. "How many of you are willing to take a bullet in the belly over a fight for something that there'll be plenty of in a day's time." She aimed the gun directly at his middle. There'd be no reason to miss this time.

"Since you put it that way," he said, backing up a step. The rest of them followed suit.

Keeping her pistol pointed at them and putting her left hand on the canoe, she waded out in the water and walked the canoe out to a sandbar, where she was able to get in and still keep an eye on the men.

During that moment she was getting in, the rough-talking one started toward her. She let off another shot, kicking the dirt up in front of his feet. He froze in his tracks.

"Missed again," she growled, putting both hands on

the gun, but no one else seemed inclined to move in her direction. "If I ever see any of you again," she called out, "I'm shooting to kill."

No one moved, so she guessed they believed her. Just to be on the safe side, she shot a hole in each of the remaining canoes. That would keep them busy for a while.

Meg reloaded, put the gun back in her pocket, and picked up a paddle. She paddled steadily on through the night, grateful that it was almost a full moon so she could see to miss the rocks, snags, and sandbars in the river. Fortunately, she was headed in the same direction the river was.

As dawn was stealing the darkness away, she saw Lower Fort Garry rise up above the riverbank ahead. She'd been so worked up last night, that she was just now starting to get tired. The thought of trying to explain to a bunch of army men what she was doing out here all alone convinced her to just keep going. She'd get her second wind before long and be down to Winnipeg before she knew it.

The real reason, of course, was that she would catch up with Robert. No doubt, he'd stopped at the fort before going on to Winnipeg. If she kept on, she stood a better chance of meeting up with him before he and Hank took off across the prairie.

It turned out to be a beautiful morning. Except for a few scattered, cottony clouds, the sky was clear and blue as a robin's egg. By late afternoon, she arrived at a collection of buildings that had to be Winnipeg. She beached the canoe, grabbed her bedroll, and started toward the main street.

Being a woman was always such a stumbling block to success. Except for this last bit of trouble, she'd done a fair job of passing herself off as a man. Disguised like this, she was sure she stood a good chance of getting out west. The more she thought about it, the better she liked the idea. Certainly, no one would question her desire to seek out a frontier life. Nearly every man she'd ever met talked about it, some constantly.

As she headed into town, she practiced walking the head-back stride that men walked, not that silly women's shuffle that was so easy to fall into. It struck her that she'd not worn a corset since she'd left Duluth and realized how grand it was to be able to take a deep breath whenever she felt like it. There were a lot of things she found appealing about living as a man. She wondered why she'd never thought of doing it before.

Winnipeg was certainly a disappointment. Somehow, Meg had been expecting more. The city was nothing but one wide, muddy street lined with shanties and saloons on either side.

Two ragged men were wrestling in the middle of the street over what appeared to be a bottle of whiskey slowly draining into the muck beneath it.

Weary onlookers stared at her, but didn't wave or nod or give any sign of welcome. The whole place and everyone in it looked pathetic. This was the Winnipeg she'd heard so much about for weeks on end?

One of the ramshackle buildings might have been a dry goods store, it was hard to tell. But other than that, none of the shacks appeared to be any sort of recognizable business such as a bank or a church or anything.

It wasn't until she got to the end of the street that she even saw a building with a sign on it. The paint was peeling off, but from what she could make out, it seemed that this establishment was known as Carina's.

Carina's what? she wondered. She hoped it was Carina's Restaurant. The smell of roasted meat and fried potatoes coming from the building was reminding her that it had been ages since she'd had a decent meal.

The mouth watering smell led her up to the open doorway where she watched a roomful of grimy men eat like this was the last food they ever hoped to see and they were worried that there wouldn't be enough to go around. They were stabbing at the meat with hunting knives. Few even bothered putting the meat on their plates, preferring just to leave it on the ends of their knives so they could rip off hunks with their teeth. It was a wonder someone didn't cut a lip, slash a nose, or put an eye out.

There were two huge bowls of greasy fried potatoes that they grabbed at with their bare hands, ignoring the forks and plates scattered about the table. The only food that was passed around was the bread piled high on the cutting board. Slices of it were tossed down the table as men yelled, "Don't hog it all," and "Throw me some of that bread down here."

As the men chewed and talked at the same time, food spilled out of their mouths, and what didn't cling to their beards fell to the table and floor. Meg's empty stomach rolled in disgust.

One man wiped a dirty finger through the butter and spread it on a piece of bread. When he noticed her standing there watching, he said, "I'll wash twice next time," and flashed a friendly grin. The man was missing so many teeth, he looked like a jack-o'-lantern.

A tall, sturdy woman in an amazingly white apron carried a skillet full of fried potatoes to the table. A man with a scar across his cheek grabbed at her. Without missing a beat, she dumped the potatoes into a bowl, then thumped him a good one over the head with the iron skillet. He sat stunned for a moment, then dropped like a rock. No one even noticed when he toppled off the bench and fell to the floor.

"You want something to eat," she yelled in Meg's direction, "then sit down."

Meg sat.

Then the woman flashed a smile so wide that it brought out two half-moon creases on either cheek before it disappeared.

"Don't give Carina any backtalk," warned one of the men.

Meg was determined not to say a word. Hungry as she was after the endless hardtack and jerky, and enticing as the aroma of the meat was, her stomach lurched at the very thought of touching any food on this table. For certain, she would do without butter.

She wondered if she shouldn't wash up or at least remove her hat. But as no one else had taken the time to do either, she imagined that it would only be thought of as taking on airs and decided to let it pass.

Carina left and came back with a platter piled with meat and a plate stacked with bread. She sat both in front of Meg, and shouted out a warning, "You boys leave this alone, you hear?"

Meg wondered if she was supposed to eat all of this by herself. Her question was answered a moment later when the hostess grabbed a plate from between the elbows of the nearest man and shoved it in front of her.

"They can just share," Carina said.

"No, really," Meg said in dismay, as she pushed the plate back in the direction it came from. "I couldn't take a man's plate away from him."

"The way these pigs eat, they don't even need plates. But if that's the way you want it." The woman said this as if it made no difference to her, she was willing to humor this particular person. "I'll go see if I got another plate back in the kitchen."

As she shuffled off, she hollered out, "You boys leave him alone, you hear."

Meg doubted that "the boys" heard a word she said above the chomping, slurping, and belching. It was the most disgusting display of sober behavior she'd ever seen.

Carina disappeared through the doors just as a nearby man choked on a piece of meat. He was gagging and gasping for air and not a soul paid him any attention. Carina came back in and gave him a good slug in the back. Otherwise, he might have fallen unnoticed to the floor like the scarred man who'd been hit with the skillet.

"I have the darnedest time teaching my boys any table manners," she said.

Meg was appalled. There were almost a dozen of them, each one worse than the next. They did act like overgrown, misbehaving boys but surely, Carina's own son hadn't tried to grope her.

"Are these all your sons?" she asked, almost reluctant to know the answer to that question.

"No, just three of them are mine by birth," said the woman, pointing to the end of the table.

Meg wondered which of the slack-jawed, slope-browed, bearded boys belonged to her. Not for the first time she questioned the joys of motherhood.

"But they've all been out in the woods too long to remember their table manners. I sort of expect they'll shape up in a week or two."

Meg wouldn't bet on it.

On the plus side, their peculiar eating habits meant that they were all finished in no time.

Amazingly enough, one of them said, "Excuse me," as he stood up to leave the table.

"Sit right back down," ordered Carina in her no-nonsense manner. "I've made up some klappgroet, and anyone who's cleaned his plate can have some."

Of course their plates were clean. Some of the men hadn't even touched theirs, preferring to eat their food right off their knives and out of their hands. Apparently, they'd been saving the plates in hopes of dessert.

Carina walked around the room with a large bowl full of thick, wine-red pudding and plopped a large wooden spoonful in the middle of each of their plates. Meg half expected to see them lower their faces and lap at it like dogs. To her amazement, they passed around spoons and ate like gentlemen.

"Berry syrup and boiled wheat middlings," the man nearest her explained as she stared down the table. Although, in truth, it wasn't the pudding she was wondering over, but rather the change in the men's behavior.

One of them even made a stab at polite conversation. The man missing every other tooth asked what had brought her to Winnipeg.

"Heading west," she mumbled, taking care to keep her voice low.

"You ought to catch up with that Mountie, that's where he's going," said the man missing most of his teeth.

Meg's breath stopped. "How long ago was he through here?" she asked, her voice hoarse from trying to make words out of so little air.

"I doubt he's left," said the scar-faced fellow. "He's probably down at the saloon still asking everyone what they know about 'conditions.'"

This brought on a round of guffaws and food spurting across the table.

"Wonder if he's going up to Swan River to ask about 'conditions'?"

The hilarity moved a notch higher.

"Never seen the likes of it," said the gap-toothed man once he'd recovered enough to speak. "It's the unlikeliest place you ever heard of for having a headquarters."

"What's the matter with it?" she asked, forgetting to keep her voice low. They didn't seem to notice.

"First off, it's way up north. There's not a damn thing nearby or ever likely to be nearby," said a man who shook his hand in the air like he was scolding someone.

Meg noticed he was missing both a thumb and a forefinger. "They built it up on top of a hill all covered with huge rocks and known to be infested with snakes. There ain't a tree in sight to block the wind nor to build with either. Every solid log had to be hauled across the prairie and up that damn hill."

"That place is the most unlikely spot I ever saw for humans to live," added another.

"Probably built it up on top of a hill so they could catch all the north wind they possibly could," said one wit. That brought on a round of table-pounding laughter.

"Don't know why they built a fort, if you could call it that, way out there. Seems like it'd make a whole lot more sense to build it where it was needed, like around where people live or over closer to the Montana Territory. At least there's a telegraph line there," said the scarred man who'd recovered from his conk on the noggin and had returned to the table.

"Now, Bill," said another one. "You know they put it way up there 'cause they're going to build the Canadian Pacific Railway through that part of the country."

"You gotta be shittin' me," said a man who then let out a long, sputtering fart, much to the delight of his companions. When the merriment died down, he continued, "They ain't going to be building no railroad up to Swan River. Who the hell wants to go up there?"

"If you ask me, I say they should use Fort Whoop-up. Now that's a prettier place for the headquarters and it's already built good and sturdy," said a slow-talking man from the other end of the table. He seemed to be the deep thinker of the crowd. Though the men had interrupted one another throughout the conversation, they waited patiently while this man paused to scratch an armpit before continuing. "More to do there, too. More people and such, and it's right on the whiskey trail."

Heads around the table nodded in agreement at the wisdom of his suggestion.

"I don't believe you could even grow a garden up at that Swan River fort," said the slow-talking thinker. "Too many rocks."

"I understand that the Mounties are going to put an end to the whiskey trading in these parts," said someone.

"Well, good luck up at Swan River. Anyone that lives up there is either drunk or needs to be," said the thinker from the other end of the table.

This brought on another round of wild hooting.

"Now you boys quit making fun of those Mounties," Carina said with a wide wave of her wooden spoon that caused a couple of the men nearby to duck. "They're doing the best they can."

She herded her boys out on the porch and sent them off with the advice to stay sober, get in early, and behave themselves if they knew what was good for them. Meg seriously doubted any of them did.

"You'll be wanting a room, I suspect," Carina said as the rowdy bunch disappeared down the street.

"I couldn't be staying here," Meg said, alarmed at the thought of her "boys" returning from a night of carousing.

"Oh, they'll be all right," said Carina. "They're just a little rough around the edges."

"They are that," she agreed. She'd seen packs of dogs with better table manners.

"You aren't a man, are you?" said the plainspoken woman.

"No," said Meg hesitantly, concerned about what might be coming.

"I didn't think so," Carina said, crossing her arms in front of her and looking like she intended to get to the bottom of this right here and now.

"So how come you're dressed like one?"

"It was easier traveling this way," said Meg.

"I won't argue with you there," said Carina as she bent to stack up the plates. "I can make up a pallet for you in a little room I have off the kitchen. Will that suit you?"

"I'm not wanting to put you to any trouble," said Meg.

"It's no trouble," she said, "and if you don't mind pumping water and carting in the wood yourself, you can have a hot bath, too," she said.

A bath would be heavenly. Meg shuddered at recalling what a cold dip in a river had nearly cost her a day ago and felt just the start of pleasure at knowing that tonight the water wouldn't be ice-cold and Carina would be guarding the door.

"Where's the pump?" she asked.

For the next half hour she carried water and wood to the stove.

"How did you know I wasn't a man?" Meg asked Carina on one of her trips in with an armload of wood.

"In the first place, your hair is all stuffed up under that hat," she said. "A man's hair would've been hanging every which way." She paused before backing through the door. "Besides, after being on the trail for a time, if you'd have been a man, you'd have stopped off at a grogshop before looking for a meal or a place to spend the night."

She was probably right about that.

Carina helped her drag the high-backed tub from the porch into a small room off the kitchen. She told Meg to be careful about splashing water, as she'd be sleeping in this room tonight.

"Would you cut my hair off?" Meg asked Carina while they were waiting for the water to heat up.

"Why, you don't want to do that," the woman said, sounding as if this was a foolish notion Meg would soon regret. "A woman's hair is her crowning glory."

"Well, my crowning glory is nothing but a bother and a mess. I've got a long summer ahead of me, and it will be a lot easier if my hair isn't hanging every which way."

"You're doing this just so you'll look more like a man, aren't you?"

"I'll be safer if I look like a man."

"Sugar, don't fool yourself. In the first place, it'll take more than short hair to fool most folks, and in the second place, women are so few and far between out here, that we're treated special."

"I'm not wanting men to bow and scrape for me. I just want to go out west, and I believe I'll stand a better chance of talking someone into taking me along if they think I'm a man."

"You want to go out west?" Carina asked, sounding as if she thought this was an odd idea. "Whatever for?"

"Opportunities," said Meg. "The same reason everyone else wants to go west." What was so odd about that?

"Just what sort of opportunities are you hoping to come across?"

"I'd like to go on stage—melodramas, dancing, singing, and so forth," Meg said.

"You'll be wanting your hair for that."

"It'll grow," Meg said, irritated with the way Carina was telling her what she should and shouldn't do with her own hair. "Now, will you cut it, or shall I cut it myself?"

"If you ask me, this is pure foolishness. But if that's what you want."

"That's what I want," insisted Meg. Seeing a bread knife lying across a cutting board, she snatched it up, pulled her one long braid to the side and proceeded to saw back and forth until she'd cut clear through.

"*Min Gud,* girl," said Carina. "Once you decide on something, you don't let much moss grow, do you?"

"What in the world?"

Meg froze. It was Robert's voice. She would have known it anywhere.

She turned and there he was, standing in the doorway with Hank right behind him. They were both gawking at her like she was an exhibit in a sideshow.

Relief at seeing him traded places back and forth with anger over his leaving her behind. Her ire was getting the upper hand.

"You cut your hair." Robert said, sounding as shocked as if she'd stripped naked and whitewashed "Go to hell," across her fanny.

"Give him first prize, Hank," said Meg as she pulled a chunk of hair from the side of her face and began to saw away at it.

Carina put her hands over the knife and pulled it away. "Here, let me," she said quietly. She took the knife to a cupboard and exchanged it for a pair of scissors.

"Your hair was so beautiful." Robert said this with the stunned disappointment of a child being told the cookies are all gone and they'd be eating liver for dessert.

"It still is," Meg said, tossing him the cut-off braid. "You can keep it as a remembrance of me if you like."

He caught it easily enough, but acted as disgusted as if she'd tossed him a dead rat. He let it fall to the floor, then he turned and, without another word, walked back outside.

"Meg Reilly," said Hank after a moment, "you're an amazing woman." He doffed his hat and followed Robert.

"Guess they decided not to have supper after all," said Carina, continuing to snip away at Meg's hair.

"Was that why they were here?" Meg asked, feeling more than a little let-down. Somehow, she'd assumed they heard she was in town and had rushed over to say hello.

Surprised or not, Robert did not seem at all pleased to see her. She realized she wasn't exactly overjoyed at the sight of him either. Whatever had been between them a few weeks ago was obviously gone. *Well, good riddance. Love, especially one-way love, is nothing but a nuisance.* They were both better off being irritated and angry with one another.

"I imagine you're the woman that's got that young Mountie all tied up in knots," Carina said.

Meg pulled away and looked back up at her. *How does this woman know about me?*

"He got in a day or so ago, and Hank took him over to check on the horses and have a few drinks. I guess before the evening was over, he was crying in his beer about this red-haired woman he'd had a falling-out with. According to Hank, all he talked about all night long was your hair, and how well you paddled a canoe, and how he regretted sending you back to Chicago but he really had no choice in the matter."

"Oh," said Meg. So he hadn't just gone off and forgotten her. Well, that was good news.

"He'll be back," Carina said, giving Meg's head a final pat. "Don't you worry."

Meg ran her hands through what was left of her hair. It felt strange, but she imagined she'd get used to it. She already liked having the weight of it gone. Twisting her head back and forth, she marveled at the feel of her hair flying through the air, at how light her head was now. First her corset, now her hair. Soon she'd be so free of things that weighed her down, she could probably just fly wherever she wanted to go.

The kettles of water were steaming, and Carina helped her haul them over and fill up the tin tub. She handed Meg a jar of soap and stack of towels before closing the door behind her.

Meg stood there, anticipating the soothing warmth and wondering whether to jump in while it was scalding hot and enjoy a longer soak, or pour in some cool water first. The second way would make it more tolerable to start out with but would bring her bath to a chilly end sooner. She decided in favor of hopping in and taking the risk of having to jump right back out again.

It was heaven, pure heaven. The hot water melted the muscles in her back and shoulders, and the steam filled her lungs and made her drowsy. She ducked under the water and came up to suds her hair and down her whole body with the soft lemon soap Carina had left her. She loved that smell and was soon wishing for a cold glass of lemonade to drink as she soaked her cares away in her lemon-scented bath.

"I wonder what the rich people are doing tonight," she said, letting out a deep sigh. Whatever it was, it could never be as grand as this.

Much as she hated to spoil her lovely soak, the thought of tomorrow weighed heavily on her mind. On the trek out, she'd whiled away the hours daydreaming about what her first meeting again with Robert would be like. At times she'd imagined she would just ignore him, show him a thing or two. He, of course, would eventually realize he was wrong about her. Other times, she saw the two of them running to each other's arms, grateful to have a second chance. Though she knew Robert didn't want her out here, in the back of her mind she'd held on to the hope that he would at least be pleased to see her. Apparently, he was not.

Well, so what? Let him be his old hoity-toity self. Who cares? Men are like streetcars. There will be another one along in ten minutes. Why, I've met at least a dozen already tonight.

This thought offered little comfort. Though Carina might think of "her boys" as merely poorly mannered, they didn't get those scars and missing thumbs from playing frog-in-the-middle. Placing her life in the hands of the likes of them would be dangerous folly.

She didn't hold any hope that the men at Fort Garry would be much better. In her experience, a uniform turned a man into a bully. There were exceptions, of course. It didn't seem to have that effect on Robert. But then he was still young and idealistic. As a whole, armies seemed to attract men who liked to lord it over other folks. She'd read the accounts of what was happening with the Indians and soldiers out west, and she took the reports about "murdering savages" with a grain of salt. The Irish had been on that same side of the coin for more years than she cared to recall. Which side has the heroes depends on who has the guns and who owns the newspapers.

But that didn't solve her problem now. *What have I gotten myself into? What if everyone out west is like these men?* That was a sobering thought. *Surely not!* Surely, it was just the less populated areas that attracted such misfits and nitwits. There was no reason to judge everyone west of here on the basis of the few she'd met so far.

But the simple fact was, she'd heard too many drunken boasts about going out west where "a man made his own law" to just dismiss the possibility altogether.

Up until now, she'd assumed that what she'd read in the newspapers about murderous outlaws and quick-to-kill gunslingers was exaggeration or outright invention, meant more to thrill readers than to stand as a true reporting of the facts.

However, it was easy to imagine Carina's "boys"

shooting and stabbing one another for no particular reason. Not that neglecting to wash or cut up your meat meant you were a murderer at heart. But still, they'd acted like heathens, and she wouldn't put it past a one of them to do harm if he felt the occasion called for it. *What if the west is full of such men?*

Now this is a pickle. Just when she should be soaking her troubles away, she was crowding her mind with worries.

She laid her head back on the rim of the tub and let her mind loose to wander. Though she'd been wet and miserable a lot the past few weeks, it was one of the few times in her life she could recall being carefree—just riding along, enjoying the journey, nothing in particular to be concerned over. Life would either work out or it wouldn't.

Why couldn't she hang on to that feeling now? If things worked out with Robert, so be it. If not, that was fine, too.

Because I will always wonder what might have been. The memory of that last night flooded over her, and she was lost in the sweetness of it all.

Over the years, whenever she'd been on the verge with a man, she'd always gotten a scared, suffocating feeling. This was understandable when he was trying to force himself on her, and she was struggling to get away.

But there'd been other times, times when the man had been sweet and loving and she was liking what they were doing. Yet she always put a stop to it when things got to a certain point. And it surely wasn't because such relations were a sin. She'd sinned plenty of times without so much as a pinch of guilt bothering her.

No, it wasn't the loving she was afraid of. It was the knowing how once you crossed over that line, you belonged to him. With or without marriage, once a man had taken you, he could take you again without a fare-thee-well. After she'd given in once, a woman no longer belonged to herself. Meg couldn't stand the thought of that. She could see where you'd have to put up with it when marriage was part of the arrangement. But without the benefits of marriage, a woman was a fool to let a man have that kind of power over her.

So why don't I feel the same way about loving with Robert?

Though she'd been sorely disappointed the night he'd refused to continue their lovemaking, there hadn't been so much as a hint of the panic she'd experienced before. All she could recall was the pleasure of their kissing, of their touching, of their holding one another.

Perhaps she felt safe because there was no way Robert was ever going to be a permanent part of her life. Or perhaps it was because he was more respectful of her than most, less inclined to order her about than others had been.

She scratched that last one off the list. Robert was quite definitely inclined to order her about. He was probably arranging for her passage back to Chicago at this very moment.

We'll just have to see about that, she thought. She arched back and shook her bosoms out like she'd seen women do when they wanted to attract attention. Her mam had always said that a man could resist temptation just so long. She wondered how much temptation Robert could resist.

She could always try to convince Robert to take her along to write his reports. On the trek up to Port Arthur's Landing, he'd taken out his packet of papers and bottle of ink a few evenings, but he never seemed to get much written down. He'd scribble away for a while, muttering and wadding up precious paper. She'd offered to help him, but he'd acted like he resented her suggestion that he might need assistance. After a while, he hadn't gotten the packet out any more and she'd been glad of that.

Since he was supposed to send back regular reports, he'd be needing to get one written up before long. And unless his writing had improved considerably over their separation, more than likely he still needed help. She'd always earned good marks in penmanship and composition. If she could think of a way to get around his stubborn pride, he might see his way clear to taking her along as his secretary.

She let her mind wander around this idea until she realized the water had turned cold. It was time to get out. It was time for a lot of things.

If Robert came back, she wanted him to find her writing out an account of her journey, not lolling about in the tub. Upon second thought, maybe she ought to go with the lolling and use the report writing as a backup plan.

But even if he was to walk through the door that instant, it was too late to entice him into the tub. The water was already giving her the shivers. She dried off quickly, wishing she had something other than her filthy pants and wool shirt to put on.

Her wish was granted. Carina had placed a folded flannel nightgown underneath the towel. She pulled it over her head and sighed as it slid smoothly across her skin and settled in soft folds around her feet.

Meg felt like a fairy princess in the billowing gown as she stepped into the kitchen to ask Carina where to dump the water. Since Carina wasn't there, she held up her hem and whirled around in the warmth of the room. Meg was glad she'd cut her hair and wondered why she hadn't done it years ago. Without that heavy braid dragging her down, she was light as a feather.

She closed her eyes and imagined that she was indeed a feather, floating along on a breeze. Perhaps she should sew a feather costume. She wondered how difficult it would be to find ostrich plumes out west.

The sound of a throat clearing caught her attention, and Meg turned and looked in the direction of the doorway.

Robert was standing there. *How awkward to be caught dancing around in a nightgown.* She felt exposed somehow, when in fact, the gown was so big it could have covered the two of them completely. That thought brought a wicked smile to her face—and an embarrassed blush. She couldn't help but notice that his face looked as flushed as hers felt.

Before she could think of anything to say, Carina came bustling back in the room.

"Good," she said. "We'll get some more hot bathwater now and have you scrubbed up in no time." She walked over to the stove and picked up a steaming kettle. On her way past them, she asked, "Where'd Hank go off to?"

Robert didn't answer. He simply stood staring at Meg.

"Cat got your tongue?" asked Carina.

But neither of them answered. They'd moved into a place of their own, where words were only a distant distraction. The smile faded from her face as Meg watched his gaze travel up and down the length of her. She could feel his eyes on her as surely as if they had fingertips of their own, tracing her hidden curves, brushing across her skin.

Goodness, it's warm in this room.

On the edge of her awareness, Meg heard the gurgling and splashing sounds of Carina dipping water from the tub and pitching it out the window. Carina's unhurried, steady footsteps as she moved back and forth between the stove and the tub reminded Meg that they should really give her a hand. Meg would have if she could've moved, if she could've so much as lifted a hand or even a foot. But she stood there like a statue, lost in time.

"Come along," she heard Carina say, and watched helplessly as Robert was pulled away. "That water should be warm enough now." Carina pushed him into the small room with the tub and closed the door behind her.

"I can see a bath did you a world of good, young lady," Carina said to her as she brought down a teapot and filled it with water from a kettle on the woodstove. "Now, would you care for a cup of tea?"

Meg gave her head a quick shake in an attempt to scatter the enchantment that had come over her. "What?" she asked, confused by the question. She knew Carina had asked her something, but for the life of her she was unable to recall what it had been.

"A cup of tea. Would you care for a cup of tea?" Carina repeated. Her words cut through the fog.

"Yes, please." *A cuppa tea would be just lovely.* It wasn't the only thing that would be just lovely, but it hardly seemed proper to bring that up.

Dazed, Meg sat at a small table and smiled up at Carina as she set down two rose-painted china cups and saucers. Meg started to compliment her on them when she was stopped cold by the sound of water splashing in the next room. Her thoughts turned to the image of Robert standing there in the altogether.

"Why don't you go in and scrub his back, dear?" Carina gently suggested.

"Oh, I hardly think that would be the thing to do," Meg said with a start.

"Why not? There's no one here but the three of us, and I assure you I don't care."

She took Meg's arm and led her to the doorway. "Go on," she urged. "Offer to scrub his back for him. That ought to do it, dear."

Carina pushed her inside, and Meg heard the solid thud of the door closing behind her. All thoughts of report writing vanished at the sight of his big, bony knees sticking out of the water.

Startled at the sight of her, Robert reached over and grabbed a towel to cover himself with. It sank into the water, leaving most of him still exposed.

Meg stood there dreamy and dazed and unable to think

what to do. Indeed, it was a moment or two before she even realized that she should say or do something.

"I'll scrub your back if you'd like," she said, rolling up the sleeves on the flannel gown.

He didn't say "no." So she reached for the jar of soap, dipped her fingers in it, and ran them across the top of his shoulders. They were so wide they touched both sides of the tub. The tub was a much tighter fit for him than it had been for her. She ran her hands down the part of his back that was out of the water, recalling all the nights she'd soothed away the ache of these muscles.

The scent of the lemon soap made her wish again for an ice-cold glass of lemonade. Or anything cool, really. She was so hot, she was practically panting. Strange, he didn't seem to be breathing at all.

She ran her palms across his slick skin and dug her fingers into the thick muscles that ran down the side of his neck out to the edge of his shoulders. What she really wanted to do was run her hands through his unruly black hair.

"Dunk your head," she told him. When he didn't respond, she pushed him under. He came up sputtering and spitting.

"Why'd you do that?" He sounded indignant.

"Didn't your mother ever wash your hair?"

"My nanny did, but she never tried to drown me."

Nanny? Her people were more likely to be nannies than have one. Yet another reminder about their different stations in life. It was like staring at a doll in a store window and knowing that even wishing for it was foolish.

"Say, are you going to wash my hair or not?" he asked,

giving his head a quick shake that sent drops of water spraying out across the room.

She dipped her fingers in the soap and began sudsing his dripping wet hair. Looking over his shoulder, she noticed that the wet towel had sunk into the tub and blocked the view.

Shoot.

She scratched her fingernails back and forth on his scalp and pressed her fingertips around in little circles. Then she massaged down the back of his neck and up behind his ears and across his forehead.

When she could think of no other way to move the soapsuds around his head, she said, "Now take a deep breath," and pushed his head back under the water. As the water swished around, the towel floated aside.

Oh, my.

It took her breath away and left her flushed with embarrassment and desire.

Robert pushed his head back up out of the water. "Just how long do you think I'm able to hold my breath?" he asked.

"I'm sorry. My thoughts wandered."

He turned back to look at her and her thoughts quit wandering. More than anything, she wanted to pull off the hot flannel gown and climb in there with him. Which was too foolish to even consider. There was barely room enough in that tub for him. And besides, he'd already been more than clear about his thoughts on the matter. Why humiliate herself any further?

But if she couldn't make a move to get in with him, neither could she leave the room. Perhaps she should just press her lips against his and see what happened. She closed her eyes for a moment and was overwhelmed by the memory of their kissing that night, the warmth, the smooth softness, the tender pressure of it. It seemed so real, she never wanted to open her eyes again.

Chapter Seven

Robert could no more resist leaning toward her than he could resist looking up at the stars on a clear night. He touched his lips against hers and nearly came undone right then and there.

He couldn't recall ever meeting a woman like Meg before. She was as carefree and impulsive as a kitten, yet as sensual as a courtesan.

Not that he'd ever actually met a courtesan, but he knew what one would be like. She'd wear daringly low-cut dresses and she'd show off her ankles a lot. When she laughed, she'd touch her tongue to her teeth. And she'd use that tongue to do all sorts of wicked, exciting things to the man who kept her. He was a little vague on just exactly what those wicked things might be, but he knew it would be enough to cause a weak man's heart to give out.

As he put his hands along the back of her damp head to deepen their kiss, he realized that Meg wasn't at all like the women of his dreams. She was infinitely better.

He felt like kicking himself every time he thought about the way he'd spurned her that last night. What had he been thinking of? Naturally, he'd been taught that a gentleman must never take advantage of a lady. But that was hardly the case with Meg. She had clearly been a willing partner that night—and, it appeared, tonight as well.

If only there was room for the both of them in this bathtub. The floor wasn't all that appealing, but he didn't see they had any other choice. He whispered, "Let me dry off, Meg," against her lips. She nodded agreement, and he reluctantly pulled away from her.

After hurriedly running the towel up one side and down the other, he turned back to Meg, wrapped his arms around her, and continued their kiss.

All he could think about was gliding his hands up her back and his tongue down it. And it was only going to get better. Any niggling thoughts about behaving like a gentleman were quickly pushed aside by how perfectly she fit in his arms. Surely, he couldn't be expected to resist such temptation forever.

At the sound of Carina's footsteps in the kitchen, Meg stiffened in his arms.

"Later," he said, pulling himself away with reluctance. "After everyone's asleep."

He watched her bare toes peek out from beneath the voluminous nightgown as she walked out of the room. She turned and smiled at him before closing the door behind her, and he felt that melting-away feeling again.

After quickly drying off, he pulled on the clean clothes

he'd brought in from the packs. He decided to forgo the long underwear. He wouldn't be needing it tonight.

Just as he stepped out of the room, Hank stepped in. It seemed like it took him forever to bathe. Carina insisted on washing out their clothes in the bathwater. Then they had to empty it all out.

By the time the clothes were pegged out on the line, the tub was returned to the back porch, and a straw tick was hauled into the little room, Robert was more than ready for bed. Watching Meg and Carina tuck sheets and blankets around the floor pallet was getting him so keyed up that when Hank suggested they take a short walk around before turning in, he readily agreed. He was all for anything that would help him calm down and pass the time until everyone else was bedded down for the night.

Just stepping out into the night helped quiet his mind. The evening breeze was cool, and the air carried the sweet prairie smell of grass and wildflowers on it. Tinny piano tunes mixed in with the raucous bragging and laughter coming from the saloons. A few faint lights in the scattered windows echoed the stars sparkling across the sky.

By unspoken mutual agreement, they both turned and walked away from the town.

"Nice night out," said Robert.

"Yep," said Hank. "I think I'll leave it out."

Hank held up an open pouch of chewing tobacco to Robert, who Robert took a pinch and pushed it down behind his lower lip. He didn't really care for the taste, and it made him a little light-headed and sick to his stomach, but it seemed unfriendly to refuse.

They walked along, spitting occasionally, until the saloon noise faded.

"Kid, you got to get a grip on yourself," Hank said finally. "That woman is just waiting for you to make your move. It don't have to be a perfect move. I suspect, just any move'll do."

"I realize she's mine for the taking," said Robert. "But it still doesn't seem quite right."

"What's not right about it? She wants you. You want her. You're both adults. Seems straightforward enough to me." The scout let fly a stream of tobacco juice.

"Well, it isn't," said Robert. He used his tongue to clear out the tobacco from behind his lower lip. When he spit, he spit the whole nasty mess out. "See, I'd be the first man for her."

"I can sure see why that would make you a little on the nervous side," Hank said, clapping him on the shoulder. "Seeing as how this is her first time, you need to be extra certain that she finds it satisfying."

"What?" This thought stopped him in his tracks. Here he'd been concerned about how this would ruin Meg and hadn't even given a thought to making sure she enjoyed herself. "How do you go about that?" he asked.

"Well, first off, you've got to understand that a woman enjoys relations just like a man does," Hank said, "only different."

When Hank didn't elaborate, Robert was compelled to ask, "What's different about it?"

"First off, most men go after it like they was killing snakes, no finesse at all."

Robert was somewhat startled to hear Hank use a word like "finesse."

"Now a woman, a woman needs to be played like a good hand of cards. There's no sense in rushing. Take your time, keep upping the ante, don't be flashing your high card around until you're ready to call." He nudged Robert in the arm with his elbow. "Know what I mean?"

Robert didn't have a clue.

"Now, you might be asking yourself just how old Hank seems to know so much about bedding females?"

Robert wasn't wondering at all. As far as he could tell, Hank knew a whole lot more about a lot of things than he did. He was willing to take his word on lovemaking. Who else was he going to ask? Carina?

"Well, look at it this way. What do I have to offer a woman besides a good time? I ain't going to be sticking around and taking care of her. All I can give her is a couple coins, and that ain't much when you get to thinking about it."

Robert nodded in agreement.

"I learned early on that if a woman wakes up in the morning with a smile on her face, she's more likely to invite me back the next time I'm through town. You keep that in mind, son."

"I will," Robert said. He wondered if that explained the easy relationship he seemed to have with Carina. He waited for Hank to continue.

"Well, guess we ought to check on the horses and turn in. What do you say, kid?"

That's it? That's all he's going to say on the subject?

"What's the rush?" Robert said, trying to sound nonchalant about it.

"You got that right. There ain't no rush. You just remember that tonight."

"Remember what?"

"That there ain't no rush, of course," said Hank, giving him another nudge in the side. "Just take things nice and easy. Women like it that way, at least most do. Take your time kissing 'em. And don't just kiss them on the mouth either. Kiss 'em all over. You know what I mean."

Robert had a vague idea. Naturally, he'd listened to the lewd talk of his school chums, but it was different when the woman they were talking about was Meg. "I'm not sure she'd like that."

"Trust me, son, she'll like it. She might be too shy to say so, but you just listen real close to her sounds and the way she breathes, and you'll be able to tell what she likes and what she likes best."

"That's it?" asked Robert. He was hoping for something a little more specific than advice to go slow, pay attention, and kiss a lot.

"Pretty much, except for the baby business. You got anything on you to keep from making one of them?"

Robert assumed he was talking about French letters, and he shook his head. He didn't have one with him and he certainly didn't know where one could purchase any in Winnipeg, not at this hour at any rate.

"Then you're just going to have to make sure you don't leave your seed in her."

"How do I do that?"

"Jeez, kid. Do I got to tell you everything?"

A few hints wouldn't hurt, but he was not about to ask. It was uncomfortable enough as it was. After all, he was the man's commander. Hank should be turning to him for advice and instruction, not the other way around.

"Just stay with the kissing, that's all."

"That's all?" He couldn't help himself. As much as he didn't want to appear foolish and inexperienced, the words just slipped out.

"Just kiss until you're both satisfied."

"Kissing is all right, Hank, but it isn't all that satisfying."

"It is if you do it right." Hank gave Robert's shoulder a light punch. "Don't worry about it none, kid. I suspect that Bess taught Meg a thing or two. You just follow along, and you'll do fine."

That appeared to be all the man-to-man advice Hank was going to offer. They circled back to where the horses were stabled. After ensuring that all was well, they returned to Carina's place and parted company at the porch. Hank gave Robert a thumbs-up sign before disappearing around the corner of the boardinghouse.

Robert stood on the porch and wondered if it was this difficult for other men. Did other men worry about whether they would be hurting the woman, ruining her good name, leaving her with the consequences to pay? Did they worry about making fools of themselves because they didn't know what to do?

He'd long suspected that most of what men bragged about was just that—brag. But what if it wasn't. Why must he go through life always trying to figure out what everyone else already seemed to know? No doubt, when he was on his deathbed, a ring of mourners would surround him, all benevolently beaming that patronizing, I-know-something-you-don't-know smile.

He ran his hands through his hair and mentally prepared himself for what was ahead. Physically, he was set to go.

"Robert, is that you?" he heard her voice from inside.

His throat was so dry he couldn't form a word in answer.

"Are you coming in?" she asked.

He was so mixed up he didn't know whether he was coming or going. He felt like he was pulling back on the reins and digging in the spurs at the same time. He'd been looking forward to this ever since he saw her lean over that banister. But he sure didn't want to hurt her in any way, and he was pretty certain this would. That she was more than willing made no difference to him. He should be protecting her, not taking advantage of her.

But didn't she have some responsibility in all of this? After all, she'd been around a bit. She'd certainly been around a lot more than he had. And this *was* the third time she'd invited him into her bed. Mountie or not, surely there was a limit to how much resistance a man should have to put up.

That decided it. The third time was a charm as far as he was concerned. He'd deal with his conscience in the morning.

Robert opened the door, hoping that Meg was already abed so he could just slip in next to her.

But there she was, sitting there at the dining-room table, writing. *Writing? What is she writing about at this hour?* Whatever it was had obviously captured her complete attention because she didn't so much as look up at him. He found this bewildering. What had happened to change things?

The yellow light from the coal-oil lamp softened the red in her hair and made shadows across her face. He liked her tousled curls. In fact, he believed he liked everything about her. It's too bad she hadn't been born into the upper class. He could think of a few people she would astound with her brash approach to life.

"There, what do you think?" She blew gently on the paper to dry the ink before passing it over to him.

Robert pulled his eyes from her and read what she'd written.

> The expedition proceeded as planned until the layover in St. Paul, Minnesota. While purchasing needed supplies, the troop met up with a group of men who had deserted the Force over the previous winter. These men voiced numerous complaints with regards to provisions, leadership, and duties of the Mounted Police. During the ensuing encounter, Inspector Parker was killed and ten men in the troop sustained injuries. Because of injuries, the demise of the troop commander, and reports about the presence of insurgents north of the Fargo railhead, all but one man decided to remain in St. Paul. Constable Hamilton traveled by rail to Duluth, Minnesota, and by canoe to Port Arthur's Landing and across the Dawson Route to Winnipeg. The trip was uneventful but rigorous. It is recommended that re-

placement troops be sent via the Fargo Route in sufficient numbers to ensure their safety.

"I'm impressed, Meg." And he was. He couldn't count the number of times he'd tried to express these very thoughts. But his attempts always came out muddled and full of too many crossed-out words and misspellings. Had he known his duties were to include report writing, he'd have brought a dictionary along.

But with the door to paradise right behind him, he wasn't in any mood to work on dispatches to headquarters tonight. That could wait until tomorrow.

Robert set the paper down on the table and put his hands on her shoulders. After all the backrubs, he knew every inch of Meg's back. He knew where that mole on her shoulder blade was. He knew how the muscles tapered down along her spine. He wanted that same familiarity with the rest of her.

"Meg?" he asked, not sure how to go about this.

"Yes?" she answered, turning to look up at him.

"I'm getting sleepy. How about you?"

"Sleepy isn't what I'm feeling, but I do think it's time to go to bed." She stood up and walked through the dining-room door without looking back even once to see if he was following her.

He swallowed hard and headed after her.

"Are you sure you want to do this, Meg?" he asked, reluctance and anticipation tugging him in opposite directions.

"Why don't you come in here and find out for yourself," she suggested softly from the darkened room.

That was all he needed. Her voice wrapped around him like that tasseled scarf in Duluth had. It pulled him inside where he quickly stripped down to his drawers. He didn't know whether it would be best to get all the way undressed or not. But since he had decided to stick to kissing, he imagined it'd probably be best to leave a little something on.

He was glad he had for she was still in her nightgown. He'd have felt ridiculous to be stark naked while she was still covered from head to toe. Even though he was as eager as he'd ever been about anything, there was no sense in announcing it.

He put his arm around her and together they knelt on the straw mattress and slipped between the sheets. He scooted around trying to get their bodies aligned, but he couldn't understand why it felt so awkward tonight. It'd been so easy all those other nights. But she'd been turned away from him then. Perhaps that made a difference.

Robert wasn't about to suggest she turn away from him. Not tonight. "I don't want to hurt you, Meg," he said softly against her ear.

"You won't," she promised. He hoped she was right.

They settled into slow kissing. Recalling what Hank had suggested about kissing her in all different kinds of ways and places, Robert began by changing the pressure of his lips on hers, sometimes pressing firmly and other times softer, just barely touching. For a while, they fought a duel of sorts with their tongues. That was fun. For a while.

He moved to kissing her cheeks, then her eyelids and across her forehead and down behind her ear and around to the back of her neck. He kissed every bit of skin he could find and then nuzzled through her damp, lemon-scented hair. He wanted to move on down as Hank had suggested, but he didn't know quite how to go about it. Kissing her through her nightgown seemed a bit bizarre, but then, so did crawling underneath it like a dwarf in some circus act.

Other than kissing him back when the opportunity presented itself, she wasn't offering him any assistance whatsoever. He finally decided that since he'd pretty well covered every square inch on this end, he'd move down to the other end and work his way up.

Kissing her toes and the delicate skin on the top of her feet was by far the most carnal experience he'd ever had in his life. He had no idea ankles could be so erotic. No wonder women went to such lengths to keep their ankles covered. Although, he had to admit, he was so worked up that even the feel of the coarse sheet beneath him was pleasurable.

His hands smoothed the downy hair on her calves as he kissed his way back up to her knees and back down again. Moving up to her thighs, the thought of where this was leading was almost more than he could bear. It was too bad it was pitch-black in the room. After all the years of listening to other men describe what a woman's body looked like, he was still left using his imagination.

Judging from her soft sighs and the catches in her breathing, she seemed to be enjoying his touch. He had entered another realm. In all his years, he'd never experienced anything quite like this before, not even close. The physical urgency was replaced by a floating sensation.

He was aware of everything at once—the pulsing warmth of his own body, the rough sheets and the hard floor against his legs and feet, her smooth skin sliding across his cheek, and the way her muscles tensed and relaxed beneath his lips and between his teeth. He made his way around the bottom of her belly, wondering if when he got to her breast he should suckle like a babe or if there was something else she'd like better. She solved that dilemma by digging her heels in against his shoulders and pushing him back down to where he'd just barely passed by.

CHAPTER EIGHT

MEG HAD NEVER IMAGINED IT WOULD BE ANYTHING LIKE this. Robert was such a fine and noble man that she knew he'd be gentle and caring, but she'd also expected him to fumble about quite a bit. He was anything but bungling. *Oh, my.* How could he know just where to touch and how to go about it?

Though she was a maid, it wasn't as if she'd never had loving encounters with a man before. Realizing the dreadful consequences of sex outside of the bonds of matrimony, she'd protected her virtue. However, that didn't mean that in her younger years she hadn't hugged about with a young fellow when the occasion rose.

But that awkward groping had never resulted in more than a mild and easily managed excitement. She'd never experienced anything like these drifting, pulsing feelings that were flowing through her now. It was as if joy had found roots within her and was beginning to bloom. There was no rush, nothing she needed to figure out, nowhere she needed to go. She trusted that he would take care of her.

Gradually, without even being aware of when or where it started, Meg noticed a change. It was as if her body had forgotten something it was trying desperately to remember. She heard a wordless chant coming from deep in the back of her throat, and for the life of her, she couldn't recall ever knowing that before. She made a feeble attempt to shush herself, but she had no more will than a rag doll.

She dug her fingers into the prickly straw padding and arched up off the mattress. The smell of dry hay and lemons came to her, and she remembered swirling her fingers through Robert's sudsy hair. She reached down to touch his hair again and realized her body was moving in rhythm with the chanting. What a curious thing this loving was.

Suddenly, the sunlit image of riding across the waves with Robert was so vivid that she struggled to tell which was the vision and which was the truth of the matter. She could see his scarlet coat as plainly as ever. His barely contained excitement brought a smile to her face. He was a precious one, no doubt about it.

That was her last coherent thought as he pulled her gently along to that mindless place where nothing seemed to matter, then everything did. One moment, she was sure she couldn't bear to have this last so much as a moment longer. Then she was certain she couldn't stand it if they ever stopped. It was all too grand, too wonderful, too intense. She realized she was heading to the edge of desire.

And then, with one gentle tug, she plunged over that edge.

She heard a cry come from low in her soul as she turned herself over to the pure pleasure of it all. The steady, deep pulsing gradually changed to rich waves that flowed from the core of her out to the end of her toes, the tips of her fingers, the top of her head.

This was like nothing she'd ever experienced or even imagined before.

As the last shudders faded, she was flooded with emotion for this man who was holding her in his arms. Without a word between them, he knew what she needed and he gave it to her. How did he do that?

How could she do it in return?

Hours later, they were stretched out side by side, exhausted and content.

"Wow," he murmured.

"Oh, my."

"Are you sure you've never done this before?" he asked, giving her hand a slight squeeze.

"Believe you me, I'd remember this," she said, returning the pressure. "Or anything even close to this."

Meg wondered why he'd never made any attempt to enter her. Though he'd obviously found the pleasure she had, still she thought it unusual that he hadn't pursued further intimacies. She recalled Bess telling her that some men preferred things this way, but she doubted that was the case with a man still learning what lovemaking was all about.

Perhaps he just got carried away with the preliminaries. Perhaps he'd held back to protect her. Perhaps he saw this as a way in which they could both enjoy themselves and yet she could remain a virgin.

Although, technically she still qualified, Meg certainly didn't feel like a maiden any longer. She felt like a woman of the world, sure of her strength and power, and definitely destined to do it again.

As they snuggled up and drifted off to sleep, Meg found contentment in knowing that she'd come upon a better way to keep his interest than telling stories and writing reports. Indeed, she had.

The next morning, Meg slipped out to the privy before he woke up and came back in to see Carina pouring the two of them a cup of tea.

"Or, perhaps after last night, I should get you something with a bit more strength to it, eh?" Carina asked with a broad, friendly smile.

Meg could just imagine what the woman had heard through the walls last night. She felt her cheeks flush in embarrassment and quickly sat down and took a sip.

"No, this is fine, really," she said.

"So, where are you and your fact-finding fellows off to today?" Carina asked.

"To be sure, they wouldn't be telling me," said Meg, secretly pleased to hear Carina call them "your fellows." Though Robert hadn't said anything about taking her along, he hadn't said anything about not taking her along either. She was hopeful that last night would make a difference in his view about her accompanying him.

"Do they even know themselves?"

"Now there's a good question. The man who knew what they were supposed to do was killed. All Robert knows is that he should be finding out about things." Meg took a sip of tea before continuing. She wasn't sure how much she should say, or if she should say anything at all. It really wasn't her place to be telling Carina what Robert was up to.

On the other hand, what difference would it make, really? She was enjoying the company of another woman after all this time. Anyway, who was Carina going to tell out here in the middle of nowhere?

"As I understand it," Meg continued, "so far, the reports don't agree in the least. The man in charge says that everything's going hunky-dory and that they should have it all under control by next summer."

"French," said Carina, practically spitting the word out. She didn't go on, but it was clear she didn't think much of the man.

"Others say the entire operation is a disaster," said Meg. "According to them, most of the horses have either died or are about to and most of the men are ready to desert or already have."

"I wouldn't blame them for a minute," said Carina. "That French hauled a group through here last fall. Those poor devils were on their last legs. If you ask me, the whole idea was a harebrained scheme from the start. What can a few hundred men do to control matters across a country of this size. And that idea of eliminating the whiskey trade is nothing short of ridiculous. Whoever heard of such a thing?"

"It does appear to be a difficult undertaking," Meg agreed.

"Difficult?" Carina rolled her eyes. "Try hopeless."

She shook her head, then added, "But you know how men are."

Meg nodded in agreement.

"And now they've sent this young Robert here to figure the whole mess out. You have to agree, he seems pretty wet behind the ears for this kind of thing."

"He wasn't supposed to be in charge. As I understand it, there was a whole troop of them, but they got into a fight in Minnesota. Their leader was shot dead, and most of the rest were hurt. Those who were still able to travel refused to go on after hearing what was in store for them."

"They were probably the only ones with a lick of sense."

"Perhaps so. But Robert seems determined to carry on. He's not one to turn tail just because of a few problems." Meg lowered her voice to keep it from carrying to Robert's ears in the next room.

"A few problems!" Carina blurted out. "I'd say losing the whole lot of them is more than 'a few problems,' wouldn't you?"

"I'd have to agree with you there," Meg said.

"It's just lucky he's got Hank along."

"Aye, that it is," agreed Meg.

"Hank knows the country, and he's a steady enough fellow. If anyone can look out after your man, he can."

"What are you saying about me now, woman?"

Meg was startled at the sound of Hank's voice and turned to see him leaning easy against the doorframe. He was shirtless and barefoot, as if he'd slept inside last night.

He strolled across the kitchen, stopping to lightly rub Carina's shoulder on his way to pour himself a cup of coffee from the pot on the stove.

"How long until breakfast?" he asked, as he sat down across from them.

From the looks they exchanged, it was clear as glass to Meg that the two of them had spent the night together. *Well, why not?* she asked herself. They were both old enough to know what they wanted, and she was certainly in no position to be passing judgment.

"It'll be a while until the boys are up and about, but I thought you three might be wanting an early start today, so I put some biscuits in the oven. They'll be ready in a minute."

Carina stood and walked over to the stove. She lifted the lid on a kettle, and the smell of simmering beef and onions drifted across the room.

"I've got some venison and gravy too if you want," she said.

"You know what I like, Carina," Hank said, with a nod and a broad wink in her direction. Carina glanced over her shoulder at him and smiled, but there was a sadness behind that smile that was impossible to miss. Meg didn't imagine that either one of them was talking about venison gravy.

Though she hadn't seen or heard him, suddenly Meg realized that Robert was standing behind her. The air was different, or maybe she was.

She waited for him to say something to her, or touch her somehow. He seemed uncomfortable in her presence this morning.

"Good morning," said Hank. "Pour yourself a cup of coffee and come on over and sit down a spell while we map out the day."

Meg turned to watch him walk over to the stove, pour himself a cup of coffee, then sit down next to Hank. She noticed he was careful to avoid looking over at her. He sat there sipping his coffee and staring into the cup without saying a word. It was too bad they couldn't be as easy around each other this morning as Carina and Hank were.

"Say, you think a person can tell the future by looking at the way coffee grounds settle into the bottom of a cup?" asked Hank.

"I think that only works with tea leaves, Hank," said Carina.

"Well, I was just wondering," he said, "what the world has in store for us today."

Robert looked up, and, for the first time, his eyes met hers. He looked liked he was pleading with her for something, but for the life of her she couldn't figure out what it might be.

"First off," he said. Then he paused to take a deep breath. "First off, we need to arrange safe passage for Miss Reilly to the railhead at Fargo."

Her breath caught in her chest. No wonder he was looking so miserable. To start the day off saying he wanted to get rid of her was making her feel miserable herself.

"I don't know about that," said Hank. "That Reil's got the Métis all stirred up around that part of the country. You might be able to arrange for passage for Meg, but I doubt it'd be safe. Not unless you hired an army to escort her, and a sizable one at that."

Meg's hopes rose. Robert would never send her into a dangerous situation.

"Of course, I could always take her back through the woods with me to Duluth," he added.

"Absolutely not." Meg stood up. She felt like pounding her fist on the table. "For weeks I've paddled a canoe, carried backbreaking loads around waterfalls and rapids, and put up with some of the worst characters you can imagine. There's no way you'll get me back to Duluth." She sat down, still steaming. "Not without an army, you won't."

"Guess that idea's out," said Hank.

No one else said a word.

"But I can't take her with me," Robert said, sounding bewildered by the very idea.

"Why not?" asked Carina.

"Because I have no idea what's up ahead. I can't subject Meg to the danger of this journey."

"Didn't they teach you about Sacajawea in school?" asked Carina.

Robert nodded yes.

"She was no more than a girl, and she walked all across the continent with that Lewis and Clark." Carina shook a finger to emphasize the point. "And with a baby on her back no less."

Meg sat up a little straighter just thinking about the woman.

"At least Meg doesn't have a baby on her back," Carina added. "Not yet, anyhow."

"She'd be a lot safer traveling west with you than with just about anyone else I can think of," said Hank.

"But I'm not going west," Robert said. "I'm heading north out of here."

"North?" Hank seemed baffled by this news. "Why would you want to head north?"

"To assess the situation at Swan River," said Robert as if that made perfect sense. "If I'm to make recommendations about the construction and operation of a headquarters, it seems essential that I at least visit the current one for myself."

"You can save yourself a trip there. I can tell you about Swan River. It's just a bunch of buildings sitting on top of a pile of rocks. There's snakes everywhere and no trees for miles. It's not only the unlikeliest spot for a headquarters, but the most unlikeliest spot for humans I ever saw," he said, as if that settled that.

"I can't just report hearsay," said Robert. "Besides, there are probably aspects of the Swan River headquarters that are worth including in the construction of the new fort."

"It ain't hearsay. I've been there," said Hank. "And trust me, son, there's nothing up there that's worth doing again."

Meg watched Robert bristle at Hank calling him "son" and wondered that Hank hadn't noticed. Perhaps he had and just did it to irritate Robert.

"Nonetheless, our troop's orders were specific about visiting Swan River and informing Commissioner French of our mission." Robert seemed determined about following through with his plan.

"You're making a mistake, I tell you."

Their disagreement could go on forever. It was clear that Robert had made his mind up on the matter, and there was no sense arguing about it.

"It's fine by me if we go north for a ways before we head west," Meg said in an attempt to get the conversation moving.

"But how would that look, bringing a, ah . . ." Robert paused, searching for the right word and was obviously uneasy about bringing the subject up in the first place.

Meg knew what word he was searching for, and she cringed at the thought of it.

"A woman along?" Hank finished. "The way I see it, you would be providing a lady with an escort to safety, which is a grand and noble undertaking. It'd be sort of like being a knight of the Round Table."

"That does put it in somewhat of a different light," Robert agreed.

"In the second place, if you run across any Indians, having a woman along would let them know that you were on peaceable business."

As Meg recalled from the history lessons she used to teach, Sacajawea had indeed convinced war parties that her companions meant no harm.

"Whose business is it anyway? I don't expect the men out here will care one way or the other, except maybe to be envious of you. And as for the reports back home—I say leave that part out." Hank leaned back and crossed his arms, clearly satisfied that he'd made his point.

"That would be dishonest," objected Robert.

"Hell's bells, you're not going to write down every

solid detail, are you? What we had for breakfast and such is no concern of those bigwigs back East. They don't care about none of that. They want to know what the North-west Mounted Police can do about settling this land and making it safe for folks. They don't give a shit about who you sleep with, son."

Robert's face flushed a furious red. Meg felt her own face heat up at the memory of last night.

"And get over that," said Hank. "Last I heard the only folks who objected to a man and a woman enjoying each other's company were the preachers. They're few and far between in this country. Out here, what you two do is your own personal business. Right, Carina?"

Carina nodded in agreement.

"Now that we have that settled, how about them biscuits, woman?"

During breakfast, Robert gruffly asked Meg if she would get the report she'd written last evening and make a copy of it. Meg was secretly thrilled that he wanted her help and hurried off to get the paper, pen, and ink that Carina had loaned her last night.

When she'd finished copying it down, he said he wanted her to add a line to each report about his intention to travel to Swan River and assess the situation there before heading west to determine a more suitable site for a headquarters.

She could see the pride glowing from him as he signed the first one, "Respectfully submitted, Constable Robert Eugene Hamilton." Carina promised to see that it was carried to the railhead and sent off to Ottawa the next time she heard of someone heading that way. Just in case the first report should go astray, he had Meg put the copy away to include in his next report.

She was pleased that he'd asked her for help, but knew if she'd offered straight out, his pride would've refused.

They were the only customers in the dry goods store that morning, and the first things they picked out were decent, wide-brimmed hats for Robert and herself. Hank didn't say a word, but it was plain to see that he thought their purchases made good sense.

Meg had money left over from the refund of the steamship ticket. She offered to repay Hank for the clothes he'd bought her in Duluth, but he said not to bother, he'd only spend it foolishly anyway. Robert suggested she tuck the money away. She might be needing it before their journey was over.

Though Robert still acted ill at ease around her, he let her know that there were sufficient funds to purchase pants and shirts as well as any other garments she desired. He said that even though she planned to continue to dress like she was, he strongly recommended that she choose a dress and the "necessary accoutrements," just in case the situation called for it. Then he turned his attention to restocking their provisions. Meg asked the clerk what "accoutrements" meant and the woman said he was probably referring to undergarments and such and was just too shy to say.

Meg felt awkward about placing her things on top of his pile. In twenty-nine years, this was only the second time a man had ever paid for a purchase of hers. Not that she had any objections to it. It was a peculiar, but not unwelcome, situation.

As they got ready to leave, Robert stopped at the doorway and told her to wait at the store as they'd be back with the horses for the supplies.

"Here," he said, handing her a folded bill. "Buy whatever else you might need." Then he turned and headed off for the stable without a backward glance.

Meg was overwhelmed with the sweetness of his gesture. She just wished he could get it out of his head that taking her along was wrong.

She ached for Robert. He was so worried about always doing the right thing. Everyone made foolish decisions now and again, everyone made mistakes. A person just had to give it their best shot and go on. Not everything would work out, of course. But to Meg's way of thinking, if you weren't falling down every once in a while, you weren't trying hard enough stuff. You picked yourself up and went on. That was the way the world worked. Life was far too short to be taken that seriously.

She knew what her mission in life was now—to lighten things up for this far-too-serious man.

Chapter Nine

"I'm telling you, these Eastern thoroughbreds won't stand up to the trip like Western ponies will," Hank said. "These horses are used to regular rations of oats. I never should have let you talk me into bringing them up in the first place. They'll drop to skin and bones on prairie grass and alkali water. I say we take that trader up on his offer."

"And I say we don't," said Robert, retying one of the packs on a bay gelding. Hank was getting on his nerves. Robert thought they'd settled this matter yesterday. "I refuse to trade fifteen good, solid, well-trained horses for half a dozen half-broke Western broncs."

"That was just the man's first offer. You're supposed to dicker with him. You come back and say you'll trade your fifteen for twenty of his and by afternoon, you'll settle somewhere in between."

"You've had these horses on the trail for the past month, and they seem fit enough to me."

"If the next three months were going to be like the last one, I'd agree with you. But we aren't going to be finding lush pasture and little creeks along the way. And we aren't going to be able to carry enough oats to last the trip either. You're risking these horses and our lives to boot with your stubbornness, son."

"Stop calling me son," Robert said with more fury than he realized he'd built up. He took a deep breath to calm down before continuing. "It's ridiculous to trade off well-trained horses for those half-wild beasts. You saw them last night. How is Meg supposed to ride one of those?" He didn't think it necessary to add that he had doubts about his own ability to keep in the saddle.

"It's a lot easier to train a hardy horse than to try and prop up a half-dead one."

"Ours are hardy," he insisted.

"You're being pigheaded about this, Robert. It's got nothing to do with who's in charge here. It's about what makes the most sense."

"And I say it doesn't make sense to trade off perfectly good horses."

"You'll come to regret this decision. Mark my word on it."

Maybe so, but I'll be damned if I'll have the man order me about like some dim-witted flunky.

They rounded the corner to the stable and didn't say another word to one another as they saddled the horses and led them back to the dry goods store.

Though the morning was a bit cool, it looked like it was going to be a gorgeous day. There were a few scattered clouds, but nothing ominous. Robert was looking forward to a lazy, long ride across wide prairie meadows.

"I'm glad you've decided to go with me after all," Robert said as they neared the dry goods store.

"Might as well," Hank said. "I've got nothing better to do."

Robert was relieved. Generally, he enjoyed Hank's company and felt it advantageous all around to have him along.

He felt his heart pick up the pace at the sight of Meg. She was standing there with the provisions stacked around her feet and the promise of adventure on her face. He'd missed her. He'd not only missed the nights, but he'd missed the days together. He'd missed her laughter, her teasing, her stories, her smile. Though he wasn't at all certain that taking her along was in her best interests, he knew for a fact he'd be enjoying her company.

They loaded up and headed out of town. Mercifully, Hank didn't question the direction they were going. Robert hoped they were heading the right way. If it wasn't, he could deal with turning around a great deal easier than listening to the old man second-guess every word he uttered.

To ease his mind, Robert turned and watched Meg trying to keep her horse from stepping on the wild roses. The prairie was carpeted with them. They grew so thick that to avoid one, she ended up tromping on two more. She finally just let her horse pick his own way.

No two ways about it, this woman was a wonder. She certainly was determined to get west. She looked up and smiled at him and he felt a jolt of joy pass through him as surely as if he'd been struck by lightning. If it wasn't that they came from such different stations in life, he could imagine being married to Meg. *Now wouldn't that make for a life filled with the unexpected?*

Just the thought of it brought a smile to his face. She was a few years older, but he'd known a number of marriages where there was a difference in ages. It didn't seem to pose a problem.

No, the problem would be in bringing back a woman who wore men's pants, cursed upon occasion, and had been born into the lower class. It wasn't just that she wouldn't know which fork to use. That would be easy enough to teach her. It was that she wasn't all that convinced the forks were preferable to fingers.

Then there was her accent, her bluntness, her wild stories. There were no end of things that would make her an oddity back in Ottawa. No doubt, people would be amused by her "quaint" behavior in the beginning. But how long would that last? How long until the cruel remarks, the cutting comments, the unkindness would start?

He didn't even want to think how shocked his uncle would be should he bring Meg home as his intended bride. Robert had never actually seen a fit of apoplexy, but he was certain this would bring one on. His uncle would see Robert's fiancée as a slap in the face after all he'd done for him. And all he intended to do.

No, his wife would have to be able to attend balls and make polite conversation on meaningless topics with boring people.

It was hard even to imagine Meg in a ball gown. Other

than that nightgown, he'd only seen her in a dress once, and she quickly switched that for a pair of long underwear with some odd things sewn all over it. Ever since, she'd been wearing pants and seemed quite comfortable in them.

As for conversation, he doubted that comments like, "Get off your arse and give me a hand here, bucko," would go far in polite society.

No, they were from two different worlds and destined to stay that way.

Meg rode up next to him, and he marveled at the way she sat her horse. She rolled with her mare as if she'd been cantering about bridle paths all her life. He wondered if it would be acceptable to reach out and kiss her. Just a quick kiss, just enough to let her know how much he enjoyed her company. He looked around to make sure Hank wasn't watching.

"Robert, I have a bone to pick with you," she said. It didn't appear she was in the mood for a kiss.

"About what?" he asked, mystified as to what she could be upset about.

"I've about had my fill of the way you've been behaving," she said.

Robert wondered what way that was but hesitated to ask. Knowing Meg, he was certain she'd tell him whether he wanted to know or not.

He was right.

"I'm tired of you acting like you're ashamed of me, ashamed of what we did. You were eager enough when we bedded down last night."

"I'm not ashamed," he said, perhaps a bit too quickly

for there not to be a touch of truth to it. "I'm trying to maintain a professional relationship here. I've got Hank telling me what to do and now I've got you thinking you can lead me around by the balls."

He instantly regretted using such a vulgar term around her, but he didn't feel like apologizing, so he went on. "I may be young, but I am the one in charge around here, and I'll thank you to remember that."

"And just when would I get a chance to forget, what with you reminding me every half hour?"

She was practically snarling at him. He wished she'd keep her voice down. The last thing he needed was for Hank to ride up and give him some more of his old-man advice on how to handle a woman.

"Listen, I'm not ashamed of what we did," he insisted. "It was rather enjoyable, as a matter of fact."

"Enjoyable? It was the most unbelievable night of my entire life, and you found it 'rather enjoyable'?"

"All right, more than enjoyable," he admitted, "but, in any case, I'm not ashamed of what we did."

"Then quit acting like you are," she said bitterly.

"What we did last night doesn't change things between us, Meg." What an awkward situation. How was he going to get her to understand that enjoyable or not, sex was a thing apart, not the focus of one's life?

"I suppose then you won't be wanting a repeat of last night."

His spirits sagged.

"Just as I thought. You didn't get quite this far in your wee plan, did you?" she taunted him. "Well, I don't care how much you *enjoyed* last night, I'll take up with the goblins before I'll let you treat me like this all day, then crawl into my bed come evening."

"Meg," he said, feeling apprehensive about the entire matter and wanting desperately to rectify it.

"You can't have it both ways," she informed him in no uncertain terms. "You can be all high-and-mighty and pretend like you hardly know me during the day if that's what you want, but tonight I'm crawling in next to Hank."

"You wouldn't dare!" Unaccustomed panic fluttered in his chest, and he struggled to keep a clear head.

"I wouldn't bet on it if I were you." She sounded as if she meant it.

"Hank hasn't shown any interest in bedding you," was all he could think to say. He regretted the words the minute they were out of his mouth. It sounded needlessly cruel and quite possibly untrue.

"I hardly think that was called for." Her eyes narrowed, and her lips wrinkled up.

It'd just popped out without any thought behind it. That was the trouble with getting overly emotional—you said and did unreasonable things. Matters should be decided intellectually, not emotionally.

"I suspect that Hank was just trying to give you first chance, seeing as how you are the *boss* and all." She emphasized the word "boss" as if to let him know how ridiculous this whole notion of his was. "Once he finds out you've decided I'm not good enough for you, I suspect he'll be agreeable to being just a mite more friendly toward me."

"Meg, you wouldn't do that, would you?" he said, dismayed at the turn in the conversation.

"What do you think, bucko? You think I should just hang around waiting for a kind word from you?" Sarcasm didn't really suit her, and he felt an immediate longing for the happy-go-lucky woman he'd grown to know those first few weeks.

"Couldn't we just go back to how it used to be?" he asked without a great deal of hope.

"You mean where you tolerate my company with the intention of shipping me off at the first chance you get? Didn't last night mean anything to you?"

"Of course it did. It was by far the most incredible night of my life. I have no doubt but that I'll recall it fondly on my deathbed." He struggled to think of how else he could express what last night had meant to him.

"That's more like it," she said with a self-satisfied flip of her head.

"But I can't ignore the fact that I have a mission to accomplish here, Meg," he said, turning away from her to stare out at the horizon. As wonderful as it'd been, he couldn't just abandon his mission in favor of passion-filled nights. "You may think of this as nothing more than a silly, misguided adventure, but it's a serious undertaking, Meg. Just because the Canadian government bought this land doesn't mean it'll belong to us. If we can't govern it, the Americans will take over or the whiskey traders and outlaws will.

"Be realistic," she said. "This doesn't all rest on your shoulders."

"It most certainly does," he insisted. "Do you think my

uncle and his cronies can figure this all out from their offices back in Ottawa? Without accurate information they are just guessing about what needs to be done."

He knew he sounded intense and self-important, but this was serious business, and he didn't understand why she couldn't seem to grasp that.

"I, for one, believe that an effective police force will ensure a peaceful settlement of this country. Or would you prefer another lawless land like the American West?" He waited for her to acknowledge what he said before continuing.

"But surely you're not the only one," she said.

"Oh, there are others sending reports back. But they're all army men. They're used to using brute force, and that won't work out here. The question is, will this? Is it even humanly possible?"

They rode silently side by side as he weighed his thoughts before continuing.

"There have been some mistakes made. Does that mean we should replace those responsible with men who'll make mistakes of their own? Or is this whole scheme doomed, regardless of who's running it? Does it have any chance at all?"

He looked at her not for answers, but for recognition that she understood the responsibility that weighed heavy on him. It was different for her. She only had herself to worry about. He had an obligation and a duty that burdened men, or at least men of his station.

"Canada just cannot afford any more protection than this. Think of what will happen if this fails, and we're forced to abandon the area."

She shrugged her shoulders as if she hadn't given that any thought before now.

"The outlaw element will move in. Murders and massacres will become common occurrences instead of occasional incidents. It's not just the future of Canada that rests on what I recommend, Meg. It's a lot of lives as well.

"And you have to figure this all out on your own?" she asked doubtfully.

"If I don't, who will? Who else is there to figure out how to salvage things? From all the conflicting reports, it's obvious the men in charge aren't up to the task."

"This seems far too weighty a task for just one man," she said.

"One young man, you mean," he said with more than a trace of bitterness.

"All right, just one young man," she admitted. "One fine and grand young man."

"Meg, how can I risk all of this to spend the night in your arms? Can I see what's going on if I'm so concerned about getting into your bloomers that I'm not paying attention to matters? Will people even take me seriously, or will they write me off as some absurd joke, a dandy and his mistress off on an adventure?"

"Does it have to be either or? Can't you accomplish your mission just as well with me along?" she asked.

"Just what do you think will be going through men's minds when they see me show up with you? I'll be a joke, and an easily dismissed one at that."

He could see from the slight grimace on her face that he was close to the truth.

"Given my age and lack of experience, it'll be hard enough to get taken seriously without having a mistress in tow."

"So what if no one takes you seriously? Use it as a disguise," she suggested. "You'll probably be able to pick up a lot more information than if they think you're investigating them."

"What?" The idea of misrepresenting his mission struck him as underhanded.

"It makes perfect sense," she said, obviously pleased with her plan. "What if you let on that you were just a pampered, rich gentleman on a lark. Instead of telling everyone that you are on a fact-finding mission and having them all start scrambling around, hiding what they can and putting the best possible face on the rest, what about letting them believe that you're a well-to-do heir out on an adventure? There's certainly no need to alert them to put their guard up. You might learn more than you imagine."

"I hadn't thought of that," he said. And he hadn't. His intention was to ride in, announce who he was and what he was doing, and take it from there.

"Well, think about it. This way, you just may end up seeing a great deal more of what is really going on and a great deal less of what they want you to see."

"Hmmm," he said, pondering the possibilities of this new approach to matters.

"I would be the perfect setup. You've brought me along since you doubt you'd be able to find suitable companions on your journey. Hank is our protector, the bodyguard hired by your family to keep you out of scrapes."

Though on the surface it made sense, he was a little leery about getting involved in any plan she thought up. From what she'd told him of her life so far, things had a way of tumbling in on Meg.

"It's perfect, I tell you. No one would ever suspect that all the writing we'd be doing is more than a young man penning his lusty adventures. Who'd be the wiser?"

"It doesn't seem quite honest," he said, uneasily weighing the drawbacks to this approach.

"You won't be hiding anything or telling any lies. After all, you *are* a young man and I *am* your traveling companion. Let them make of it what they will. Just because you won't be blurting out the entire story every time you run across anyone with ears doesn't mean you're dishonest. 'Keeping your own counsel' would be a wiser way to think of it."

His mood improved as he considered the advantages to this take on their situation.

"I could be asking around as well. People tell a lot of things to a woman, you know."

"It might work out," he said, feeling his reluctance fade away.

"Just remember who suggested it," she said, putting the spurs to her mare and galloping ahead. Since he had a string of packhorses tied to his saddle, he couldn't keep up with her without scattering their provisions all over creation. He plodded along at a steady pace. The burden of responsibility was a heavy one.

Evening found them at Lower Fort Garry, where the fort commander was rousted out of bed for an indifferent introduction. The man's speech was slurred, and he had to grab onto the porch post to maintain his balance. He was clearly in his cups and by six o'clock, no less. Controlling the whiskey trading in this country was going to be a difficult undertaking indeed if even the army commanders themselves couldn't stay sober.

After seeing to the horses, they retired to the quarters they'd been assigned. Apparently, their attempt at subterfuge had been lost on the commander as he had obviously not even grasped the fact they had a woman traveling with them. Why else would he assign them bunks in the main barracks?

Robert planned to straighten the matter out directly after dinner. But they ended up staying in the mess hall, sitting around talking with the men. Since Meg didn't do more than mutter a word here or there, no one paid much attention to her. Hank had introduced her as McReilly and Robert suspected most thought she was a boy they'd hauled along to help out. The rest probably didn't care one way or the other.

When the talk turned to horses, he was surprised to hear that Commissioner French had chosen horses for the march across the prairie based on their colors.

"Yep," said one old codger, "I saw it my own self. Each division of fifty had their own color horses. One troop was mounted on dark bays, another on chestnuts, the next on blacks. Damnedest thing I ever saw, I'll tell you that."

"Instead of picking out pretty horses," said a stout man from the far end of the table, "he'd have been better off picking horses that didn't scare quite so easy. First night off the train, they got spooked by lightning, broke out of that makeshift corral and ran all over the country. If it hadn't been for those steady Western broncs that Steele fella had with him, they'd still be out wandering the prairie."

"French ought to have learned his lesson right then and there and got his men some decent mounts. Things might have turned out better all the way around if he hadn't turned up his nose at them Western ponies," said a gaunt-faced man across from him.

Robert cringed at remembering how he'd refused to trade for sturdier mounts yesterday. He glanced in Hank's direction and noticed he was nodding in agreement with the man.

"French had more show and less common sense than any grown man I ever run across," said an older man with a raised, red scar running from his forehead to his neck. "He didn't even bother to get his men decent gear. The cheap saddles broke down and rubbed sores on the horses. The guns were all busted up. And they forgot to bring anything to carry water in."

"What?" Robert couldn't believe this.

"You heard me right. They headed across the prairie with not a damn thing to carry water in, nary a canteen or a barrel. Nothing."

"Well, how did they do it?" This was inconceivable. Robert glanced over at Meg, hoping she was remembering all of this so they could get it written down later. She nodded her understanding of his unspoken request.

"They did without, that's how they did it. The bugler's lips were so swollen and blistered that he couldn't blow so much as a note."

"Surely, they found water along the way."

"They did indeed. But a good deal of it was that alkaline water, and everyone knows that'll give you the runs in no time."

"That French didn't know the territory, didn't know horses, and didn't know men. Worse yet, he was too damn proud to learn," said the scarred man.

By now, Robert had ceased keeping track of who said what. Everyone around the table was adding his take on the situation. There appeared to be little disagreement about the facts of the matter, and none of the facts were good.

"But according to the reports," interrupted Robert, "they went all the way to the Rockies and back."

"Some made it the whole way because every once in a while, French would divide off the weakest men and horses and send them off in another direction. I'll tell you, it was a sorry mess."

Nods all around the table confirmed as much.

Apparently, the men could go on all night and probably would. But Meg looked exhausted, and he realized he needed to bring the evening to an end soon.

"I still don't understand how he ever completed such a long march under those conditions."

"*He* didn't do it. The men did." The man across from him practically spit the words out. "Men so sick and weak they could barely put one foot in front of the other. During freezing rainstorms, they covered the horses with their own blankets and then huddled together for warmth. They'd rub the horses' joints in the morning to help them get up and then walked alongside, leaning on those poor, skinny beasts to keep them from falling over. That's how they did it."

Robert looked around the table. He appeared to be the only one who was astounded by this sorry story.

"My brother Teddy said it was a pitiful sight, them horses staggering along and falling in the mud and the men not much better. Toward the end, the only way they could keep some of those horses upright was by putting a pole underneath them and a man on either side to help it walk along. My brother said that when he signed up for this business, he thought he'd have an easy ride to the Rockies, with a fine horse carrying him. Instead, he had a rough walk to Edmonton with *him* carrying the horse."

Bitter snorts of laughter around the room confirmed the truthfulness of the tale.

Robert was overwhelmed by all he had heard. He'd thought the deserters in St. Paul were exaggerating, as slackers often do to justify their behavior. But according to these men, the former Mounties hadn't told the half of it.

"Where's French now?" he asked.

"He's up at Swan River. If you don't believe us, go see for yourself."

"I intend to."

"So what other facts do you want to know for this report of yours?" asked the scarred man.

"How did . . . ?" Robert looked from Meg to Hank. Why'd they give it away? He thought they'd agreed to keep things under wraps for the time being. "How did you know we were gathering information?"

"Hell, it was easy enough to figure out," said the

scarred man. "There's just you and your two partners here. What else would you be up to—taming the West? An army man with a troop of men came through a few weeks ago. We figure he was getting the official version, and they sent you out to get the real story."

"Son," said a grizzled old-timer who'd been silent up until now, "you tell them Ottawa politicians that in spite of the worst leader I've ever seen or heard of, those men prevailed. They gutted it out, and they're here to stay. You tell them those Mounties can handle anything you throw at 'em, but they deserve a better leader than that fool French."

"And how about those ridiculous little pillbox field caps? Now you want something worthless, there you go," said a skinny old man. "Out here you need something that'll keep the rain off your neck and the sun out of your eyes."

A decent hat was at the top of the list of the things Robert intended to recommend. He himself felt ridiculous wearing the little pillbox field cap and much preferred the pith helmet. But while there might've been some benefit to wearing the pith helmet in a hot climate, it was no use at all in this country. A hat with a brim was what was needed.

Except when they rode into the fort, he had ceased wearing any of his Mountie uniform. The coat was filthy and far too warm for the heat of the day and he much preferred the wide-brimmed hat he'd purchased to either the field cap or the pith helmet.

Robert bid the men good night and the three of them went in search of someone with enough authority to assign them more suitable quarters. Unfortunately, none could be found. As much as he dreaded sleeping in the barracks, they could hardly just go about pounding on doors and peering into places looking for an empty room with a bed. They couldn't even find a decent place to sit down and write up the reports before the details slipped their mind.

So, the three of them made their way to the end of the barracks and stretched out on the bunks they'd been assigned. Meg was in the bed nearest the wall and Robert slept across from her with Hank up above.

It was frustrating to be this close and not be able to nuzzle his face into her hair, not be able to inhale her rose-lemon scent, not be able to feel her skin on his lips. Though the day had started out with a disagreement, that hadn't lasted long, and by afternoon she'd been teasing him about tonight. It was damn disappointing to have to lie by himself with her no more than an arm's length away. He'd have settled for just holding her. But that was hardly possible, not with a barracks full of men snoring and snorting all around them.

Apparently, both of them were as uneasy as he was about undressing in this barracks full of strangers. They'd all left their clothes on and kept their boots nearby. Meg had her quilt with her, of course. She hated to let that thing out of her sight. Tonight she was using it as a pillow.

Moonlight flowed over her face and sank into the quilted flowers beneath it. He wished he were better at drawing because he'd like to have remembrance of what she looked like tonight. Her features were so expressive, she couldn't hide her emotions if she tried. If she felt joy, it showed. Irritation, anger, happiness, contentment, excitement . . . it was all written on her face for the world to see.

He watched her lips move, and it seemed as if she'd whispered "Robert." He hoped so. He hoped she was dreaming of him because he would surely be dreaming of her before long.

It was hard to believe none of the soldiers had caught on that she was a woman. He was glad they hadn't as they probably avoided a certain amount of unpleasantness this way. But even covered up by that jacket, it was plain as day to him that "McReilly" wasn't a man.

He drifted off to sleep, grateful that they'd be spending tomorrow night on the trail.

They nearly beat the sun up the next morning. It was so early, the cook appeared to be the only one stirring about. He ladled them out some cornmeal mush and wished them a safe journey.

It didn't take long to get the horses ready to go. Meg slipped on the halters and bridles while he and Hank cinched down the saddles and tied on the packs. They headed out the gate before the sun was even half above the horizon.

Wispy clouds slowly shifted high in the sky, and the scent of springtime hung in the air. It was the kind of day that made a person glad just to be alive. Robert felt like giving out a whoop and galloping across the grass. He didn't, of course, but he felt like it.

Meg seemed to be in a grumpy mood. He tried to get her to laugh a few times but all he could get from her was sort of a tolerant amusement. When they stopped for their noon break, she walked up along the creek and disappeared.

She acted like she was upset over something, but for the life of him he didn't know what it could be. Perhaps she was peeved because he hadn't paid much attention to her last night when they were all sitting around talking. Or maybe she was mad because he hadn't been able to do anything about her sleeping in that barracks with all those men. Possibly she'd had a change of heart about sharing intimacies with him. Women were a struggle to understand under the best of circumstances, and theirs was hardly an ideal situation. Perhaps she was waiting for him to make some sort of declaration of his affections or, at the very least, his intentions.

What could he say? He had no intentions at all. Other than enjoying the pleasure of her company, of course, and that seemed ungentlemanly to say out loud.

Now, his affections were another matter entirely. He could declare them quite openly. If that's what she wanted.

The question remained as to just how to go about it. Perhaps she'd gone off into the trees hoping he'd follow. One could hardly launch into kissing with Hank nearby mumbling advice and the occasional obscenity.

Nothing ventured, nothing gained, Robert decided as he put down his tin cup and headed off in the direction where she'd disappeared.

"Where you going?" Hank asked.

"Thought I'd check and make sure Meg's all right," he

answered, trying to sound nonchalant. *Why didn't the man mind his own business?*

"I wouldn't do that if I were you," Hank warned.

"Fortunately, you're not me," Robert said tersely and strode off.

That man got on his nerves. Maybe he should tell him about how scouts are supposed to ride out ahead, then come back and report, not sit around the campfire giving out advice all the livelong day.

As he followed the trail around a bend, he caught a glimpse of Meg, and the sight of her lying there, dozing in the deep grass took his breath away. She was beautiful, absolutely beautiful. The sun reflected off her tousled curls, giving her hair the appearance of a fire that had died down to tumbled embers.

Now that he'd grown used to it, he found he liked her hair cut short. It made her look like a stained-glass angel he'd once seen in a church window.

Meg herself did not remind him of an angel. She was the focus of all his fantasies lately, and she was not an angel in any of them.

A movement of her hands caught his attention and he glanced down to see that she was pressing in on her stomach and softly moaning. He hoped she hadn't gotten sick from the venison jerky. Then the thought hit him that this might be some sort of erotic thing women did to themselves.

He felt his own face flush and decided he'd better take it nice and easy so as not to scare her. Unfortunately, she heard him approach and her eyes flew wide-open.

"What are you doing here?" she asked, clearly annoyed at seeing him.

"I came by to keep you company," he said.

"I don't want your company," she said irritably. "Just go on and leave me alone."

Robert was disappointed. What was the matter with the woman? Wasn't he the man who'd given her the most incredible night of her life?

"Meg?"

"What?" She stared up at him as if he was trying her patience.

"Are you mad at me?"

"No, I'm not mad at you. Now go on."

He left, feeling like he'd just been given a scolding for no good reason.

"She didn't want you around I take it?" he heard Hank say as he walked back to sit down and pour himself a cup of tea.

"How did you know she didn't want me around?" Robert asked. "Did she say something to you?"

"She didn't have to. I know what's going on," Hank said with assurance.

Robert waited for him to continue. It was irritating to have to ask, "Would you mind filling me in on it?"

"Not at all," said Hank. "It's that time of the month."

"She's acting like this because it's the end of June?" This didn't even make sense.

"Not our time of the month, *her* time of the month," said Hank, acting as if Robert should know what he was talking about. "Didn't your papa ever tell you anything about women?"

"Not much," Robert admitted.

"I guess not, if he didn't tell you about this," Hank said. "Now pay attention."

Robert was.

"Once a month, women turn crabby and cranky. It's their time. Usually it's somewhere around the full moon. But not always."

"All women?" It seemed strange he'd never heard of this before.

"Every woman I ever met."

"How do you know when it's their time?"

"You don't need to worry about that, kid. They'll let you know all right."

"How long does it last?"

"It varies. A week or so for most of 'em."

"A week!"

"Sometimes longer, it all depends."

"Depends on what?"

"I don't know, son. I wish I did."

This was the strangest way to find out about the world—little hints here and there. In school, the professors would lecture for hours and hours on something you weren't even the least bit interested in, and then there'd be the text to study as well. Now here was information that a man ought to know and all he could get was a few vague comments from an old-timer who might not even be all that knowledgeable on the subject. He had to admit, though, the kissing advice had worked out rather well.

"Well, is there anything I can do?"

"Hang on for the ride is all I can say," said Hank. "There's the possibility that it won't be too bad. Meg doesn't seem the excitable type. Some women will run you ragged, but Meggie just seems to want to go off by herself. In my opinion, that's to be commended."

"So we just carry on like normal and after a while she'll come out of it?" Robert asked.

"Near as I can tell that's how it works."

"I don't suppose she'll be in an affectionate mood until this passes."

"I don't suppose."

Now that was disappointing information.

"However, if I was a young man trying to make a good impression on a lady, I'd do everything I could to make this time bearable for her."

"Like what?" At this point, he was willing to try just about anything to stay in her good graces.

"For one, don't fuss with her about a thing, not a thing. If she says she wants you to go catch her some frogs because she has a hankering for fried frog legs, you get yourself over to a swamp and start searching for them croakers. If she burns them to a crisp, you tell her that's just the way you like 'em. And if she throws the whole mess out in the weeds, you say that's fine, you never cared much for frog legs anyway. Sometimes they'll just get the craziest notions, and then you go right along with it. It only lasts a week, then they're back to their old affectionate selves," he said. "If they were affectionate to begin with, that is," he added after a moment's pause.

"It's good to know you only have to make it through a week," Robert said. A week wasn't all that long.

"Unless, of course," Hank paused.

Robert waited expectantly.

"They're in the family way. Then you got nine months of nastiness ahead of you."

"Nine months of this?" That'd be hard to take.

"Give or take a few weeks here and there. Of course, in their minds, they're all sweet and loving and, if anything, just a touch more emotional than usual. I once rode twenty miles to get a jar of pickles for a woman who ended up throwing the whole mess in my face." Hank shook his head at the memory of it. "And it wasn't even my child. I could see it if she thought I was the cause of all her misery, but I was just trying to help her out."

They nodded in shared understanding over how there was no way either one of them was ever going to be able to figure out women.

Robert was glad not to have the worry over whether Meg was carrying his child. He knew there was more to lovemaking than what they'd done together, but he thought he'd stick with the kissing just the same. What they'd worked out was enjoyable, and it wouldn't put him in a bind. He hated the thought of being forced into a hasty marriage, but neither would it be right to leave Meg with the burden of a child of theirs. They were better off sticking with kissing. He was certainly looking forward to a repeat of the other night, and he imagined that once Meg was in a better mood, she would be, too.

Much to his disappointment, Meg was short-tempered all day. When they sat down that evening to write up what they'd learned from the men at Lower Fort Garry, they disagreed about nearly everything that had been said. In the interest of harmony, he finally decided to have her write down *The soldiers were unimpressed with the oper-*

ations of the Northwest Mounted Police. Base commander was not available for comment. They left it at that.

The only time she didn't snap and snarl at him was when they laid down to sleep and he pulled her in close and rubbed her belly like he'd seen her doing that afternoon. It relaxed her, and she murmured, "Thank you," before falling asleep. He was disappointed but knew there would be other nights.

Just as Hank predicted, her temper steadily improved over the next few days. However, she still wasn't encouraging any affection between them at night. He had hoped things would be back to normal before they arrived at Fort Swan River, but that was not to be.

They arrived early in the afternoon, recognizing it from the description he'd heard in Winnipeg. One could hardly apply the term "fort" to a collection of buildings strung out across the top of a hill. *Whatever possessed someone to lay it out this way?* he wondered.

On the only close-to-flat area around, a tall man was arrogantly ordering men on horseback to move into various formations. First he'd insist that they all get into a straight line, then he'd want them to split in half and circle back until they formed an equal-sided cross. The poor bugler was trying to keep his own horse under control while playing some tune Robert didn't recognize. While the mounted men milled around, their commander cursed them soundly with nearly every breath.

Huge boulders poked up out of the ground all over the place, making the operation ridiculously difficult. The riders had to detour around them, throwing off both their formation and their timing. The men were surly and slow, and the horses stumbled about, so malnourished that their ribs were visible even from a distance.

The whole performance reminded Robert of lunatics on the loose.

As they rode forward, he and Meg kept looking at each other as if to assure themselves that their eyes weren't playing tricks on them. This was almost too bizarre to believe.

When the commander saw them approaching, he called a halt to the drill and shouted out a booming welcome. But after a brief introduction, he ignored the three of them completely as he rode around them, admiring their horses.

"Where are the rest of them?" Commissioner French demanded after he'd taken a good look.

"We had some difficulties in St. Paul and were forced to leave the injured behind to heal." Robert felt this was the best explanation for the time being. He could fill in the details later. "I was left to carry on alone."

"Surely, their injuries have healed by now. We shall make our way to St. Paul with the utmost haste and retrieve the remainder of the mounts," said the commissioner.

"Sir, there are no more horses," said Robert.

"No more horses?" He seemed truly disturbed by this news. "And here I was expecting over two hundred head. There aren't even twenty here. What am I to do? I have nearly three hundred men needing mounts."

"I don't know anything about that, sir."

"Commissioner," Hank said, speaking for the first time, "we've been sent to report on the condition of the trails connecting the forts. There will be others following along behind us with the remounts."

If there were, this was the first Robert had heard of it.

"Somehow, I doubt that," said the commissioner with a resigned shake of his head. "We've had to practice the strictest economies out here. How does Ottawa expect us to patrol with these?" He swung his arm in a wide arc. "They're nothing but skin and bone."

And barely that, thought Robert.

"How did this happen, sir?" he asked, realizing that he could be referring to the skinny men as well as the scrawny horses.

"Fire!" he yelled out, as if he smelled smoke at this very moment. "After the hardships of last summer's march, they needed to spend the winter fattening up. But a prairie fire destroyed over half the fodder, and they were on thin rations all winter because of it."

"Tough situation, sir," was all Robert could think of to say.

"And getting tougher by the day," said the commissioner. "But thank God you've arrived. I can put these horses to good use."

This caught Robert by surprise. Things looked as if they were going to get increasingly difficult from here on out.

"Sir," he said quickly, "as much as I'd like for you and your men to have fresh mounts, we can hardly give you ours. It would leave us afoot."

"Which is more important to our mission here?" French demanded to know. "Whether we are able to carry out successful patrols or whether you are able to report on the conditions of the trails?" He shook his clenched fist. "I think we both know the answer to that, don't we, son?"

"Commissioner French—" Robert started to protest, but was cut off.

"Call me Colonel French, if you would," said the commissioner, leaning toward him as if he were going to let him in on a little secret. "The men understand army ranks better than they do police titles."

That was fine by Robert. He briefly wondered why the commissioner hadn't chosen to call himself a general while he was at it.

"Colonel French—" he began again.

"Subconstable Ryan," French ordered, "see that these mounts are stabled and given a thorough examination by the veterinarian. Bugler, sound the dismissal."

The man tooted out a couple of notes, and the men rode off in the direction of the buildings. Robert pulled out the orders he'd taken from Inspector Parker's coat pocket, but the commissioner waved them aside, refusing even to look at them.

Robert not only *felt* helpless, he *was* helpless. As they stacked their saddles and piled their packs in the corner of the tack barn, he comforted himself with the knowledge that at least the commissioner hadn't commandeered their gear as well. For all the good that did them. Without decent horses, they were stuck at the fort for the foreseeable future.

If you could even call it a fort. He was appalled at the condition of the buildings. They'd been built with freshly cut timbers that had dried and left cracks big enough to put a fist through. A good many of the holes were stuffed with rags, but it was easy to see from what the men were wearing that there weren't all that many rags to spare.

The Mounties wore a wide assortment of tattered clothing and most of it wasn't even government issue. Some men still had regulation boots but the rest wore moccasins or gunnysacks wrapped around their feet. It was pitiful.

There was a vast variety of headgear as well, including any number of fur hats with tails hanging down the backs. If he hadn't known better, he might've mistaken this group for a Davy Crockett brigade instead of a contingency of Northwest Mounted Police.

How had things deteriorated so drastically in just one year?

Dinner was a dreadful experience. The beans had been simmered to a tasteless mush, and the bread was filled with brown specks.

"Weevils," explained one man. "Can't do nothing about 'em."

Mercifully, there was no dessert.

It was a wonder the men's ribs didn't stick out like the horses' did.

They were assigned their own separate building to sleep in. It was hard to say if that was a blessing or not. Robert had never seen a structure lean so many ways at one time in his life. Both the floor and the roof let in light and, judging from the damp places in the dirt floor, moisture as well.

At least they weren't sharing quarters with a brigade of men. There hadn't been the opportunity for Robert to explain the gentleman-on-a-journey cover story. Hank had slurred Meg's name to sound like McReilly, but no one seemed to notice or care one way or the other.

Which Robert found astounding. In his opinion, she oozed sensuality. When she bit through a bread crust, he had to close his eyes, so strong was the memory of her nipping his shoulders in just the same manner. When she accidentally brushed against his wrist, shivers ran up his arm and down his spine. Just the thought of lying next to her later that night was enough to make him anxious for the evening to end.

Just his luck, right after dinner, Commissioner French called him to his office to inquire about the mood of the officials in Ottawa. He wanted to know if they still supported the idea of a police force, if they were going to appropriate additional funds to support it, and when he could expect replacements of both men and mounts.

But every time Robert attempted to answer, the commissioner launched into another long, rambling tirade about what a struggle the whole operation had been, how there'd been no precedent for such a police action in the history of mankind, and how damnable it was that they received such minuscule support from the prime minister and his minions.

"Do you know what we need more than anything?" French asked at one point, stopping his pacing to stare Robert straight in the eye.

Robert couldn't imagine pinning it down to just one item—horses, food, uniforms, building materials, a new commander—what could it possibly be?

"A piano," the commissioner said, pounding his fist on the desk.

A piano? Of all the things that might be of use out here, a piano was clear at the bottom of the list as far as Robert was concerned.

"A piano, sir?" asked Robert, uncertain that he had heard correctly.

"Yes, my good man, a piano. Actually, I'd like a variety of instruments so that we could form a band. I think it would improve the morale of the men to have musical performances, don't you?"

Decent food might go a long way toward improving the men's spirits, or warm clothes, or perhaps a place to sleep protected from the wind and rain. But a piano!

He was at a loss for words. Robert knew it was never a good idea to fuss with one's superiors, and he'd hoped that by being agreeable, he could convince the commissioner to allow them to continue on with at least a few of their horses. But to encourage the man in forming an orchestra seemed unconscionable.

"I have this idea for a mounted band," French said, throwing his arm through the air as if he was already leading a spirited selection.

A mounted band! Surely, not! Robert could see it all now, frightened horses charging this way and that while their equally terrified riders attempted to blare out tunes on trumpets as they dashed about. This was madness.

"Sir," he said firmly, "I believe there are more important matters to consider than forming musical ensembles to pass the time."

"But think of it," French continued enthusiastically, waving his fist back and forth in the air. "A parade ground of crimson-coated riders on prancing dark bays and golden chestnuts, going through their drills while mounted musicians play 'God Save the Queen.'"

God save us all! The man was deranged. Robert wondered if he'd even noticed that his troops were not only out of uniform but out of a good deal of the necessary gear altogether. Personally, Robert thought he ought to put some effort into getting boots for his men instead of dreaming of a piano.

A fury was building in Robert. He felt like hitting something—or somebody. *Who had put this incompetent fool in charge? They ought to be out here trying to keep warm with burlap bags wrapped around their feet.*

He took a couple of slow, deep breaths to calm down and made one more attempt at convincing the commissioner to allow them to continue on their journey.

"My uncle Walter has supported the idea of a mounted police force for years. He believes in it so strongly that he's even turned over the management of his shipping business to allow him time to—"

"Bully for him," French said, not allowing Robert to finish. "We need more clear-thinking men like that in this world." Then his eyes narrowed in thought. "He isn't one of those cigar-smoking, tightfisted politicians is he?"

"No, sir," Robert agreed. "And if we could only continue on our journey, I'm sure I could convince him of the need for—"

"By any chance, do you play an instrument, Constable?" French asked, his mind back on the band business.

Robert gave up. For the rest of the conversation, he nodded in agreement but declined to make any comments of his own. What was the use, really?

His anger slowly faded as the commissioner rambled on. The man was mad as a hatter. In a way, Robert felt sorry for him. French had been assigned a duty he was incapable of carrying out. The dreadful responsibility had obviously unhinged his mind or else he'd been daft to begin with. Either way, the results were the same. His men were left to fend for themselves while he obsessed over forming a mounted band. *Perhaps I'd have done the same if I'd had this overwhelming responsibility and so few resources,* Robert thought. *No, I'd have seen that there was decent food and warm clothes at least.* The commissioner was derelict in his duty. He ought to be court-martialed.

To control his anger, Robert turned his thoughts to Meg. He wondered if she might be feeling chipper enough to consider some serious affection tonight. He was fairly certain that Hank would make himself scarce if he knew what was going on. He wished Hank would offer more unsolicited advice about women and less about horses and so forth.

"What do you think of that, son?" French asked suddenly.

"Sounds good to me," Robert replied, and hoped he hadn't just agreed to a squad of performing monkeys or perhaps the addition of feathers to those silly pillbox field caps.

"I think we'd better call it a night," said the commissioner. "Don't you?"

Robert jumped to his feet before French launched into another tirade against bureaucratic bungling and political shenanigans. He opposed both but could see no sense in discussing it with this man. Who knew where such a conversation would wander?

After French's lengthy parting remarks about their noble undertaking, Robert all but ran over to the building assigned to them. It was after dark, and he hoped Meg was in bed. He hoped Hank wasn't.

To his disappointment, neither one was there. He worried about Meg wandering alone amidst all these rough frontier men. Hank would look out for her if she only had the good sense to stay with him.

Since Meg's good sense was not something a man could count on, he immediately took off in search of her. He was certain that he'd find the two of them within a short time. The fort wasn't that big.

But after covering the length of the compound three times, searching every building and scanning every group of men he came across, he still hadn't found them.

As the mournful notes of taps signaled lights out across the compound, Robert reluctantly made his way back to their assigned quarters. His last slim hope faded as he opened the door to the still-empty room.

Surely, they hadn't taken off without him. Robert couldn't believe they'd actually do that. But since they were nowhere to be found, he had to at least consider the possibility.

The most telling evidence was that Meg's quilt was gone. If that green quilt had still been on the bed where she'd thrown it earlier in the day, he'd have felt better about the situation. With her quilt missing, it was hard not to reach the conclusion that she was gone as well.

Robert slumped down on the pine bed, too discouraged

and disappointed to think straight. After all they'd been through, she'd left him here at the mercy of a deranged man.

"Psst, psst."

It sounded like her voice, but he was certain there was no one in the room. Unless she was hiding under the bunks. He leaned over to check, but the moonlight didn't do a thing for under-the-bed investigations.

"Robert, come around back," he heard her whisper through one of the countless cracks in the walls. "Don't tarry."

He didn't. He was around the back of the building in no time. Meg was standing there holding the reins to two scrubby-looking horses. He was far from astounded.

"Where did you get these?" he asked, as she handed him the reins to one.

"We'll talk about that later," she said, throwing her leg over the back of her horse. "Come on. Let's go."

He mounted up and followed her over a rise and down a gully to where Hank was waiting for them with four other horses. At the sight of them, Hank took off, and the three of them loped along at a steady pace for better than an hour. The excitement of making their getaway from that delusional man's clutches was tempered by the knowledge that how they were going about it was hardly ethical or legal.

When they finally stopped for a rest, he couldn't help but ask how they had acquired the horses.

"Traded for them," was all Hank would say.

"Commissioner French wouldn't trade for those horses." Robert knew for a fact that French would not willingly part with any of his horses. He'd insisted repeatedly that he was in desperate need of mounts as it was.

"I didn't do my trading with French. He didn't seem to be strung too tight to me," said Hank.

Robert had to agree with him there.

"So you stole the horses," he said, resigning himself to the simple facts of the matter.

"No, I traded for them. In return for these fine Western broncs, I promised that you would get those poor men out of their sorry situation. I told them your uncle was a bigwig back in Ottawa and that once you told him what was going on, he'd get this all straightened out and they'd have some decent food and warm blankets by next winter. Believe you me, they were more than willing to trade a few horses for a promise like that."

Robert did not share Hank's optimistic view of the situation.

"They'll be after us by morning," he said. It was discouraging to be hunted down by the Mounted Police. He'd taken such pride in belonging to the Force, too. Robert wondered if they hanged horse thieves or merely put them in prison and if there would be a court-martial along with the trial.

"Not to worry," said Hank. "They're brushing out our trail tonight and laying another one that'll make it look like we're heading back to Winnipeg. That'll keep them occupied until we can get over to the South Saskatchewan. We'll follow that river across and down to the Montanas."

What could he say? And what difference would it make anyway? Going back was out of the question.

They loped along at a steady pace until dawn. Robert tried not to think about their situation, but it wasn't all that easy. Even thoughts about Meg couldn't keep his mind off the fact that he had just committed a criminal act.

Hank found a stand of trees at the bend in a small river, and they stopped to rest for the day. With the weather warming up, it made sense to travel at night, he said.

Robert knew it made sense from the standpoint of staying out of sight, too, but he didn't say anything. Being a fugitive didn't sit well with him. Even in school, he'd never been one for getting involved in pranks. He couldn't see the point to it. It was depressing to realize that depending on how well connected French was, this escapade of theirs might well be regarded as a good deal more serious than a prank.

Later, resting in the shade of a stand of cottonwood trees, Meg attempted to snuggle up next to him. But he turned away. In broad daylight there was little hope of more than a stolen kiss. Besides, he just wasn't in the mood.

"Why don't I get out the paper and ink and you can tell me what you want written down about Swan River?" she offered.

"How can I report that the leader of this entire operation is an incompetent ass?" he asked, amazed that she would even suggest such a thing. Maybe she didn't understand how things worked. "French has influential friends, or he wouldn't have been given this command.

For all I know, anything I say will be dismissed as disgruntled ramblings and wild rumors."

"Surely, your uncle will believe you," she insisted.

"He's only one man and, in any case, he's likely to be viewed as biased," he pointed out.

"You've got a point there, Robert," she admitted.

"But if something isn't done and done quickly, there'll be no choice but to disband the Northwest Mounted Police. It's inconceivable that those men at Swan River are going to establish any sort of law and order. And they're the best of the lot. You heard them tell how the weaker men are scattered at various forts and outposts across the prairie."

"Aye," Meg agreed. "They'll be lucky to make it through another winter."

"If they're disbanded, I doubt they'll try anything else for some time."

"Well, Robert, what if you modify things a wee bit?" she suggested.

"Not tell the truth?" That didn't seem right.

"Don't lie, but write about need for supplies and horses. Leave off mentioning French's leadership ability."

"Meg, if I don't report the situation honestly, I'll hardly be fulfilling my duty."

"And if you do, they're likely to throw all your recommendations in the trash heap," she pointed out.

"I'll have to think about it."

Indeed, it was all he could think about. Meg tried to distract him with her shameless flirting, but he couldn't seem to summon the interest. There was a time when he would've followed her around all day with no more encouragement than a smile. But now, her hints about the passion they could be sharing did little to excite him.

He had weightier concerns. Despite his exhaustion, he was unable to do more than doze off occasionally.

That evening the tension eased somewhat when they were unable to detect any sign of pursuit, no clouds of dust, no riders in the distance. Either the false trail had worked, or Commissioner French did not hold these Western broncs in high enough esteem to put forth a great deal of effort in getting them back.

As they rode through the night, Robert's respect for the horses increased. They might not look as grand as the blooded thoroughbreds he and his companions started out on, but they were easy to ride, and they were making excellent time.

The next day, they camped on the edge of a blackened stretch of prairie. Though the ground was cold and there was no evidence of fire anywhere nearby, the harsh stench of burnt grass hung in the air.

Hank said that sometimes the fires were started by lightning, but just as often the Indians lit them to run the buffalo where they wanted them to go or to scare off people they didn't want around. He told them that the Blackfoot Indians got their name because of the color of their moccasins and feet after traveling across burnt prairie land like this.

All that night, they traveled across the charcoal-covered ground. The horses' hooves stirred up the soot, and the riders tied handkerchiefs over their faces to make it easier to breathe. When they hadn't reached the edge of the burnt area by morning, they decided to travel on through the day. There was no pasture for the horses, and none of them wanted to sleep on the charcoal and cinders.

By noon, they reached the jagged edge of the burn. Robert wondered out loud about whether a rainstorm had put it out or the wind had changed directions.

"Hard to say," said Hank. "Not everything has a reason."

Robert was beginning to think that there was no rhyme or reason to a lot of things. Like how had he ended up plodding along in the middle of nowhere on a stolen horse with a woman who only flirted when he wasn't in the mood?

The whole situation was depressing. It wasn't at all what he'd expected when he'd started out. The entire plan was ill conceived from the very beginning. He'd been traveling for better than a month, and according to their map, he wasn't a fourth of the way across the country yet. This land was vast. It was all well and good to argue back in Ottawa that a well-trained police force could do what an army couldn't, but they hadn't seen this land yet. Looking out across the prairie made all that brash talk sound like a lot of balderdash.

He'd do the best he could in assessing the situation, but he wasn't Hercules. He wished he had better advisors than a man who seemed intent on taking the easy way out and a woman who didn't appear to have the sense God gave a goose. It was difficult to envision their venture turning out well.

Though they'd ridden all night and half the day, Hank urged them to keep going. He said there was a lake up ahead, and they could camp there for the night. After that, they'd be traveling through the hills they'd been skirting all day, and it was probably better to do that in the daylight anyway.

Robert just shrugged. It made no difference to him. Now that they were in grass again, the horses kept trying to stop and graze as they went along. It was fine by him. He was in no hurry to get anywhere.

About an hour or so later, Hank called out, "Hey, lookie over there." He pointed to a small brown area where the top of a nearby hill met the sky. There seemed to be some movement, but it was hard to tell. "Are those wild Indians coming over the hill?"

That's just what they needed now—to be attacked by wild Indians. That would round out this adventure.

Robert pulled out his spyglass to take a look. The Indians were quite a distance away. Maybe he and Hank and Meg could make a run for it. Or perhaps it would be better to stand up to them right here.

There were about a dozen people on the horizon, but they appeared more pitiful than wild. They were sort of running along, their tattered clothes flapping in the breeze.

"I wonder why they're running," Robert said as he passed the spyglass to Hank.

Hank took a deep, noisy whiff of the air before checking things out with the spyglass.

Robert and Meg sniffed, too. The burnt smell was there again, but something different, too.

"Fire," said Hank. "That fire must have circled around, and now it's coming back toward us. It's hidden down behind that hill, but it'll be on us in no time. We better high-tail it to the lake."

Hank pulled the reins over on his horse, but Robert reached down and grabbed onto them to stop him.

"What about those people up there?" he asked, pointing toward the ragged bunch.

"What about them?"

"We can't just leave them," Robert said.

"Why not?"

Robert was astounded that Hank would even suggest abandoning these people to such a grisly fate. He looked over at Meg and saw the fright on her face.

"Listen, they're used to living like this," said Hank. "If we go after them, there's a good chance that none of us will make it out alive. You've never seen the way the wind can push a fire down on you. It's a frightful thing. I feel sorry for them. But I'm supposed to be looking out for you two, not the Indian nation."

"Then you take Meg and head for safety. Leave the packhorses here," Robert ordered as he let loose of Hank's reins and jumped off his horse. He was as clear-headed as he'd ever been about anything in his life. It reminded him of the night in the bar when Inspector Parker had been shot. There was no need to think things over. He knew what had to be done then just as he knew what he had to do now.

Grabbing the lead rope from Hank, he tied it to his own saddle, then went down the line uncinching and pulling off the packsaddles. When he'd thrown the last one on the ground, he mounted up. The horses were all shying around. No doubt, they'd smelled the fire in the air.

"Get her to safety," Robert ordered Hank as he dug in his heels and took off in the direction of the Indians. He felt his heart keeping time with the hoofbeats beneath him. The urge to let out a wild yell welled up inside of him.

"I'm coming with you."

He looked over to see Meg flying alongside. "Go with Hank," he shouted. She shook her head no and kept right on coming. He wished she wouldn't. There was no way he could protect her from what was ahead.

But he had to admit it was exhilarating to be doing what he knew was right with her at his side.

They headed across the prairie to the foothills. A flash of movement on his other side caught his attention and Robert realized that Hank was riding along with them.

"What the hell," Hank shouted and shrugged in answer to his unasked question. They were all grinning like they didn't have good sense.

Robert felt the surge of exhilaration. The Three Musketeers had nothing on them.

By the time they reached the Indians, the horses were getting hard to handle, jerking around as they tried to turn away from the danger ahead.

Meg and Hank held on to the reins, while Robert got down and boosted the children and the older folks up. He untied the lead reins on the pack animals and handed them over before remounting his own horse. Then they all dug in their heels and headed down the hill.

Hank had an old man hanging on behind him and a kid up in front. Meg had an old woman hanging on to her and a child in her lap. Robert had a young boy clinging to him and a babe that had been shoved in his arms.

Though the fire itself was some distance back, the smell and the sound of it were strong on them. They settled the horses into an easy lope. When the horses began wheezing, they slowed down to a walk. It was easier on the animals, but harder on the riders, who bounced up and down, clinging to one another to keep from falling off. They alternated paces until the wind whipped up and they could see the fire gaining speed behind them. The horses needed no urging to break into a gallop. They all hung on for dear life.

The Western broncs might not look as fancy as the blooded thoroughbreds they'd started out with, but Robert doubted those horses could have covered the miles like these magnificent animals. When he considered that except for a few rest stops along the way, they'd been moving for almost twenty-four hours now, he couldn't help but be impressed. He was amazed that the horses hadn't panicked. No wild snorting or running off as one would expect. A man couldn't help but admire them. He only hoped they had the stamina to get everyone to safety.

The wind was filled with smoke and cinders that stung his eyes and burned his throat. The occasional deer or prairie chicken they'd seen before had now swelled to a stampede of small animals racing by. With the flames crackling no more than fifty yards behind them, they reached the edge of the lake.

He led them right into the water and kept going until it was nearly up to the horses' bellies before he jumped down. They all did the same. Meg and Hank helped him pull the bridles and saddles off and turn the horses loose.

He trusted they'd be smart enough to stay in the water until the fire had burned its way around them.

Just before he tossed Meg's saddle down into the water, he grabbed her bedroll and pulled that old quilt of hers off. He knew it meant a lot to her, and it would be safe down in the mud.

To his surprise, she pulled it out of the water and held it up over the heads of some of the women. They gathered the kids and the old people in and soon all of them were wading out into the deeper water with the wet quilt protecting their heads.

One by one, the smaller children were picked up by the adults. Meg had a little one in her arms, and Hank had another in his. Robert still held the baby he'd carried to safety, and he knelt to let a young boy climb up on his back.

The Indian women started a low, soothing chant to calm the frightened children. Robert found it eased his mind as well. Amazingly enough, though he knew they had to be scared, neither the children nor the women showed any outward signs of fear—no shrieking, no crying, no carrying on. Even Meg was just doing what needed to be done without a lot of fuss and bother. This was the way men were supposed to behave. He was surprised to see women demonstrate the same commonsense approach to dealing with what could have been, and might yet be, a disaster.

The quilt formed a cave above them that they lifted from time to time on the lake side to let in the air. It was hot and smoky and sooty, and they could hear the fire snapping along the edge of the water. Some of the older people were wheezing and gasping. But otherwise they were safe for the time being.

The water was cold, and he could feel Meg shivering next to him. He wrapped his free arm around her and pulled her in tight. There was something about being under that blanket with Meg that made him feel on top of the world.

His life was beginning to read like one of those five-penny Westerns. Here they were surrounded by fire and Indians—with no provisions and probably no horses.

What next?

Chapter Ten

It was such a relief to be safe in the water that Meg didn't give a thought to what they were going to do from there on out. At least this time there hadn't been people screaming and burning timbers toppling over like that nightmare fire in Chicago.

Leaning into Robert, she felt his strength surround her. Maybe the reason she wasn't scared out of her wits was because of this man standing next to her. She'd been so terrified wading around Lake Michigan that dreadful night. How she wished she'd have known him then. Then she realized that he would've been about fifteen at the time.

So what? She'd never met anyone, no matter how old, who was as brave, and honest, and honorable as the man standing right next to her. And if they got out of this with any skin left, she was going to love it right off him.

It was strange how she truly wasn't scared this time. There wasn't a doubt in her mind that they'd make it through somehow. She leaned her head on his shoulder and felt his confidence and warmth flow into her. *What would it be like to face life head-on with this man? To hold his children in her arms? To grow old with him? Heavenly,* she decided, but not likely to happen on this earth.

Looking at the faces around her, she was surprised to realize there was no panic or terror on any of them. Just a calm acceptance that as soon as the fire swept around them, they'd come out of the water and take up their lives where they'd left off.

It seemed forever until Robert said that they could come on out. They walked along the edge of the lake and sat on the sand, grateful for the warmth it offered.

It was witches' country all around them, desolate, black, and burnt over.

The sun was setting behind the thick, shifting gray clouds. They had nothing to eat and only wet bedrolls to keep them warm. Who knew when, or even whether, they'd ever see the horses again.

But Meg knew they'd done the right thing. She wouldn't have been wanting to come out of this knowing they'd left these poor people back there to burn.

One of the women took the child from Meg. She'd been holding her for so long that her arms felt empty without her.

Then another woman pulled out a leather pouch of soggy brown chunks and passed a piece out to everyone.

"Pemmican," Hank explained.

It tasted like gritty tallow. But still, she was glad to have something in her stomach.

A little girl twirled around, making faces, and waving her arms up in the air. Meg chuckled and heard an old woman cackle next to her. Within moments, all the children were giggling, mimicking, and dancing about. They all began laughing like they didn't have a care in the world.

And for the moment, they didn't.

In a ritual as ancient as time, they celebrated making it through this ordeal together. Belly laughter eased the tension knotted in their stomachs and created a bond of understanding among them. Soon they'd need to worry about what to do next. But for now, it was enough to enjoy the moment and appreciate the lives they still had.

Hank was making faces at a little girl, pulling out his lips and eyelids to look frightening. The child was trying to copy him and giggling up a storm.

Meg made a fish face at Robert, poking her lips out and pretending to blow air bubbles. The next thing she knew, his mouth was on hers, kissing her for all she was worth. She felt his arms reach around her and pull her in tight to him. Holding on to one another, they created their own world, safe from the dangers surrounding them.

She wanted so much more than a kiss. But since that was out of the question, at least for the moment she rejoiced in the feel of him next to her.

Eventually, the laughter died down, and they all realized they needed to see to a few matters before night was upon them.

Meg and Robert each took one side of her quilt and wrung out as much of the water as they could, then they laid the poor cinder-spotted thing in the sand to dry. Working together, they pulled the saddles, bridles, and bedrolls out of the water and spread them out to dry as well. He left the guns underwater. Cleaning them in the coming dark was out of the question, and there was no sense in letting rust get started.

It was discouraging to find that water had leaked through the rubber sheeting wrapped around Robert's report. Though they could still make out a good deal of it, it would all have to be recopied.

While they were doing that, the Indian women began digging pits in the dry, warm sand. Meg had wondered how they were going to stay warm tonight. Digging themselves down in the sand made perfect sense.

The sunset was covered by smoke, but as darkness gathered around them, the women stretched out in the pits two or three together, scattering the children among them. They'd rubbed mud all over their own faces and patted her face and Hank's to show that the three of them should do this as well.

Meg realized that the breeze was keeping the mosquitoes away for now, but they couldn't count on that lasting. Well, they'd take care of that when the time came.

They helped cover the last group up to their necks before climbing into their own pit. It was an odd sight to look around and see heads sticking out of the sand, like marbles scattered about the beach.

Meg encouraged Hank to get in next to her and Robert. But Hank declined, saying he didn't think it was going to get all that cold tonight, and, besides, he wasn't ready to go to sleep just yet. He told them to get comfortable, then covered them in sand until only their heads stuck out.

They were snuggled together when they saw Hank pick up a couple of halters and start down the beach.

"Think I'll go see if those horses are looking for me yet," he said.

"Just a minute, and I'll come with you," Robert called after him as he moved to get up, shifting the sand off of them.

"Don't bother," said Hank. "Like as not, them broncs are a hundred miles from here. Even if I do run across 'em, it'll be a whole lot easier for one of us to sneak up on them than two. You just stay here and take care of the women."

Meg knew which woman she wanted him to take care of. Robert settled back in. She turned her head and rubbed her nose slowly back and forth across his, inhaling his scent along with the smell of smoke and ashes.

"Meg," he asked, "just how tired are you?"

"Not very," she said and realized it was true. Given the ordeal they'd been through and the fact that she'd not had so much as a wink of sleep the past twenty-four hours, she ought to be exhausted. But she wasn't, not really.

"How cold are you?" he asked in that same soft, low voice of his.

"Not very," she answered.

"Would you have any objections to lying on your quilt for a while?"

"Not at all," she said, feeling a smile spread across her entire body.

Together, they pushed up out of the sand. Robert picked up her quilt and folded it over one arm. He draped the other arm over Meg's shoulders.

They strolled along the beach like lovers on a holiday until they were some distance away. The waning moon shone through the haze, lighting the path for them.

When they found another open spot of sand, Robert spread out the quilt and, without a word, began to undress. By unspoken agreement, she did the same. Since their clothes were wet, it really wasn't much cooler with them off than on.

She stood in the moonlight, appreciating the sight of him. His familiar face was streaked with soot, and she resisted the urge to wet her fingers and wipe the black marks off. That seemed too motherly, and motherly wasn't at all the way she was feeling tonight.

He swallowed and she watched his Adam's apple bob up and down in the shadow of his neck. She recalled how nervous he'd been that first night at Bess's and wondered briefly if he was nervous now.

Her gaze traveled down past his shoulders and collarbone to the mounds of muscles on the top of his chest. A sprinkling of hair gathered to a dark line in the center. She followed that dark line to his belly button and on down.

Oh, my.

"Scared?" he whispered.

"No." And she truly wasn't. She trusted him completely. This man would no more hurt her than he would suddenly sprout wings and fly away. But what had sprouted up was a vision to behold, for sure.

They sank down to the quilt, and he suckled her while she toyed with him.

But not for long. The urge was too strong within them, and neither felt like denying themselves. With a groan he eased into her and she was surprised to find that it hardly hurt at all. She let out a little yelp, but it was more from surprise than the wee stinging she felt.

"I'm sorry," he murmured as he arched into her and held still.

"Don't be. I'm not," she said, marveling at the feel of him.

"Meg," he groaned, "don't ever leave me."

"You needn't worry there," she murmured as she moved her hips up just the teeniest bit. *My, that feels fine.*

He responded with just the smallest movement of his own, and she replied. They rocked back and forth, gaining confidence in their rhythm as they went along. She ran her hands along his spine, feeling each wale and hollow along the way. As she couldn't reach his lips with hers, she kissed his chest, settling in on a nipple when she found one. His moan of pleasure reached to the very core of her.

She knew where they were going this time, and though she was enjoying the journey, she could feel it tugging at her, pulling her along.

And then she was there. And it was doubly sweet because he was flying with her. His moans, his body, his soul melded with hers.

If she could wrap up a moment and keep it for later, this was the one she'd choose. She'd tuck it away to take out during those times when the world was too much to bear. When she was an old lady, all bent over in her rocking chair, she would pull back the corners of this memory and hold it close.

How can I go on knowing that life will never be as grand as this ever again?

She felt hot tears against her cheeks and a sob strangle in her chest.

"I didn't mean to hurt you, Meg," he said, pulling her tight against him. "I'm sorry, I didn't mean to hurt you."

"You didn't hurt me," she said softly, knowing she'd pinned a lie to her lips.

He'd shattered her heart. From now on, when anyone asked her what was the best time of her life, she couldn't say that it was still to come because that wouldn't be true. This would be it. She'd cherish this precious memory for as long as she lived. And weep in the night because it was gone.

"Marry me, Meg," Robert asked.

His words caught her by surprise. He was such a dear one. In his mind, he'd ruined her, and he was doing the honorable thing. Though she'd give anything to spend the rest of her life at his side, she knew as well as anyone what a foolish notion that was. How would that be for a young gentleman like him to marry a woman like her? It would be a shameful disgrace that they'd both live to regret.

Though she ached to say yes, she decided that it would be kinder to make light of his proposal, to treat it as the offhand remark it probably was.

"Oh, you wonder of a man," she said, pulling up to

kiss him. She tensed as she felt him slip loose from her, but it was too late. "And just who would you be thinking of asking to marry us out here in the middle of nowhere—Hank?"

She tickled his sides a bit and tried to bring a jolly feeling to the two of them. "Or perhaps you've spied a minister among these mosquitoes?"

The evening breeze was dying down, and the bugs were biting again. They rolled themselves up in her wet quilt, shoving their feet into the sand so there'd be enough to tuck in around their heads.

When they were snuggled in against one another, he said, "I know you think I'm too young to take on the responsibilities of marriage, that I wouldn't be able to support you. But I'm not just a dollar-a-day constable, Meg. I'm only doing this for a year. When I finish college, my uncle has a position in his shipping business waiting for me."

He said this as if his words would persuade her that he was a serious suitor. But it was all the more reason he shouldn't even be considering a marriage with her. How would that be for a man of importance to have a wife who was raised in a brothel? That would never do, not in the least.

But that didn't mean they couldn't enjoy the time they had together. And more than likely, the less talking they did, the more enjoying they'd have.

She ran her fingers lightly across his chest until she found that little nubbin she was looking for. Then she followed with her lips to it and was pleased at his response.

For a time, they were lost to the world.

Before exhaustion finally claimed her, Meg's last thought was that this was the happiest night of her life. She'd had nothing to eat for days except hardtack biscuits and a ball of gritty fat. She'd escaped a prairie fire by the skin of her teeth, and there was a good chance that tomorrow was going to be even less pleasant than today.

And still she was smiling.

Chapter Eleven

ROBERT WOKE UP TO THE CHATTERING OF CHILDREN ALL around them. He poked his head out of the quilt to see them running down the beach, splashing and giggling and generally behaving as if they were on a holiday outing.

He hurriedly pulled his clothes on and urged Meg to do the same. As she was dressing, she blushed like a new bride. He rather liked that image of her.

It looked to be a reasonable day. The sun was shining, and though the breeze still carried the strong smell of smoke, at least there wasn't any soot or cinders—or mosquitoes either, for which he was exceedingly grateful.

The first order of the day was going to be cleaning and drying out the guns. Hand in hand, he and Meg walked back to where the saddles were drying in the sand, and he retrieved their weapons from the water. He hoped the water hadn't ruined the saddles, but there'd been no option other than throwing them in the lake. Undoubtedly, their packsaddles and supplies were burned beyond salvage out on the prairie, where he'd dumped them yesterday.

They shook out the quilt and he sat down and proceeded to take apart both the rifles and the sidearms, while Meg went to meet with the women.

He watched her pick up the child she'd held yesterday and whirl around in a circle. Both seemed delighted and comfortable in one another's company. Why not? An experience like yesterday's did away with a lot of shyness.

Meg pantomimed brushing the sand off of herself. Apparently, the Indian women thought this was funny. They chattered among themselves, including Meg in the midst if not their actual conversation. Robert turned his attention back to the guns.

A few minutes later, Meg came back with a chunk of suet for him. It wasn't all that tasty, but it was better than nothing at all.

By the time Robert had the guns all cleaned and reassembled, who should show up but Hank riding one gelding and leading another. The rest of the horses were following at a distance. After saddling the first two, he and Hank were able to round up and get halters and bridles on the other four as well.

At first, the women didn't want to go with them, insisting through an exchange of hand signals with Hank that their men would be angry with them for leaving the area.

Robert had Hank show them that they would leave a trail that a blind man could follow and that they needed to find some shelter and food for the children.

They all mounted up much as they had the day before

and set off. The two little boys were obviously pleased to be riding with him. He had to admit, he rather enjoyed the way they looked up to him.

Late that afternoon, just as they were leaving the burned-over area, their men caught up with them. From the scowls on their faces, it was clear they were none too pleased to see their women and children riding along with strangers. Their suspicions were eased when the women explained what had happened. This was followed by an exchange of hand signals with Hank.

Though Robert kept his rifle close and stayed alert to any changes in the situation, the ragtag band bore little resemblance to the murdering savages he'd been led to expect. It was hard to imagine this pathetic group massacring anything bigger than a rat or a rabbit. They appeared to be more in need of protection than policing.

Hank and the Indian men traded various gestures back and forth for nearly half an hour. Robert couldn't make out what they were discussing, but they seemed perfectly willing to continue signing until the sun set. He grew weary of waiting for an explanation and asked Hank what they were saying.

"They're plenty glad to see you," Hank said.

"That's all?" *Surely, they hadn't taken them all this time to say they were glad to see them.*

"That's the gist of it. Then I asked them if they'd show you and Meg the way to the Sweet Grass Hills, and they're still trying to decide whether they want to do that or not."

"Where are you going?" This was the first time Hank had mentioned anything about not going with them.

"I think I'll head back to Winnipeg. Last night got me to thinking about things."

"Can't you do that at the end of the summer?" The thought of being totally responsible for Meg out here was unsettling.

"Just feels like time for me to go," the old scout said. "You'll do okay, don't you worry none. You got a strong sense of what's right and what's wrong, and you got the courage to act on it. That's the core of a good man and a good leader. You just keep following that, and you'll make out fine. You can pick up the rest of what you need to know along the way."

Robert would miss Hank's advice and company, but maybe it was time for him to go, time for him to be standing on his own two feet and not always checking with Hank on every little thing. He wouldn't mind being alone with Meg again either.

They followed the Indians to a stream with a few scattered trees along its banks and set up camp for the night. As they sat around the campfire, Robert asked the chief of the band to help him learn the hand signs. He'd have Hank ask the Indian men a question, then follow closely how Hank moved his hands and the response from the Indians.

It seemed that any question, regardless of what it was about, always began with the right hand at about shoulder height with the fingers separated and pointing upward. He tried that, twisting his wrist back and forth as he'd seen them do. They all nodded encouragement, so he imagined he had it right.

One of the younger men pretended to drink out of his

cupped hand and then pointed to the water nearby. That made obvious sense.

He pointed his hand down in front of him while closing it into a half fist, then quickly raised it and snapped his fingers open, imitating flames going up into the air.

The man combined the signs for fire and water again, then staggered around, bumping into things. The rest thought this was hilarious. Robert didn't know quite what to make of it until Hank explained that the whiskey traders often put cayenne pepper and the like into their liquor. Because of that, the Indians had taken to calling it "firewater."

Robert asked about the sign for whiskey trader, and Hank held up both hands, pointing to the sky with his index fingers, then dropped his arms until they crossed in front with the fingers pointing in different directions.

"Does this mean the traders travel in different directions?" he asked Hank.

"It might," the scout said. "It could also be explaining how traders often say one thing but mean the opposite. Hard to say."

Robert had him ask how long it'd been since they'd seen a whiskey trader.

"Too long," Hank said, translating a rather lengthy response.

It seemed the men had left the women behind while they'd gone off hunting. They signed hunting by putting the first two fingers of each hand in front of their eyes and wiggling in imitation of eyes looking out across the land. Robert thought it wouldn't be too long until he could converse in sign language.

Apparently, the hunting had been good, for that night they ate slow-roasted chunks of buffalo.

Robert asked Hank how to say "Thanks for the good buffalo," and Hank had him hold both hands palm down in a sweeping motion toward the ground. He explained that "good" meant "on the level of the heart." Of course.

He swung his arm out in an arc for "good." For "buffalo," he took a chance and curved his pointer fingers up above his head like buffalo horns.

Apparently, he'd guessed right because the men accepted his thanks with solemn faces. But the old women standing around the edge giggled behind their hands when he did this. Robert wondered if he'd made some error.

"Don't mind them," said Hank. "They're thinking you're a fine young buck and since you're learning their language, maybe you'll be wanting one of their women for your own."

Robert quickly asked Hank to teach him the sign for "no," which involved holding his hand palm down on the left side and then swinging to the right, turning it up and then back down again on the way back.

He did it twice, just to make certain they understood.

"Tell them I already have a woman," said Robert.

"I think they can see that for themselves," said Hank, tilting his head in Meg's direction.

Robert looked over and was caught by the sight of her running barefoot in the grass along the edge of the creek. The children were chasing after her or, more likely, after the feather she was holding above her head. They were all laughing and squealing, a picture of exuberance and joy.

Sometimes it seemed to Robert that he was the older one, always weighed down with responsibilities and worries whereas she flitted through life carefree as a butterfly.

She looked up at him and stopped in her tracks. There she stood, still as a statue—a long-limbed, peach-skinned, red-haired statue. Everyone else faded away, and for a moment they were the only two beings in existence. Then the children caught her and pulled her away. But for a moment she was his. He was struck by what a gift it was to know Meg Reilly.

It was too early to take her to bed, so he did the next best thing. He bid his farewells to the men, retrieved the packet of papers, and spread it out on a rock ledge. He hoped that would call her to him. It did.

"So, what did you decide to say?" she asked.

"The truth," he answered.

"Aye, that's best. Let them make of it what they will." She sat down next to him.

For the next hour, they talked of what needed to be said, and she wrote it down. Often he would find his thoughts had strayed to the way her hair curled about her ears or how her fingers curved around the pen. She would tease him back to reality, and they'd continue, only to find his thoughts wandering off a moment later.

They finally finished the report, dried it off, and wrapped it in a rubber sheet. The paper was crinkled from the water that'd seeped in, but the words were plain to read. He hoped his thoughts were as clear. He hoped they were convincing.

Hank and the Indians were circled around the campfire, signing to one another. They were finding considerable amusement in the topic. The warmth and friendliness drew the two of them over.

"We'll send this report back with Hank," Robert said. "He's leaving for Winnipeg tomorrow."

"And why would he be doing that?" Meg asked.

"I imagine he's had enough adventures for the time being," Robert replied. From the way she tightened her mouth, he could see that Meg didn't like the idea of Hank leaving any more than he did.

Two of the women moved aside to let them sit down. Whatever point Hank was making at the time tickled their funny bones, because they all burst out laughing.

"Meg," he said when the laughter died down. "Good to see you. Too bad you don't know the lingo yet. I'm sure they'd like your stories better than mine."

"I could tell you, and you could do the signing for me," she suggested.

"Now why didn't I think of that?" From the way he said it, it was clear he had.

"In the long time ago," she began.

Robert could feel the familiar rhythm of her words pulling him along with her.

"In the land of Tir-nan-og, there was a warrior called by the name Cuchulain. And even when he was a young boy, the warrior Cuchulain never took the easy path, but always chose the road to glory, whatever the risk." She looked daggers at Hank, clearly conveying what she thought of his reluctance to assist them on this difficult journey.

"Then the man was a fool," said Hank. "But then, who wants to sit around a fire and listen to tales of how cautious men keep out of trouble?" He winked at the two of them, and Robert couldn't help but accept the man for who he was. He didn't fault him for wanting to turn back. Hank had never agreed to stay to the end. Maybe this trip was just more than he was up for.

Meg continued with her story of how Cuchulain had been warned by Cathbad the Druid that if he should take up arms, the time of his life would be short but his name would be greater than any other in Ireland.

Robert wondered if that would be his own fate, destined to accomplish remarkable deeds but live only a short time. If that was the case, he wanted to live life to its fullest while he had the chance. He looked over at Meg, who was sitting beside him. It was hard to imagine how life could be any fuller than it was right now.

His mind wandered from Meg's story to the report they'd just written and to what he hoped awaited him later that evening.

The sun was certainly taking its own sweet time to travel that last distance to the edge of the horizon. Robert wondered why it seemed to just pop up in the morning, like it was on a spring. But in the evening, it was as if that invisible spring was stretched out all across the sky, and the sun was just barely able to overcome its force.

When he saw one of the women yawning, Robert made a great show of yawning himself. All the men followed suit and the women laughed, but he noticed everyone wasted no time in getting to their feet. As they were gathering their bedrolls, one woman handed them a buffalo robe and gave them a push as if to tell them they needed to find a spot off by themselves. Robert thought that was a great idea.

He and Meg walked up the creek a ways before finding a flat, protected spot to settle in for the night. He spread the buffalo robe on the ground, then she snapped her quilt above it and let it float down over it. Without a word between them, they stripped off their clothes and slipped naked under the covers.

They came together as if it had been years and not hours since they'd last touched. She ran the arch of her foot down his calf, sending shivers up his spine. He caressed his cheek against hers, wanting to kiss her but knowing it would be too much right now. Their hands were everywhere, touching, exploring, checking to see if everything felt the same as last night.

It did.

But last night's urgency was gone. There was no rush now, no reason not to enjoy every step of the way home.

Home? Now why had that word come to mind? But it fit the way she belonged in his arms and he belonged in hers. He tried to recall when he'd ever experienced this feeling of being wanted and of being delighted in before. Nothing came to mind. A responsibility, a duty, a nuisance—that's what he'd always been to others.

There was a doubt niggling around the back of his mind about how Meg delighted in a great many things. He buried the thought. She desired him now. That's what counted.

They wrapped their arms and legs around one another as if trying to merge through their skins. When their lips finally met, the sweetness of it all stole his breath away.

Time came to a halt. Or perhaps it flowed endlessly, like the stream that gurgled alongside of them. He really didn't know, or care. All he was interested in was how her breast filled his mouth, how her behind felt beneath his fingertips, how her sighs traveled the length of him. His senses seemed all mixed up. He could feel the sound of her voice on his skin, like a gentle vibration. He could hear the way she moved against him, a low humming that followed the rhythm of their joining.

They were slippery with sweat when he kicked the covers off. The breeze cooled his skin, but it was no match for the heat that kept pouring from inside. It seemed that the slower they moved, the hotter they were. Every time he felt the end approaching, he held himself still until it passed. There was no rush here. If this lasted all night, it would be all right by him.

Inevitably, the intensity became too much to put off. They were both holding still when it happened. He felt her give a little gasp. Then, knowing that once she went over the edge there was no way he could keep from following, he pulled loose. She rocked against him as if seeking his return. But it was too late. The exquisite sensations pulsed through them, flowing back and forth, and out then into the universe, leaving them limp and wondering at the magic of it all.

If this wasn't paradise, he didn't know what was.

They were a tangle of arms and legs when they woke up in the morning. It would've been so easy to slip back into lovemaking. But from the sounds of things, the rest of the camp was already up and about. So they did a quick wash-up in the stream, donned their clothes, and joined the rest near the fire.

Hank was already saddled up and ready to go.

"You'll do all right, Robert," he said, clapping him on the shoulder in a gesture of farewell. "They'll take you as far as Fort Qu'Appelle and get you pointed in the direction of the Sweet Grass Hills. It's good country, and you'll not be too far from the Whoop-up trail. I'd say that'd be as good a place as any to find a spot for that headquarters of yours.

"Meg, you take care now." He gave her a long hug, and even though Robert knew it didn't mean anything more than friendship, it still bothered him to see it.

"Why won't these people guide us all the way there?" he asked in an attempt to get Hank's attention off Meg.

"They're Cree, and that's Blackfoot country," Hank explained, backing off from Meg but not totally letting go. *What is the matter with the man?*

"Thanks for seeing that report gets sent to Ottawa," he said in another attempt at turning his attention from Meg.

"No problem," Hank assured him. The man still hadn't let go of Meg. Was there something going on here that he should know about? It was an irrational thought, but then things weren't always what they seemed.

"Say hi to Carina for me, will you?" asked Meg.

"I'll do that," he said. "In fact, I may be saying hi to her from now on."

"Thinking of settling down, are you?" Meg said, teasing him.

"That fire sort of opened my eyes," Hank said. "And I

decided I'd best get back there and see if things might work out for Carina and me before it's too late."

"What brought that about?" she asked. "This is the first I've ever heard about you wanting to settle down."

"Oh, I'm getting a little long in the tooth for the adventuring business."

"You seem spry enough to me," she said.

"I guess I still got a few good years left in me," he said with a half smile. "It's just that Carina and I used to be like you and Robert here. We came to a parting of the ways because she didn't want to roam, and I didn't want to nest. It hurt like hell when she married that dry goods man and had those boys of hers. He's dead and gone now, but Carina's still a desirable woman. Who knows how long it'll be before someone else takes his place? I guess I want that someone to be me."

"Well, good luck," Robert said, and he meant it.

"You two take care of each other," he said as he mounted up. Then he leaned down and took Robert's hand in his for a firm handshake. "You got yourself a job ahead of you, son."

Robert wondered whether he was talking about figuring out the Mountie mess or taking care of Meg. Hard to say which one would be more difficult to accomplish.

He put his arm around Meg and they watched Hank ride off. Robert regretted his leaving but realized it was time for him to go.

"He's been a good friend," said Robert.

"Aye," Meg agreed. "He has at that."

* * *

The next few weeks were like nothing Robert had ever experienced before. He was more deeply alive than he'd ever felt in his life. Each moment was meaningful. It was as if someone up above had cranked up the intensity of the world. Colors were brilliant, with deeper, richer hues than he'd ever recalled seeing. Sounds had a ring and resonance that he hadn't been aware of before. He even savored the smells, the sweet scent of wildflowers on the afternoon air as well as the rank odor of the decaying buffalo carcasses they came across.

Meg was gently teaching him to cease judging things as good or bad, better or worse, but just to enjoy them for what they were. Could a person really say that the bluebells growing along the streams were prettier than the yellow buttercups out in the meadows? Were the puffy clouds that floated above them better than the wispy mare's-tail clouds? Was kissing his ear preferable to whispering in it? She urged him to use that same reasoning other places.

It worked. He had a tendency to look down on the Indians they were traveling with. They lived such a precarious existence, it was easy to view them as simple, backward, and altogether inferior.

But the more he was around them, the more he appreciated their ways. Though they might not have much, what they had they shared. They cared for one another, laughed easily, and calmly accepted adversities that most others would have railed against. Who was to say which ways were better?

They knew a great deal about their world and gladly taught their new friends. They showed them how to look at signs in the trampled grass for what was happening around them and how to watch the way the clouds formed in the sky in order to predict the coming weather. Patiently, they taught the two of them how to speak their sign language. Hank had told him that this was a universal means of communication among the plains Indians and that once he could talk with this tribe, he could talk with any of the others.

Robert could see that learning this sign language should be an essential part of every Mountie's training, and he and Meg spent hours every night writing down and organizing what they'd learned during the day.

They also noted what things seemed to offend and what was the best way to confront someone. It really wasn't that difficult. Like himself, the Indians valued honesty and courage and were offended by disrespect and discourtesy.

And naturally, they recorded what they saw of the land they were traveling through, the streams and rivers, the crossings and the trails.

Sometime it seemed as if there was too much to take in. By nighttime, his brain was filled to capacity.

Fortunately, he didn't have to do much thinking at night. He and Meg spent those hours exploring the world of sensual pleasure together. In his wildest imagination, he'd never thought lovemaking would be anything like this. There were so many more dimensions to it than he'd thought possible.

Who would've guessed that so much of the body would be so sensitive or how much depended on timing? What felt grand one moment was annoying the next. Blending into one another and then into the universe only to drift off to sleep was becoming as natural as breathing, as easy as gazing at this wonder of a woman he held in his arms.

Their lovemaking wasn't confined to the hours of darkness either, but happened throughout the day as well. One moment he'd be setting a rabbit snare and look up to see her watching him. He'd be caught in her spell, unable to move or think beyond the need to touch her, hold her in his arms. Or he'd be staking out the horses, and she'd walk past and touch her fingers to his neck and he'd melt. Or they'd be sitting around a campfire, and she'd send a slow wink in his direction. All of a sudden, he wasn't hungry anymore, at least not hungry for the rabbits roasting over the fire.

Odd that though this was a time apart from the world, he'd never felt so deeply immersed in it. If he lived out his days like this, he suspected he'd die a happy man.

Just as time was ceasing to have any meaning, they reached Fort Qu'Appelle, an old Hudson Bay trading post. He bought packsaddles, tools, and supplies for Meg and himself. For their traveling companions, he bought iron pots, striped blankets, and sticks of candy.

The men were insistent that he buy them liquor, repeating the upward hand-flicking and drinking motion for firewater over and over. Naturally, he refused. Naturally, they were disappointed. They couldn't understand why he'd deny them such a simple request, and he didn't know enough sign language to explain it.

After watching the endless back-and-forth over the matter, one of the traders talked with them in their language and they let the matter drop after that. Robert asked him what he'd said that had made such a difference.

"I told them it was against your religion," the trader said.

"It isn't against my religion," Robert protested.

"You're a Mountie, right?" the man asked.

Robert nodded in agreement.

"Then it's against your religion."

The man wasn't quite right, but he was close. The more Robert saw of this country and the people in it, the more he believed in the mission of the Northwest Mounted Police. He was no longer just going along with what others had told him; he could see it for himself.

That night, Meg taught the women how to fix biscuits. For their farewell dinner, they feasted on buffalo stew and biscuits and the warmth of friendship.

It took forever to leave the next morning as each one had to say a lengthy good-bye. Often as not, these silent speeches were accompanied by a gift. The children gave Meg feathers and pretty rocks, the women a hand-woven grass basket and a buffalo robe.

The sun was high in the sky before they were finally on their way. Robert was anxious to get going. Not only was it nearly midsummer and he still had quite a bit to do before winter set in, but he was uncomfortable with the amount of alcohol consumption that seemed to go on at the fort. He knew he was supposed to do something about it, but he was at a loss to know what that might be. He could hardly arrest anyone who looked intoxicated. For then what would he do with them? There were no jails or judges anywhere. This was something he needed to include in his recommendations. Surely the Mounted Police couldn't be expected to do it all. There must be a system set up to handle lawbreakers once they were apprehended.

But that was a worry for tomorrow. Today, blue sky stretched from one end of the earth to the other and he was heading off to do his duty with the woman he loved at his side. *Does life get any better than this?*

Whenever possible, they followed the meandering rivers across the country. They could probably have made better time by heading straight across the prairie, but he thought it was safer all the way around to stay close to water.

But Robert had to admit, the real reason he was content to take their time was that he didn't want these days to end. He felt like he was coming into his own. Instead of always turning to others for advice and direction, others were turning to him. He liked that.

Nor was he anxious to change a thing between himself and Meg. He'd not asked her again to marry him, but he intended to, just as soon as they reached Fort Macleod in the fall. It was the only honorable course of action.

Not that he had any objection to being wedded to her. He did dread introducing her to his uncle Walter. He was fairly certain that his uncle would find neither her outrageous behavior nor her fanciful stories as amusing as he did. No doubt, there would be a grim lecture on the duties and responsibilities of their class of people. Perhaps even a stern reprimand on his impetuous behavior and the impact it would have on his business and political career.

He'd deal with that when the time came. Meg was a

stimulating companion in more ways than one. She enjoyed his tales of horrible headmasters and foolish houseparents and would, often as not, respond with funny stories of her own. He'd never seen anyone enjoy life the way she did, and he loved the way she would just throw her head back and let the laughter bubble out of her.

He taught her how to tie knots and she taught him how to play poker. Robert decided that knowing how to keep track of who had what as well as how to bluff out a poor hand would be useful skills in the years to come. Actually, it was probably more useful knowing this than knowing how to tie a bowline in a bite or a half hitch. It was hard to imagine that Meg would be tying knots once they returned to society. Unless she planned to kidnap someone, of course.

With a sinking feeling, Robert realized that wasn't beyond the realm of possibility. Judging from what he'd observed, morality was a flexible concept with Meg. Try as he might just to accept things as they were, there were certain behaviors that he put under the criminal category. Horse thievery for one. Cheating at cards, for another.

No doubt, she would curb her criminal tendencies once earning a living was no longer her burden but his. But he wouldn't put it past her to become involved in embarrassing, even scandalous behavior, without realizing what it would do to his career.

He would just have to deal with it when it happened, for he saw no way around the situation. He could hardly ask her to be his mistress. That would never do. Not only would she be dreadfully hurt by such a request, but it would make their children illegitimate—neither an appealing prospect.

He realized that his future would be compromised with her as his wife. He could only imagine her regaling his colleagues with tales of working in a brothel or the disastrous end to her riverboat-gambling scheme. What was hysterically funny out here sipping tea under the open sky would no doubt be considerably less amusing told in a drawing room over sherry. He could already envision the pinch-faced, disapproving responses to how they'd slept on a smelly buffalo robe or shared pemmican with their Cree friends around a fire. Nor could he imagine Meg keeping those stories to herself.

Well, he would just have to deal with that when the time came. Others had survived less-than-fortuitous marriages. He would, too.

Today the breeze was blowing away the bugs, the woman beside him was laughing up a storm, and, if all went well, they wouldn't have to worry about polite society for some time to come.

Chapter Twelve

The next few weeks were heavenly. As they rode along, they talked about everything under the sun. Meg told all sorts of stories about her life, mixing in a few extra details here and there to make them more interesting.

Robert talked a little about his life, but only when she asked and only in answer to direct questions. He didn't add anything on his own. Meg didn't feel he was hiding anything, just that he didn't find it all that interesting or pleasant to talk about his life. There were a few funny things that happened to him at boarding school and in college. But for the most part, it seemed a dreary existence full of overbearing adults and cruel classmates. From what she could tell, his father had been a self-indulgent wastrel and his mother had bats in her belfry. He didn't say much about them or about his uncle, who was apparently a nice man but too busy with his own endeavors to spend much time with Robert.

However, he did talk endlessly about the Mounties—how critical the success of the Force was, how important it was to avoid the mistakes of the Americans, and, of course, how essential his reports would be in all of this. She just let him go on. It was easy enough to turn her attention to the wildflowers, the distant foothills, and the cottony clouds that followed along above like guardian angels.

At the first sign of rain, they'd head for what shelter they could find and set up camp. Usually, by the time the thunderstorms rolled across the plains, they'd be snug as bugs in their tent, counting the time between the lightning flashes and the booming thunder. They'd play poker and parlor games. And they'd make love.

Meg prayed for rain.

Despite the almost continual bother of mosquitoes and black flies, the only real unpleasantness they encountered was during the crossing between the headwaters of the Qu'Appelle and the South Saskatchewan River. It was a substantial distance, and Robert insisted that they cover it in the least amount of time possible. It took them days of hard riding to cross, and they were uneasy the entire time. One harrowing experience with a prairie fire was all either cared to go through.

They followed the river down to a settlement they were certain must be Medicine Hat. From the sounds of all the shouting and shooting, it appeared there was some sort of drunken celebration going on.

"I say we go on to the Sweet Grass Hills," said Robert. "I doubt we'll find anyone here sober enough to give us useful information."

Meg nodded in agreement. They were doing fine all by themselves. As far as she was concerned, regardless of what they were celebrating, there was nothing to be gained by going anyplace where drunken people were shooting off guns.

Besides, the snow-topped Trois Buttes Mountains were calling to them with promises of cool shade and green pasture in the foothills before them.

The closer they got to this hill country, the stranger it seemed. They'd been warned about this area back in Fort Qu'Appelle. According to the Indians, powerful spirits lived here in the slopes and valleys.

Meg believed it. In the distance they could see a huge rock wall that looked too orderly to be there by accident. It almost seemed to have been built by a clumsy giant.

The afternoon they rode into the first valley, he passed her the spyglass and pointed to the top of the hill. She nearly fell off her horse at the sight of the animal he was pointing out. They'd seen creatures all along the way, everything from toads to buffaloes, and they'd heard wolves howl off in the distance, but this was the first time she'd seen one.

Pictures in the storybooks didn't do this animal justice. All of a sudden she didn't feel so safe and snug in that tent of theirs.

Meg scanned the surrounding areas with the spyglass.

"I wish I could find a cave," she said. "I'd rather spend the night in a cave than in that flimsy tent of ours."

"Wolves don't eat people, Meg. That's just in fairy tales," he reassured her. "A wolf would have to be desperate even to come around a campfire."

"Well, maybe that one's a desperate wolf," she said, not convinced in the least by his argument.

She didn't find a cave, but she did see some smoke rising in the distance. Apparently, they weren't the only ones in the valley.

They rode up the side of the hill to where they could get a better view. From there, they could see that the smoke was rising from a spot that was overgrown with leafy trees and lush bushes in various shades of green.

"Might be a hot springs," Robert said, looking at the map in front of him. "It's too billowy for smoke. More likely it's steam. According to this map, the mountains to the west of us are riddled with hot springs. I suspect that this could be one of them."

"Let's go see," she urged. Hot springs meant a hot bath. They'd taken brisk dips in the rivers along the way, but the water had always been far too chilly to allow much more than a quick jump-in and a fast scrub. She could do with a nice long soak.

"What about the wolf?" he asked, teasingly.

"A wolf isn't going to jump into a pool of water. Haven't you ever read about wolves?"

He threw up his hands as if bowing to her superior reasoning ability, and they set off through the trees.

About an hour later, Robert was in the middle of a tale about a hard-of-hearing housemother at his boarding school when Meg noticed that the faint odor of old eggs was mixed in with the smell of the pines and the grass. The trail passed through the trees into an open meadow with a blue-green pool of water. Without a word, they both stopped to stare.

It was like something out of a fairy tale. Water bubbled out and flowed down a gray mound into the pool. Steam rose gently and hovered around before drifting off to disappear. Tall grasses, strewn with white and yellow wildflowers, lined the banks and bent down to brush their tips along the glassy surface of the water.

Meg held her breath at the beauty and peacefulness of it all. It was so perfect, she almost expected to see the wee folk peeking out from behind the bushes.

The silence was broken by the loud, "whick, whick, whick," from a woodpecker, followed by the scratchy, "chip, chip," of an unseen bird. They reminded Meg of an old married couple carrying on a familiar argument, one in which neither listens to the other or really expects any change to come about, but they go through the motions anyway, just out of habit.

A small sadness came over her. She and Robert would never be having old-married-couple arguments. Likely they were coming to the end of their time together. The snow on the distant mountain tops was a reminder of how short a time they had left. She glanced over at him and felt such a bittersweet pain at the sight of that cowlick of black hair that was forever falling over his forehead.

They dismounted and went over to put their hands in the water. It was almost too warm on her wrist, and Meg could hardly wait to sink down into it. Maybe she'd sleep right out there in the middle of it tonight. She cupped her hands together and bent down for a drink.

"With a pinch of tea, it wouldn't be too bad," she said once she'd had her fill. She glanced over at Robert.

Clearly, neither one of them was thinking about tea drinking.

The anticipation of the night to come had them exchanging grins while they hobbled their horses.

Meg couldn't get out of her clothes fast enough. She took a flying leap into the lower pool and floated back to the top. The water was just deep enough that if she stood on her tiptoes, she could keep her nose out of the water—barely. She spread her arms out and waved her hands around in fishtail figure eights to keep herself upright.

The tension eased from the muscles in her shoulders and back, and when she began gently kicking her legs around in a circle, she could feel their ache ease away as well. It felt so grand after all the hours in the saddle. It was too bad they couldn't have found a spot like this every night.

But they were here now, and she was going to enjoy it to the fullest.

Relaxed and light-headed from the hot water, she let her thoughts run in wicked ways. When Robert reached out to lick the water from her lips, she couldn't help but imagine the feel of his tongue along her neck, down her spine.

Passion flowed thick between them until she would not have been surprised to see it crackle in the air, like sparks flying up from a quick fire.

Her gaze was locked with his. What was between them grew more powerful with each passing day—and each passing night. She'd carefully avoided attaching the word "love" to it, preferring to think of what they shared only as physical passion, but she knew that wasn't true.

All of a sudden, she couldn't bear the sweetness of it all a moment longer. She felt that overwhelming panic and lightness that comes from looking over the edge and knowing it's a long way down.

Meg pushed away from him and moved over to where she could reach bottom. The rocks were slippery, and she had to move carefully over to the edge of the water. She pulled her quilt around her and walked down an animal trail without looking back.

Within a short distance, Meg reached a rocky point and climbed up on it to watch the sun set. This peaceful, in-between time was always her favorite part of the day. She loved the way the coral rays gradually filled the sky, then disappeared into steel blue and finally black.

In the past, she'd occasionally considered taking up art. Now she wished she had. She would love to sketch Robert—his determined expression when he dug in his heels, his excitement at seeing a buffalo herd for the first time, his frustration when things didn't work out the way he wanted them to. He would never be much of a poker player. His thoughts and feelings were as clear on his face as if he'd written them there with pen and ink. He simply wasn't devious enough to hide his thoughts behind a blank look.

She heard him climb up behind her and sit down. One nice thing about Robert, he didn't crowd a person.

"What's the matter, Meg?" he asked after a time.

"Just a little sad tonight, Robbie," she told him. It was true. Meg wasn't real sorrowful. That would come later. She was just coming to terms with what was to be.

"You go on back," she told him. "I'll be there in a little while."

He put his hand on her shoulder and kissed her neck before leaving. *Oh, is he a sweet man or what?*

Twilight was settling in like a comforter that had been snapped in the air and was floating down to cover everything beneath it. Meg realized that if she wanted to see the passion on his face tonight, she'd best get back.

She walked around the bend and into the meadow, where she saw Robert floating out in the deep end. Without a second thought, she dropped her quilt, ran up to the edge of the water, and jumped into his arms.

The two of them rolled around like a couple of otters, giggling and carrying on. Finally, he found his footing and stood up with her in his arms. It felt so grand bobbing about with him that she couldn't wait to feel him inside of her. Obviously, neither could he.

Gently, almost reverently, she turned to face him, then slowly slid down until the two of them were joined. Wrapping her legs around him, she started to gently rock but stopped when he groaned, "No."

"No?" Surely, he didn't want to pass on this and return to huddling under their blankets.

"Not yet, at any rate," he said with just a bare hint of a smile.

She clenched down and watched the way his eyes melted and his mouth quivered.

"I love you," he said softly.

"You love this," she replied quickly, unwilling to get serious, not tonight. Tonight they'd play. They'd save serious for later.

"That too," he said with a broad ear-to-ear grin.

She loosened her arms from around his neck and reached down to tickle him. Robert jumped in response, but held on tight to her.

As the twilight changed to darkness, they kissed and laughed, and tickled and talked. With his feet firmly planted on the bottom, he lifted her up, then pulled her into him ever so slowly. They had all night to get there, there was no need to rush.

But it was steadily building. She could feel it in herself and in him as well.

"Last one there's a rotten egg," she said, tickling him ever so gently under the arms in an attempt to slow him down. He tickled back, and, in the midst of their laughter, rapture overtook them. Wondrous, glorious, unbelievable pure bliss—it rocked her to her very core. The shudders of release combined with the tremors of laughter and flowed through her in an endless stream. It was the best, just the best.

Meg collapsed back to float on the water. When she finally found the strength to open her eyes, she was astounded to see that they'd lit up the universe. Amazed at the sight, she blinked and gave her head a quick shake to make sure she wasn't just imagining things.

She wasn't. In the middle of the night, the sky was filled with an awesome display of light and color. Waterfalls of rose and orange and red flowed into green and cream-colored light. Then it all swirled in on itself in a rush and slowly drifted apart to begin all over again. The hair stood up on her arms at the very sight of it.

"Aurora Borealis," she heard him whisper as he pulled her back against him.

"What?"

"According to the legend, since we made love under the Aurora Borealis, our love will last throughout eternity."

Unwilling to discuss legendary love or any other kind of love, for that matter, she quickly asked, "What does Aurora Borealis mean?"

"Aurora was the Roman goddess of the dawn," he said, turning her around to face him. "Borealis means 'of the north.' It's also called the Northern Lights."

He was quiet for a moment. Then he turned her to him and looked deep in her eyes. "Marry me, Meg," he said out of the clear blue.

She felt her chest tighten in on her. "Marry you?" she asked. "Where did that come from?"

"It came from the bottom of my heart. This is a good omen for us, Meg."

"And here I thought I was the superstitious one!" was all she could think of to say.

Why does he have to bring this up again now? Her feelings of joy were being rapidly replaced by a sense of dread and doom.

"I'm superstitious enough to know that you're the best thing that ever happened to me," he said.

"Can't we just go on the way we are?"

"I'm afraid you'll leave me, Meg," he said earnestly. "I realize I'm not the most exciting man you've ever run across. And I know I've got a lot to learn about the world, but you're the most wonderful woman I've ever known, and I want you at my side the rest of my life."

"Robert, I'm practically the only woman you've ever known," she pointed out.

"Nonetheless," he said with a broad smile and an even broader wink, "you're the best."

"What would your uncle Walter say?"

"He'll be green with envy."

"I'll bet."

"It doesn't make any difference what he thinks. It's my life, and I'll live it the way I see fit."

"Robert," she said, trying to talk some sense into him. "I'm practically old enough to be your mother."

"That'd make me sort of like Oedipus then, wouldn't it?" he said with just the start of a smile teasing around the edge of his mouth.

"Never heard of the fella, but that's another reason we wouldn't make a good match. I can read and write well enough and I have my teaching certificate, but I don't have anywhere near the education you do. I'd be an embarrassment to you."

"Ah, Meg. I'd never be ashamed of you, never."

He was so earnest, so naive about what the future would hold. What could she say that would open his eyes?

She twisted around and leaned back on his shoulder. They both stared up at the swirling, whirling colors, at the stars peeking out around the edges. Meg tried to lose herself in the magnificence of it all.

"It's because I'm a bit of a plodder, isn't it?" he said after the longest time.

She could feel his discouragement and longed for things to be different. Might as well wish for the moon.

"That's got nothing to do with it," she insisted. "We're just not suited to one another."

"We seemed suited well enough these past two months," he pointed out.

She rolled her head to the side and kissed him in that gentle spot beneath his ear before saying anything.

"Robert, this has been a grand and glorious time. I love riding alongside you. The country is breathtaking, our conversations have been anything but dull, and the nights have been pure magic." She kissed him again. "But it's just been us. Let's wait until we get back to reality before we make any grand plans, shall we?"

She could tell by the stubborn set to his lips that he wasn't at all pleased with her suggestion.

"You know I'd always take care of you, Meg. You'd never have to work in a bawdy house or on a riverboat or anything like that ever again."

"But the fact is, I once did. And though you might be willing to forget whatever happened in the past, I doubt those society folks back in Ottawa will be that generous."

"No need to tell them."

"They'll be able to tell by the way I talk that I'm not fresh out of finishing school."

She felt so safe and secure wrapped in his arms, and she'd give anything to be able to say yes. But she would never fit in his world. Why lead him on? Why lie to herself?

No doubt, she could learn to talk better and use the right fork and all, but she would always be shanty Irish.

Eyebrows would be raised, invitations delayed, and his future would be hostage to a foolish decision made in the heat of passion. Even that would cool down, and then what? Would she have to stand by and watch younger, more attractive women capture his attention?

In ten years, he'd be just coming into his prime, and she'd be plucking out gray hairs. She ached at the unfairness of it all.

Hot, thick tears tried to burn their way out. "Let's not let tomorrow ruin tonight," she said quietly, doing her best to keep her voice even. "Please, let me have you to myself for just a while longer."

He started to say something, but she kissed him into silence.

After a time, the lights faded. Hand in hand, they waded out of the water. After drying one another off, they rolled up in their blankets and snuggled in for the night.

When the stars were fading and the sky was soft and pink with the dawn, Meg slipped back into the water. The morning had a chill to it that made floating in the hot springs even that much finer. She filled her lungs with the moist air hovering above the surface and gazed around at the mountains that protected this valley.

This was the safest she'd ever felt in her entire life. Even knowing there was a wolf out there hadn't kept her from a good night's sleep. She knew Robert would protect her.

"Penny for your thoughts." She heard his voice, deep and rich, coming from behind her.

"You would get change for a penny, that's for sure,"

she said, settling back in against him. "I was only thinking about how easy it is to feel safe around you, Robert."

"I guess that thought's worth a penny," he said, wrapping his arms around her and pulling her back into him.

"And what might you be thinking?" she asked in return.

"I just realized how your belief that I can take care of you helps me believe it, too."

Then, as if he'd decided this was getting far too serious to start out the day, he reached across a little farther and playfully tickled her under the arms.

Meg twisted around and tried to grab on to his hands. She wondered how long she'd been ticklish. When had that been turned back on? She was jumping and squirming all over and in order to get his mind off tickling, she planted her lips on his and gave him a toe-curling kiss.

When they came up for air, he laid his head alongside hers, and whispered, "You're the best, Meg."

She melted at the words. *If only things could always stay this way.*

"I say we stay here for a few days."

"Really?" She was overjoyed at the possibility of holding off the world for just a few days longer.

"Really," he assured her. "The horses could use a rest, and so could we. I'll scout about a bit, but we'll use this as our base camp. Do you think you'd like that?"

"I think I'd *love* that," she said, throwing herself back on the water with her arms outstretched. Just think, days and days of this. It'd be enough to carry her through a lifetime of troubles. No goblins about today.

They were wrinkled as raisins when they finally

emerged from the water. He spent the day cleaning his weapons and rubbing neat's-foot oil into the saddles and bridles. She spent the day washing. The stream running out of the end of the hot springs was the perfect wash hole, and her quilt was the first thing she dunked into it.

When the water was finally running clear of soap and dirt, she had Robert help her wring it out and hang it across the rope he'd strung between the trees. The intertwining vines of flowers practically glowed in the sun and brought back the memory of her mother and how they had worked and laughed and cried over this quilt.

It was a difficult pattern to keep straight. Every time they had to rip out stitches, her mother would say, "That's why it's called the Wedding Knot, because it's a lot more complicated than it seems at first."

Isn't that the truth!

But it was grand having it sparkling clean again. One of these days, she'd have to cover over the places with the cinder holes in them. Or, maybe she wouldn't. Perhaps she'd keep them as a reminder of this summer.

The days passed like shooting stars—wonderful in the moment, but gone before she knew it. The more Meg tried to hang on to this time, the faster it seemed to go.

"Let's come back here and build a cabin someday, Meg," Robert said one evening. He was stirring the fire around with a stick, and from the way he kept looking at that fire and not at her, she knew it was time to go.

Her chest tightened until she could barely get a breath of air. She'd been dreading this moment.

"Aye," was all she could say. *If only it were so.*

They lingered way into the night making love, as if both knew their time was coming to an end.

Without actually talking about it, they packed up and headed out after breakfast. Meg kept turning around to get one last look. Even when it was no more than just a dot of light green amidst the darker green of the surrounding valley, she couldn't keep her eyes from it. *If I were Lot's wife, I'd be a pillar of salt by now,* she thought.

They came across a trail that Robert was certain would lead them to Fort Macleod. Sure enough, it did. They topped a low hill one morning and there was a fort rising out of the river mist below.

It was just what she'd always thought a fort should be. Pointed upright logs formed a stockade fence around an orderly collection of buildings. There was an open area in the center where a group of men were standing at attention around a flagpole. Bugle notes rang out from the fort. It looked like a place of protection, somewhere to go for safety.

No doubt it was—for everyone but her. For Meg Reilly it was the beginning of being back on her own.

Her downheartedness must have shown because she heard Robert say, "Just give me a chance, Meg."

She'd been dreading this moment. If she was ever granted one wish, she knew it would be to go back and relive these last months. If she were granted two, it would be to do it twice. The urge to turn her horse around and put her heels to him was almost overwhelming.

Robert might have believed that they could continue on as they were once they reached civilization, but she never had. It would be different at the fort with others around. They would have a lot less privacy, and he would naturally want to spend more time with the men. The gradual pulling-apart would help when it came time for him to return to Ottawa. She'd stay with him until then, of course. But when he headed east, she'd head west. See what's what out there.

The sadness hit her with such force that she pulled at the reins and dropped back so he wouldn't see her face.

Not that it would have mattered. His heart was already flying ahead. Back at Swan River, they'd heard nothing but grand things about this Major Macleod. Apparently, he was the only one with sense enough to arrange for wagonloads of oats when the horses were near starved. Although Meg didn't think that such a remarkable thing to do, the men had talked about him with never-ending admiration, making a point of saying how they'd follow Macleod to hell without a second thought. More than once, Robert had talked of how much he was looking forward to meeting the major.

By the time they reached the great log gates, she'd managed to pull herself together. She was heading on to a new adventure in life. As much as she hated to say good-bye to this time alone with Robert, perhaps better times were ahead. Who knew?

Meg had a hard time coming up with much enthusiasm for this prospect. What could be better than the last few weeks?

Time rolls on, and we roll with it. Before she was anywhere near ready, they were getting a hearty welcome from Major Macleod.

The major certainly was an impressive man. His full

beard parted in the center, and he had a massive mustache with long curling ends that he twisted as he talked to them.

"So you're the young man who saved Flying Eagle's women and children," he boomed out in greeting. "It took you long enough to get here."

As soon as they'd dismounted, he clapped his arm around Robert's shoulders, and said, "I've got to hand it to you, son. That did more to prove to the Indians that we're here to protect them than all the presents and pow-wows put together."

She could see Robert's shoulders straighten just the slightest bit and realized that he wasn't offended to have this man call him son, but proud of it.

"It was really a small matter, sir," Robert said. "I'm amazed that you even heard of it."

"You'd be surprised what travels on the moccasin telegraph line," he said as he loosened his grip on him and turned to give Meg a short bow. "And you, my good woman, must be the McReilly I've heard so much about. Hard to imagine how the commissioner could've mistaken you for a man. The light must've been dim." He let out a loud and rowdy laugh. Meg guessed that the light wasn't the only thing Major Macleod viewed as dim.

"Then I imagine you know about the horses," said Robert. Meg could see that this was far from an easy topic for him to bring up. She had to admire him for getting it out in the open right at the start.

"More than I care to know," said the major, shaking his head. "Some weeks ago, I received a lengthy telegram from the commissioner." He paused and rolled his eyes to let them know exactly what he thought of the message. "But the way I see it, you rode into Swan River on horses belonging to the Force and you rode out on horses belonging to the Force. I suspect there was some mix-up in the procurement procedures, but I've got more important things to worry about than straightening out paperwork all across the continent."

Meg could see the way the tightness eased from Robert's face and shoulders. *Imagine being so worried about something as petty as trading fifteen horses for six?* She hoped he'd learn to loosen up over the years.

There was a great deal of activity and commotion going on at the fort. The major explained that a patrol was getting under way to apprehend a band of whiskey traders they'd gotten word on.

"With your permission, sir," Robert said, pulling his shoulders back even further, "I'd like to accompany this patrol and see for myself how such operations work."

"I think that would be a fine idea, young man," said the Major, "a fine idea."

So the separations begin, thought Meg, her chest tightening in around the hurt. She knew it would be coming, she just hadn't thought it would be quite so soon.

Major Macleod assigned a man to help Meg carry the gear to their quarters, then told Robert to take the horses to the stables and choose a fresh mount.

Meg picked up what she could and followed the man to a lean-to built on the end of a long building. The room wasn't much, but it would do. There didn't appear to be any holes in the roof or the walls, and it didn't smell all that musty. She'd slept in worse places.

"Just throw it there next to the bunk," she told the man without really paying much attention to him.

"Hey, you're a woman, ain't you?" he asked.

She looked at him in the doorway and could see his eyes get squinty as he stared at her. He was a sturdy-built man with a scraggly beard.

"What's a woman doing out here dressed as a man? You ain't Calamity Jane are you? I hear tell she's one wild gal." He wiped the chewing tobacco spittle from beneath his mouth and kept staring at her.

"I'm traveling with Constable Hamilton," she informed him. Surely, that would be enough to settle the man down.

"You his wife?" He asked this as if he wouldn't believe her even if she said she was.

"No," and not likely to be either.

"In that case."

To Meg's shock and disgust, the man kicked the door shut behind him and grabbed her. He tried to kiss her, but she turned her head aside and ended up with him slobbering all over her cheek. Apparently, it had been a while since he'd been around a woman. Either that, or he had peculiar notions about seduction.

"You better let go of me," she warned, struggling to loosen his grip on her.

"Come on, what's that young pup got that I don't have?"

"Decency for one," she said, kicking him in the shins. She frantically twisted and shoved against him. "If you know what's good for you, you'll let loose."

"Oh, I know what's good for me, and believe you me,

sugar, you're it." It was disgusting the way he was rubbing up against her.

Meg tried to knee him where it would do the most damage, but he kept his legs close together and pulled her in tight so she couldn't move. She was suffocating in his bear hug and bit down hard on his neck to get him to back off.

The door flew open. Relief flooded through her at the sight of Robert. It was followed by shame at what this must look like with them hugging and her with her mouth on his neck.

"What's going on here?" His voice was so cold there could've been icicles hanging from it.

"We was just—" explained the man, throwing his hands up and pulling his head into his chest like a turtle. He glanced over at Meg with a foolish grin, trying to make it seem as if he was embarrassed at Robert finding the two of them in such a compromising position.

Robert didn't wait for the rest of the explanation. He hauled back a fist and hit him in the face so hard that the man had to step back to keep from falling over. And Robert kept hitting him until he was cowering in the corner, blood streaming from his nose and forehead.

At first, her attacker made a feeble attempt at defending himself. But he soon gave that up and settled for using his hands to protect himself as best he could from the blows.

"What in the bloody hell?" It was the major in the doorway now. The room was getting crowded.

"Stand aside, Major." Robert grabbed the man by the

shirt and the back of his pants and pitched him out in the dirt where he fell to the ground and stayed there.

"She was asking for it," her attacker said in his defense.

Robert stood over him and glared down. "You ever get within ten feet of my fiancée again, and you better have your funeral arrangements made."

The major motioned to the men standing around gawking. "Take him to the stockade."

"Are you all right?" Robert asked, putting his arm around Meg.

"I'm better now, I'll tell you that." And she was. Her stomach was settling down, and her breathing was returning to normal.

"Major, I think I should pass on this patrol," said Robert.

"Now that's nothing but foolish," said Meg. "You can't stand guard over me for the rest of my life." Though the thought did have a certain appeal.

"I can assure you that Subconstable Ingersoll won't be bothering Miss Reilly again," said the major. "And I will personally see that she is protected from any further such encounters."

"Major, I hadn't given much thought before to her being alone here at the fort and all," said Robert. "I think it best that I stay here until the situation is well under control."

Meg could see the major bristle at the idea that he might not have the situation at his fort under control.

"Robert," she said, looking up at him, "I'm certain that word will spread about what's in store for anyone who bothers me." She tried to smile, but she was still a little jittery for that to be believable. "And I'll be under the major's protection."

Meg could see that she hadn't convinced him. "And besides," she continued, knowing this would do it, "you'll be wanting to write about the patrols in your next report."

She could see the stubbornness soften on his face. After a few more assurances that they'd be back in three days at the most and that she would be safe in his absence, Robert kissed her and mounted up. It was a mere touching of the lips, nothing especially romantic, just enough to let everyone know whose woman she was.

Meg yearned for a real parting kiss, but after a summer of loving like they'd had, what difference did one little kiss make?

She stood at the gates and watched him ride away with the rest of the young red-coated Mounties. If she could have died right there, she would have.

He was magnificent, simply magnificent. Before they'd set out this morning, he'd brushed his uniform and polished his boots in anticipation of making a good impression when he reported to Major Macleod. He'd certainly done that.

But it was more than the glory of his uniform and the sheen to his boots. Robert had lost that air of hesitancy he'd had when she first met him. He was a sight to behold, all right. She doubted she'd ever forget what he looked like this day as he rode away with his red-coated companions.

Just before the trail disappeared over the top of the hill,

Robert turned and waved at her. Then his hand brushed across his forehead and she could see that lock of stubborn hair in her mind's eye.

Meg waved back and tried to smile, but she just wasn't able to pull up the corners of her mouth. Her body refused to allow any parody of false cheer on the outside when it hurt so much inside.

Suddenly, she knew that this would be the last time she'd ever see him. Remaining at the fort would mean endless encounters like today. It was no wonder men thought she was a loose woman, the way she traveled about with a man who wasn't her husband. Dressing like a man offered little protection once they realized she wasn't one. Robert would be torn between the need to defend her honor and the desire to be part of this great adventure.

Staying here would also mean endless farewells, nights spent worrying whether he was safe, and days spent scanning the horizon for the sight of his red coat.

No, it was time to go. Staying around would only be leading him on, pretending that things would work out for them when she knew there was no way it ever could.

Imagine him bringing her back to the lords and ladies in Ottawa! Might as well bring an old Indian woman as an old Irish one. Either one would be equally ridiculous.

From time to time, she had imagined herself as his mistress, set up in a fine apartment with scheduled visits. She'd have gladly settled for that arrangement back in Duluth.

But the thought of Robert marrying and raising a family with someone else always put an end to those imaginings. She could never bear that, not in a million years.

No, the best course would be to head west just as she'd planned all along. She'd much rather have the parting clean and quick than to gradually fade out of his life, one missed meeting at a time.

Meg tried time and again to come up with the words to say good-bye. But how could she explain that she wasn't good enough for him, wasn't good enough to stand beside the grandest man she'd ever met or ever hoped to meet. It wasn't the difference in their ages, although that certainly didn't help matters any. It was the difference in social classes that sealed their fates. She could no more hobnob with the gentry than she could grow fins and swim with the mermaids.

Oh, they might find her an amusing creature for a season, the cause of a lot of chatter and gossip. But after that would be the snubs and the pitying glances and the invitations that never quite got there.

During her brief employment as a lady's maid, she'd watched how it all worked.

"So dreadful that you didn't receive your invitation, my dear," Mrs. Worthington would say to someone who'd come calling only to find out she'd not been invited to yesterday's party. "You know the post is *so* unreliable these days."

Over the years, Robert would come to resent how their marriage affected his career—promotions that weren't offered to him, opportunities he'd hear about after they were gone. Eventually, he'd come to resent her as well.

If their infatuation lasted that long. It had been her experience that the first bloom of love rarely lasted through the summer. Why not have the memory of its budding rather than its faded glory? She could keep their time away from the world pressed in her book of remembrances, to be pulled out on a winter's night and cherished before a warming fire.

Though she knew what needed to be done, she didn't look forward to the doing. She dreaded the inevitable pleas about how they could work things out. More than anything, she dreaded that last bittersweet night in his arms.

It would be better all the way around if she would just slip away now. She'd leave him a message. She ached to have a letter from him to keep close to her heart. But that was, of course, impossible. A note from him would mean that he would have to know ahead of time that she was leaving, and if he knew that, he would do everything he could think of to prevent her from going. He was a young man and sure of his power to change the world.

In another ten years, he would have a more realistic view of just what one person could accomplish. She would give anything to spare him the heartbreak and disillusionment ahead of him—the concessions he'd be forced to make, the ideals he'd have to modify.

He was out of sight now. Even the dust behind them had settled. She dropped her hand to wipe the tears from her cheeks. She knew what she had to do, and she'd best do it before she lost her nerve.

"Major Macleod," she said, in a voice so quivery she had to stop for fear she would break into sobs. That would never do. She squared her shoulders and took a deep breath. "Would you be so kind as to arrange an escort for me to the Montana Territory?"

He seemed puzzled by her request. "But I was under the impression that you and young Robert were to be married upon his return. He asked me to help you make arrangements for the wedding."

"Which is why I must go," Meg said, wishing for all the world that she could just throw herself on a bed somewhere and pull up the covers. "You and I both know that marriage to me would be a reckless and unfortunate move on his part. He's a bold man with a fine future ahead of him. I would not be much of a helpmate in what lies ahead for him. Indeed, I'm certain I would be more of a hindrance than anything else."

"I don't know about that, young lady," said the major. "Think of how disappointed he will be when he returns and finds you gone."

"Better a disappointing experience than a disappointing life, Major." She continued to stare at where he'd gone as if she could conjure him up one more time by the force of will alone.

"Miss Reilly," he said gently, "it is a brave and honorable thing you're doing."

Why did the first honorable act in her life have to be one she'd regret until her dying day? She'd spent her lifetime looking out for herself, and it surely was tempting to think of letting Robert take care of her. But at what price?

Heartsick as she was at the thought of leaving, it really was for the best. He'd be blue for a time. Then one day he'd find a fine young woman, someone his equal, someone who could entertain his class of people, someone whose family connections would prove valuable. Meg hoped she could make him laugh.

"Do you have a destination in mind?" he asked.

She stopped and shook her head, not daring to speak, afraid it would break the tight rein she had on herself.

"Then I have a request," he said.

She nodded to let him know that she was listening. Her lips were pinched tightly together, and her eyes squinched shut in an effort to contain the pain. In spite of her efforts, thick tears forced their way out, wetting her cheeks before dropping to the dry ground below.

"Would you be kind enough to hand-carry my report back to Ottawa? I fear that my missives have been waylaid or misinterpreted. What with Alexander Mackenzie's party being in power now, the political climate has changed a great deal since we departed. I'm not exactly sure which way the wind blows these days, nor am I certain that officials are receiving accurate reports about the situation out here."

Meg could tell him for a fact that if they were reading Commissioner French's reports, they didn't have a clue about what was going on.

"In addition," he spoke slowly and paused, as if weighing his words carefully, "there are some matters that are best not committed to paper, if you know what I mean."

"I think I do, Major," she said, recalling the sad state of affairs at the Swan River Fort. At best, it would seem self-serving to tell such tales about his commanding officer. At worst, it might be grounds for a court-martial.

"If you would carry my report back and personally speak with Undersecretary Hamilton, I would be most appreciative."

She nodded. What did she care where she went from here? It made little difference to her now.

"I would, of course, pay all your expenses, including a train ticket to wherever you wished to go after you handed over the report."

She bobbed her head again, but felt no joy or even satisfaction at finally getting her passage west.

"Perhaps we could dicuss this further over tea?" he suggested. "I could arrange an escort tomorrow morning for Fort Benton, Montana, where you could take a steamship downriver, then catch a train back East."

Fine by her. If he'd suggested tying her to the back of a mule, she would've offered no resistance. It really made no difference how she traveled, just as long as she left.

"I only have one request, Major," she said.

"Anything you want," he offered.

"I beg you not to tell Robert where I've gone."

"But surely—"

"No. I fear that out of a misguided sense of honor and loyalty, he would abandon his duty and follow me." Her voice seemed surprisingly clear. Her mind was made up on the matter.

"Surely, you can see that he belongs here. His mission is to report on the situation and make recommendations as to the best course of action. He is quite suited to the task and more than eager to see to it. There's no reason to distract him for what will be, in the end, a pointless endeavor."

"You're a brave woman, Meg Reilly."

"No, Major," she said sadly, "only a realistic one."

Meg turned and, without looking back at him, walked

to their quarters. She threw herself down on the hard bunk and bawled like there'd be no tomorrow. Which there wouldn't be for her. Her life had ridden over that hill in a red coat today. From now on, she'd just be waiting until it was time to cover the clocks.

She bit down on her quilt to keep from howling over the injustice of it all and sobbed until her head hurt, until her chest ached, until she didn't have a tear left in her. Then, so drained and exhausted that even breathing seemed to be too much of an effort, she fell asleep.

She was curled up holding her knees when there was a knock on the door and someone called out that the major requested her company at tea within the hour.

Meg usually felt better after a good cry, but today it hadn't seemed to work. She was worn-out and empty and not the least bit interested in making conversation with the major over tea. It was too bad that dress Robert bought her in Winnipeg had burned up in the fire. She didn't have the energy to get tidied up now anyway, so it was probably just as well.

After she washed her face in the bucket of water someone had thoughtfully left outside the door, she went in search of Major Macleod. She found him in his office reading the reports that she and Robert had written along the way.

"Astounding," he said. "I had not realized conditions had deteriorated so at Swan River."

"I worded it as kindly as possible," Meg said. "But Robert and I believe the man has gone around the bend."

"You must be careful about who you show these reports to, my dear," he warned. "Political connections are more important than competence, and one never knows who belongs to whom."

"My understanding is that these will go directly to Walter Hamilton," she said.

"Who is blind as a bat," said the major. "His secretary will read them, then the scoundrel will pass them along to whoever he's in league with."

"What would you have me do?" All along, she'd assumed that Robert's uncle would champion his reports. It hadn't occurred to her that he might be prevented from doing.

"Read the reports to him yourself and keep your own council, lass."

That made sense to her.

"Now, tell me, did Colonel French make any mention of magistrates?"

"Magistrates?" Meg repeated, puzzled by what Colonel French would need magistrates for. He seemed perfectly willing to decide everything himself.

"We need magistrates to rule when there are decisions to be made. You can't expect these men to be magistrates as well as constables. Somebody needs to preside over differences of opinion."

"Perhaps he discussed that with Robert, but I don't recall any mention of magistrates," she said, searching her memory.

"How about training for the men in the basics of wilderness survival?"

Meg shook her head. The men she'd seen could've used training in how to survive in a fort first. That in itself seemed a nip and tuck operation.

"I suppose he's still training the men to arrange themselves in orderly formations so they can charge into battle, line by line?"

"He was trying, sir," she said, feeling just the slightest start of a smile as she recalled the sullen men attempting to rearrange themselves around those ridiculous boulders.

She described the scene to the major, and he let out a great resounding belly laugh that spurred her on to describe the fort, the food, the complaints of the men. It seemed funnier now that she'd seen a real fort.

"Tell me, did he ever hire a scout?"

"Not that I'm aware of, sir," she answered.

"I didn't think so. Did you know that when we started our march last summer, he didn't bother even to meet with the scout from the boundary-blazing expedition?" The major shook his head in disgust or maybe amazement. "Didn't even bother to meet with a man who had traveled the length of this country, who knew every watering hole, every good pasture along the way."

"That doesn't even make sense," she said, not particularly surprised.

"Not a lick of sense. We headed out across hundreds of miles of prairies, and he didn't even bother to ask advice or directions. Can you believe that?

She could. She'd met the man.

"The colonel's a fool for not trying to hire that scout to lead us and a damn fool for not at least talking to the man before we set out."

It was a couple of heartbeats before he continued. "You realize that what I'm saying here, lass, is mutiny. Men have been court-martialed for less."

He stared her straight in the eye. She returned the look.

"But they can't court-martial *me* for telling the truth, now can they?" she said.

She was glad to see the wrinkles across his forehead relax and the ones around his eyes tighten. He seemed a good man, a bit on the blustery side, but nonetheless a dedicated, fair-minded man. It would do her no harm to help him and might be of great benefit to a lot of others.

"These are courageous and trustworthy men, lass. There is no doubt in my mind that we can make peace with the Indians and establish the rule of law here in this Great Lone Land," he said, pointing to a map pinned to the wall.

"But for the Northwest Mounted Police to bring about peace and order," he continued, "we need small bands of well-trained men who can travel quickly and act effectively."

He paused to twirl one end of his waxed mustache before continuing. "Large groups of men dragging worthless cannons about the wilderness are doomed to failure. Do you understand that, lass?"

She did.

"This grand experiment will never have a chance to succeed if we don't get a leader who realizes what needs to be done and has the ability to do it. Purchasing a commission may be all well and good for the British army, but it'll be the death of us all out here."

At that moment, the image of her Robert facing charges of horse thievery with Colonel French as judge and jury flashed in front of her eyes. She was flooded with the desperate importance of what he was asking her to do.

"Major, believe me, I realize how necessary it is to have a sensible man in charge. I'll do everything I possibly can to explain the situation in Ottawa. Who should I talk with and what should I tell them?"

"Aye, you do understand, don't you?" he said. He seemed more sad than relieved.

They spent the rest of the evening writing up a report that explained the situation as fully as possible without actually accusing French of incompetence or worse. The major listed all the people she should get in touch with and what she should say to each one, starting with Walter Hamilton.

They worked at it until they were both too exhausted to think straight, before heading off to bed. She'd hardly fallen asleep before reveille sounded.

After a hasty breakfast, she wrapped the reports in a rubber sheet and tucked them carefully in her saddlebags. As he bid her farewell, Major Macleod pressed two packets of money in her hands.

"This is for the journey," he said, handing her the first one. "And this is to buy whatever clothing and such that you'll require," he said, handing her the second.

"I hardly think the Dominion of Canada should be buying my petticoats, Major," she said, trying to add a note of levity to their parting.

"My good woman, you are the answer to a thousand prayers. For the service you are about to do for this country, we should be buying you an entire trousseau. My discretionary funds are somewhat limited, or I would double the amount and still count it a bargain."

She felt like Joan of Arc, off to fight the forces of evil. After giving him a quick hug and a peck on the cheek, she mounted up and rode out the gates with the troop of men he'd assigned to escort her.

It was as if she'd been jerked awake from a lovely dream and forced to face the day before she was either rested or ready. The lack of sleep would account for some of this, as would the worry she had over whether she'd be able to accomplish what needed to be done.

Her regrets included saying good-bye to the major. Though she'd known him for less than a day, Meg found she admired the man and what he was trying to do. She so hoped that the vision he had for this land and his courageous Mounties would come to be.

But more than that, there was the burden of saying farewell to the most incredible time of her life and the most glorious man she ever hoped to meet. These past weeks had been a dream filled with grand days and wondrous nights and she'd been awakened far too soon.

Most of her sadness was saved for bidding Robert farewell in her heart.

I should've left him a note, she said to herself as she watched the sun set that evening. She'd tried but hadn't known what to say. It wouldn't have been fair to tell him how she truly felt. That would only have led him to believe he should follow her and convince her it would all work out. Nor could she bring herself to lie to him, to tell him this summer had meant nothing more than just an enjoyable way to pass the time on her way out west. Better to let him hurt for a while, get over it, and go on. He deserved that at least.

Tears spilled over and trickled down her face. She didn't bother to wipe them away. *What's the use?* She couldn't hide the sorrow on her face or in her soul. A hawk and frog might fall in love, but how could they ever build a life?

The men kept a respectful distance both on the trail and once they reached Fort Benton. Though they were always nearby, they left her to her sorrow. It was for the best. She wasn't in any mood to talk with them, and they probably weren't in the mood to cry with her.

Meg purchased a navy blue traveling outfit. She probably should've bought black, for that surely fit her mood. She tried to pull herself into a corset, but gave up on it in the fitting room. It was hard to believe that up until a few months ago, she'd tucked all her organs up into her lungs and gone about her way. Well, she sure couldn't do that now.

It felt odd enough walking around as it was. She had to constantly remind herself to take smaller strides in order to keep from stepping on her hem and tripping. Someday she might go back to dressing as a man, for the ease of movement if nothing else. But for now, it seemed foolish to do so.

Meg bought two valises and stuffed her quilt in one and her undergarments in the other. She probably should've bought another outfit or two, but that would just be more to lug around. Not that it would've mattered in Fort Benton, because her Mountie escorts wouldn't let her carry so much as a single parcel. In a way, she rather enjoyed walking about the fort with six young men in attendance.

The morning the steamboat pulled away, they were all standing at the dock waving good-bye to her. She waved back and hollered out her thanks for their help. As the line of red coats disappeared in the distance, she had the wild urge to jump over the side and swim back to them. So what if things weren't going to be happy ever after with Robert? She was a fool to pass up what time she could have with him.

But she didn't. This might not be the best for her, but she knew it was the best for him.

To be sure, the goblins were dancing tonight.

CHAPTER THIRTEEN

"AIN'T THIS THE LIFE?"

Indeed it is, Robert thought as he lifted his hat up off his eyes to see who was talking and if the man was speaking to him. It was a Mountie about his age from Toronto, and his comment didn't seem to be directed at anyone in particular. It was merely an observation about life in general.

Robert nodded his agreement, then pulled his hat back down over his eyes. Like most of the rest of the troop, he was sitting on the ground with his back against a tree. They were giving the horses a break, and those that weren't on guard duty had all found a spot of shade to rest in.

He wished he could doze off for a while but knew that was unlikely. He was far too keyed up for that.

The troop had been doing some hard traveling. They'd trailed the band of whiskey traders right into an encampment of Blackfoot Indians.

They were heading back. Tonight he'd be holding Meg in his arms. It was hard to wait. Strange how you could sleep alone your whole life and think nothing of it. It seemed like such a waste of time when you could be sleeping with the woman you loved.

He hoped that their time apart would help her realize how much she needed and wanted him. She'd always made light of the subject of marriage whenever he'd brought it up, but perhaps a few days apart would help change her mind.

He hoped he'd be able to convince her that what she thought were insurmountable barriers were no more than minor differences, nothing that would affect the success of their marriage one way or the other. He could think of any number of gentlemen who'd married women of a lower social class, and their matches appeared to work out reasonably well. What difference did it make anyway? It was whether you felt comfortable with someone, right? Whether your temperaments were suited. Whether you could build a life together. That was all that mattered.

He couldn't fault her for her reluctance to place her future in the hands of someone as young as he was. But he'd had more experiences than most men twice his age. He could handle himself in the world and protect and provide for her. That's what counted. Certainly, she could see that.

Robert couldn't rest for imagining how excited she'd be to see him again. Knowing what the situation was, he hoped Major Macleod would be able to perform the wedding ceremony as soon as they returned. It was one thing to cohabit out in the wilderness, quite another to do so once they were back in civilization.

He trusted that the major had the necessary authority to perform marriages. If he didn't, Robert would find someone who did.

As they rode toward the fort, it was all he could do to stay at the pace of the troop. He had to keep reminding himself to calm down, not to go racing back ahead of the rest of the men.

She'd be there waiting for him. He was certain of it. Excitable as she was, she'd probably run out to greet him, and he would pull her up in front of him and the two of them would ride together through the gates.

Or maybe he should dismount, take her in his arms, and, after a kiss or two, walk arm and arm after the troop. Either way would be fine with him as long as they turned in early tonight. He hoped she missed being in his arms as much as he missed having her there.

But it appeared that she wasn't looking forward to their reunion as much as he was. At least not enough to come out to meet him. Everyone else at the fort had stepped out to see how things had gone on the patrol, everyone but Meg. He scanned each and every face, hoping the next one would have her green eyes and her playful smile.

It was disappointing that she wasn't there, but perhaps she was involved in something and didn't know they were back yet. Any minute now she'd realize there was something going on in the yard and would come running out.

But she hadn't come running out by the time they'd dismounted and the major was congratulating them on a job well-done.

Where was she?

He handed his reins over to someone and took off for their quarters, hoping that she'd fallen asleep. She did that sometimes in the afternoon.

Perhaps she wanted their reunion to be a private, not a public, affair. It would be just like her to be waiting for him under that quilt of hers.

Robert threw open the door and stood there staring, unable to believe what was right in front of his eyes. Or rather, what was not right in front of his eyes. Her quilt was gone. He tore through the room, kicking over packs and checking through everything, but he knew as he was doing it that it was no use. She was gone.

His hands chilled and stiffened up as he realized that she'd gone west. She'd said all along that's what she wanted to do. Now she had. He felt like a fool with a schoolboy infatuation. No wonder she'd always turned aside his talk of love and marriage. She'd not been planning to stay.

Though he knew what the answer was going to be, he couldn't keep from going to ask the stableman if he'd seen Meg around. Perhaps he'd saddled her a horse for an afternoon's ride.

"She's gone riding, all right," the man said. "Rode to Fort Benton the morning after you left."

He had a hard time believing she'd just up and left. She hadn't even bothered to leave a note. He went back to the lean-to and checked through everything again—

nothing. A person would think she'd at least have had the decency to leave a farewell note even if she wasn't planning to say good-bye in person.

After all the wonderful times they'd had, she'd just up and left. *She's probably off having wonderful times with someone else.* The thought of it made him sick to his stomach.

All that nonsense about how they weren't suited for one another was just her way of letting him down easy. She said she was heading west, and, obviously, she meant it.

He joined the rest of the men for dinner, but he spoke only when asked a direct question and even then his voice sounded like it was coming from inside a barrel.

Morose didn't begin to describe his mood as he headed out that evening for a walk along the river. He'd hoped to find a measure of peace with the sound of the water rippling along and the night calls of the birds. Instead, everything, even the steady croaking of the frogs, brought back memories of being with Meg. How could she do this to him?

He heard footsteps and turned around to see Major Macleod walking along the path behind him. Maybe he, too, liked to settle things with a walk before turning in.

"You don't seem to be in very good spirits, Constable Hamilton," said the major as he came abreast of him. "What's on your mind, lad?"

"Nothing really," he said. He was not going to pour out his personal troubles to his commanding officer.

"I suspect you're feeling low over Miss Reilly's departure," Macleod said.

"I'll admit I'm somewhat disappointed." Disappointed? He felt like throwing himself in the river, but that sounded like something his mother would do, not him.

"I could tell she hated to leave," the major said.

Robert rolled his eyes at that one. "She couldn't have been too reluctant to go," he said bitterly. "She didn't waste any time getting out of here."

"She doesn't believe she's right for you," Macleod said.

"How does she know what's right for me?" He turned back to face the major, his anger keeping the heartache at bay. "If she doesn't want me, that's all well and good. But it isn't because she isn't right for me. That's horseshit, sir."

The major nodded, then said, "So, what are you going to do about it?"

"I don't know yet. Maybe nothing. Why should I chase after a woman who obviously doesn't want me?"

"Now, I don't know about the lass not wanting you," said the major. "That's not the impression I got."

"Well, if she wants me," said Robert, turning on his heel, "she knows where to find me."

He knew he was right in this. Meg Reilly was a resourceful woman with a mind of her own. She'd had no trouble catching up to him in Winnipeg. If she wanted to be with him, she'd find a way to do it.

Anyway, what kind of a man would go chasing after a woman, begging her to come back when she'd said all along she didn't want to stay?

Robert headed off by himself to think things over.

Much as he wanted to go after her and talk some sense into her, he had a mission to accomplish here, a duty he'd agreed to. A man couldn't just walk away from that, now could he?

Chapter Fourteen

On the journey to Ottawa, Meg spent endless days staring out across the landscape. She tried to focus on the future, but her mind always filled up with images of Robert. She could see him standing outside Bess's, too hesitant to knock and too determined to leave. She could see him riding wild across the prairie, determined to rescue those women and children or die trying. She could see his face first thing in the morning when he was reluctant to leave the warmth of her arms yet eager to see what the day would bring. And she could envision him as he rode off that last time with the sun at his back.

The ache was so deep that, at times, it was all she could do to keep from rolling up and clutching her knees to her chest. It was a sorrow beyond words.

The steamship passengers had kept their distance, but once she transferred to the train, people kept trying to get her to talk with them. Apparently, without the decks to wander about, their only source of amusement was one another. But she couldn't summon the interest to do more than ask them to please leave her alone.

Compared to Robert, the men seemed puny and frivolous, intent as they were on discussing the weather or what did she think of President Grant and wasn't it a scandal the way that man drank so much? She didn't care one way or the other about any of it and told them as much.

One matronly woman was particularly persistent about drawing her into a conversation. She announced that she knew a broken heart when she saw it, and she wouldn't rest until she'd convinced Meg to join her in the parlor car. Reluctantly, Meg finally gave in. However, she refused to tell her about her troubles, so they whiled away the time playing whist.

In the middle of that afternoon, they were joined by four gentlemen. One of them gaily suggested they switch from whist to poker, keeping the stakes moderate, of course.

Of course.

By early evening, every third pot was reaching better than a hundred dollars and Meg was winning most of them.

She had no trouble bluffing her way through even the least likely of hands. She displayed no emotion because she felt none.

The other players were so easy to read it wasn't all that much of a challenge. They gave away their excitement over a good hand, as well as their disappointment over a poor one, with annoying little gestures and what they mistakenly believed were guarded expressions. They were so obvious that they might as well have shown everyone their cards before placing their bets.

The middle-aged woman got off in Chicago and wished her luck on the way out. By then, Meg had won close to three thousand dollars and none of it due to luck.

By New York, she'd more than doubled that. *If Black Jack could only see me now,* she thought.

And she wasn't even cheating. No slipping cards from the bottom of the deck, no hiding aces in her garter, no small fingernail marks on the edge of the face cards. Just straight-ahead poker. Read 'em and weep.

Meg feared she was turning into a better woman than she had ever intended to be. *If only Robert could see me now.*

She played poker all the way to Canada. Two of the gentlemen were so determined to win back their losses no matter how long it took that they even exchanged their tickets in New York so they could accompany her all the way to Ottawa.

As she boarded the last train, she was grabbed by the sudden urge just to turn around and go back. It was only a wild notion, a way of dulling the pain. She knew that sorrow's sharp edges would soften after a time. But she wondered how long this longing for Robert would continue—months, years maybe—surely, not a lifetime. Even goblins couldn't be that unkind.

At the Ottawa train depot, she walked away from a disappointed group of poker players with a valise stuffed full of money.

Where's the excitement, she wondered. Six months ago, if she'd had nearly ten thousand dollars in her possession, she'd have been dancing and shouting in the streets. Today, it brought little more than the grim satisfaction that at least she wouldn't have to go searching for a job anytime soon.

She climbed into a waiting cab and gave the driver the address of Walter Hamilton's office. It was the only place she knew to go.

Her eyes were so strained from being up all hours with the near-constant card playing that they felt as if someone had thrown sand in them. She'd taken short naps when absolutely necessary, but she always ended up dreaming of Robert. At least playing cards kept her mind busy.

She arrived at Mr. Hamilton's office and was greeted by a pipsqueak of a man. He informed her that he was the assistant to the undersecretary, then rudely refused to let her in to see the undersecretary without an appointment.

"There are absolutely no openings in Mr. Hamilton's schedule until late next week," he informed her. His lips were pinched together so tightly that it was a wonder he could get any words out at all.

"I simply must see Undersecretary Hamilton this afternoon," she insisted. "It is a matter of great urgency."

"Whatever your business is, Miss Reilly," said the assistant, peering over the top of his glasses as if he had his suspicions about what that business might be, "it will have to wait. There are no appointments available today."

He braced himself on his desk and leaned forward in an obvious attempt to intimidate her.

Hah! She'd faced down barrooms full of drunken rowdies. This self-important character wasn't about to send her packing, not in this lifetime or the next.

"Listen, bucko," she said, lowering her voice to a near growl. She leaned over the opposite side of his desk until their noses nearly touched. "I have vital reports regarding the Northwest Mounted Police. I've traveled across the continent twice for these reports. I've written them huddled under a canvas during a hailstorm. I've recopied ones that were ruined in a prairie fire and I've ridden half-wild horses, storm-tossed steamships, and endless trains to get them here. I am going to hand them over to Walter Hamilton if I have to strangle you to do it."

That seemed to take some of the wind out of his sails. He backed away from her.

"I assure you that you may leave the reports here and I will see that Undersecretary Hamilton receives them," he said in a much more reasonable tone of voice, but he was still looking down at her like she was dirt.

"Nothing doing," she told him. "Major Macleod was quite clear on this point. I was instructed to hand them over personally to Mr. Hamilton. I intend to do just that."

"Then you will have to wait," he informed her with a toss of his head. "After all, you can't expect to just walk in off the street and be shown right in to an undersecretary's office. It just isn't done. You must make an appointment first."

"Fine," she said. "I will wait for an appointment, and I will wait right here."

She picked up her valises, marched over to a chair, and sat down.

"You can't stay here," he protested.

He looked like a startled weasel. If she'd had a gun handy, she'd have shot him.

"What's going on, Oliver?" An elderly gentleman poked his head into the room. He looked just as Robert had described him—a bushy-haired gentleman with a thick mustache that grew right into his muttonchop whiskers. The all-in-one mustache and sideburns gave him a rather foolish appearance in Meg's opinion.

But he was anything but a fool.

"This woman," Oliver said, putting such contempt behind the word "woman," that it was easy to hear that what he really meant was "this dreadful woman," "insists she has to hand over some sort of reports to you personally." Oliver tossed his head, as if this was the most ridiculous request he'd ever heard.

"Send her and her reports in then, Oliver," said the old man, clearly unable to grasp what Oliver was in such a twitter about.

"I don't know what gets into him," he muttered as Meg walked past him into the room. "He's always been as incompetent as the day is long, but now I'm beginning to suspect he's a saboteur of some sort."

His office smelled faintly of leather and strongly of cigar smoke. Everything in it looked as if it'd been built for giants. The desk was bigger than any bed Meg had ever seen. The chair behind it was large enough to be a throne, and the windows stretched from floor to ceiling. So did the bookcases.

But it was the huge painting of a Mountie on horseback that caught her by surprise. It looked so like Robert that she wanted to run over and lay her face against it.

Get ahold of yourself. It's only a picture.

"Are you all right?" she heard the old gentleman say.

Though she could hear the words, she struggled to make out their meaning.

"Perhaps you should sit down," he suggested in a worried tone.

She was so light-headed she could have floated away and so weak-kneed she had to lean on his arm to get across the room. He guided her to an overstuffed chair. Meg sank into it, thankful for its comfort and security.

"I'd forgotten how trying traveling can be," she heard him say. "Would you care for a drop of brandy?"

Meg wanted to say yes but was unable to form any words. When he handed her the rounded glass, she drank it down, hoping that its searing warmth would chase away her sudden chill.

"Oliver," he called out. "Bring us a pot of tea and some scones or sandwiches."

Food sounded good to Meg. She couldn't recall when she'd eaten last. No wonder she was feeling faint.

But she knew the real reason was the painting behind her, and she wondered if she would always miss him like this. Would she always be at the mercy of any stray reminders?

"That's better now," Mr. Hamilton said. "For a moment there, I was afraid you were going to swoon."

Meg nodded and waved her hand away to let him know there was no chance of that. She was not a swooner, never had been. This was just temporary weakness due to hunger.

"The reports are in my valise," she said as she pointed to the bags she'd dropped in the doorway. "I'll get them for you."

"That's not necessary," he assured her. "We can examine them later. Right now, I'd rather hear about matters directly from you. I assume you are the Meg Reilly that Major Macleod spoke of in his telegram?"

She nodded yes.

"I understand that you accompanied my nephew Robert on his expedition."

She nodded again, unable to sort through the flood of images to find a reply.

"It must have been quite an experience," he said.

It was indeed.

"How is Robert?"

How is he? He is honorable, and brave, and heart-stopping handsome. He's the most wonderful man I've ever met or probably ever will meet.

"Fine," is what she said, amazed to find there were no tears slipping out. Perhaps she'd used them all up. "He's fine."

"That's good to hear," he said, "I'll have to admit, though, I worried about sending the boy along on that expedition. But I thought he deserved a bit of adventure before settling down."

Not knowing what else to say, she merely nodded.

"I thought this would make a man of him," he continued.

An image came to her mind of Robert sitting around the campfire with a council of Cree men watching and nodding as he spoke to them in hand signals. She wished she had words to describe what an incredible man his nephew already was. But this wasn't a topic she could speak of today.

They sat in awkward silence until Oliver appeared in the doorway with a tea tray. Meg was glad for the interruption. She decided it would be best to stick with the details of what they'd heard and seen and stay away from talking about Robert.

As soon as she had eaten a butter sandwich and had a sip of tea, she said, "Mr. Hamilton, how much do you know about this expedition?"

Oddly enough, he put his finger to his lips and went over and quickly jerked the door open, as if he expected to find someone leaning against it and listening. There was no one on the other side. The old fellow seemed disappointed.

He closed the door firmly, then pulled a chair up next to Meg before urging her to tell him all she knew.

She started by describing what Robert had told her about his encounter with the deserters and how he'd hired a scout to take the horses to Winnipeg while he traveled up to and across the Dawson Route. She left out the part about Bouncing Bess's and merely mentioned that she was heading west and had joined up with him along the trail.

She spent a great deal of time describing Commissioner French and what she'd heard and seen at Swan River.

"I was afraid of that," he kept muttering.

Occasionally, she would ask if he would like the reports for himself, but he declined, saying he would rather hear it directly from her. The reports could wait until later.

It all went fairly smoothly until she told of Robert's

rescue of the Indian women and children. The memory of that time was more than she could bear. Tears trickled down, then turned into torrents that her handkerchief couldn't keep up with. She covered her face with her hands as her stomach clenched into spasms of sobbing. Her throat and chest tightened. Hoarse gasps of air forced their way from her throat.

"There, there," Mr. Hamilton kept saying, until, overcome by it all, she buried her face in his waistcoat and sobbed herself into hysteria. "There, there," he kept on, as he patted her on the back.

It was a dreadful display of emotion and had clearly made the old man uncomfortable. She wished she had gotten a room for the night and come back when she was rested and more in control of herself.

"I am so sorry," she said when she finally managed to pull herself together.

What must he think of me sitting here and bawling like a baby?

"It's been a very trying journey, Mr. Hamilton." *To say the least!* "Could I trouble you for directions to a respectable place where I could spend the night?"

Why she said respectable was beyond her. It made no difference to her whether it was respectable or not.

"Certainly, certainly, my dear," he said as he continued his patting her on the shoulder. "Miss Agatha Crosswell is a dear friend of mine, and I've no doubt that she would put you up for as long as you wish."

"I have money, Mr. Hamilton. I can afford suitable accommodations."

"Nonsense, Miss Reilly. Agatha would be sorely put

out with me if I were to leave you at a hotel. I would offer you accommodations myself, but I live at a gentlemen's club, and that would hardly do, now would it?"

He seemed to think that was an amusing suggestion. Meg tried to smile back, but it just wasn't there.

Within the hour, they were standing on the steps of Miss Agatha Crosswell's stately mansion. Meg was overwhelmed and intimidated by the three-story brick building with its porches, columns, and gardens. She knew she didn't belong here and tried once more to convince Mr. Hamilton that she would be quite comfortable in a hotel.

"Nonsense," he said as he pounded the brass knocker loud enough to be heard across the street. "You will love it here at Agatha's."

She already did.

A lovely, little white-haired lady with a Scottish accent answered the door. She greeted the both of them with a warm hug. Upon hearing that Meg had just arrived in Ottawa, she directed Mr. Hamilton into the drawing room and led Meg upstairs to a bedroom with a view of the park.

"You can tidy up and leave your things here, dear," she said, taking Meg by the arm. "Then come on down and let me introduce you to my friends."

Her friends turned out to be two other ladies of similar age who insisted that she call them Aretha and Alice. Miss Aretha was on the quiet side, but Miss Alice was bold as you please. She handed Meg a glass of sherry and announced that she, for one, was quite impressed with her.

"I understand from Walter that you've traveled across

the continent with his nephew, Robert," said Miss Alice with an obvious wink. "I'll bet you have some tales to tell about that." She winked again.

Meg wondered if the dear woman had a tic or if this was her way of encouraging Meg to spill the beans about what had gone on between her and Robert.

"Alice, really," said Miss Agatha. "Miss Reilly has had an exhausting journey." She patted Meg on the shoulder. "We can wait until tomorrow to hear all the details."

Though Meg was grateful for the reprieve, she was certain these three little old ladies would be scandalized by the details of their journey.

She was so tired and groggy from the lack of sleep and the long trip that she soon couldn't keep track of which one had the nephew who was a barrister in Boston and who had just had yet another dispute with a shopkeeper over shortchanging her. While they were all nodding in agreement that a woman had to look out for herself these days or she'd be cheated every which way she turned, Meg excused herself and made her way up to her room.

Meg stripped down to her chemise and pulled her quilt out to cover herself with. Though she'd just washed it at the hot springs, it seemed dingy compared to the boiled white curtains behind it. Like a lot of things, clean depended on the circumstances. She'd done the best she could.

Though she wanted to wrap herself in its protection, she decided that it would probably be best to wait until she had a chance to give it another washing. No sense in getting this dirt all over the sheets.

But the real reason she put it away was that it brought

back memories of being wrapped in that quilt with Robert's strong arms around her, sheltering her from the night. She'd felt so safe, so protected. He was so determined, so sure of what needed to be done. She hoped the realities of life didn't wear him down, that he kept that courageous core of himself untarnished. And she wished desperately that she could see him mature into the man he was destined to be.

But that was just foolish thinking. From here on out, the less she thought about Robert Eugene Hamilton, the better off she'd be.

Lying in the plump feather bed, Meg stared up at the ceiling. She was so weary, so weary.

The next thing she knew, the maid was tapping at the door, telling her it was time to get up as breakfast would be served shortly.

But no sooner had she sat down to eat than the serving girl announced that she had a gentleman caller, a Mr. Hamilton.

Her heart skipped a beat, and for just one joyous moment, she imagined that it was Robert, that he'd followed her and found her. She jumped up, foolishly hoping to see his red tunic in the doorway.

To her disappointment, it was the older Mr. Hamilton standing there. Of course. What had she been thinking of? Robert's pride as well as his sense of duty would never allow him to chase after her.

"Would you care to join us for breakfast?" she asked out of politeness.

"I appreciate the invitation, but I'm on my way to a meeting, and I mustn't tarry." He paused for a moment and cleared his throat before continuing, "Miss Reilly, I find myself in a rather awkward position. Would you consider joining my employ as my assistant?"

"What?" She couldn't have been more surprised if he'd announced he was giving up public service to join a troop of acrobats.

"I've recently received information that Oliver is not as loyal or discreet as I'd hoped. I have no choice but to give him his notice."

Meg couldn't say as she found the news distressing.

"As you well know, my work as the liaison for the Mounted Police is at a critical juncture. I have even handed over all the managerial duties of my shipping company so I can devote my total attention to these matters. There are sensitive political negotiations going on now, and we simply cannot afford to have the reports that are coming in blabbed all over Ottawa."

Meg could certainly understand that. A good deal of what she'd reported could well be used to discredit the leadership or even disband the Force altogether.

"Not only do you have firsthand knowledge of what the frontier is like, but as far as I'm concerned, if Robert and Major Macleod can place their trust in your discretion, I certainly can."

"Mr. Hamilton, I hardly think—"

He interrupted her before she could finish. "I know it's unusual, but the circumstances are unusual as well. There is a handsome salary that goes along with it as well as the knowledge that you will be serving your country."

This wasn't even her country, and with nearly ten thousand dollars in her possession, for the first time since she could remember, employment was not a problem.

However, the thought of being able to hear about Robert was too tempting to pass up.

She nodded yes and hoped she was doing the right thing.

"Splendid," the old gentleman said, slapping his leg. "I shall give Oliver his notice today, and you can start training tomorrow. Will that give you enough time to settle in here?"

Meg couldn't imagine what settling in there was for her to do. Then she realized that a position of this nature would require the purchase of suitable outfits. Shopping could take up most of the day.

"You're not going to turn Oliver out, are you?" Though there was no love lost between the two of them, she hated to see anyone put out of a job on mere suspicion. It had happened to her on more occasions than she cared to recall. She wouldn't wish it on anybody else, no matter how disagreeable he was.

"The man's worthless," he said, leaving no room for argument.

"Surely, he must have some good points." She hadn't seen any, but there were bound to be. How else had he gotten the position?

"You have no idea how little he can accomplish. He doesn't know his elbow from his ear and he treats *me* like I'm in my dotage. In any case, he won't be unemployed, merely shifted to another office where someone else can wonder whether he's an infiltrator or an idiot," Mr.

Hamilton said, thumping his cane a good one on the floor. "Nonetheless, it's sweet of you to worry, my dear."

She hadn't really worried. But it did ease her mind to know that he wasn't going to be thrown out in the street.

Being a secretarial assistant was a career she'd not ever considered before. She'd always thought it was a man's job, but perhaps it might be just what she was looking for, at least for the time being. Mr. Hamilton seemed like a pleasant enough employer, and it was clear he needed more help than what Oliver was willing or able to offer.

"I'll pick you up on my way to the office tomorrow morning," he said as he headed out the door.

Miss Agatha, Miss Aretha, and Miss Alice were all delighted that Meg was to be Mr. Hamilton's secretary. "Women can do that job just as well as any man, and it's high time we were given a crack at it," were Miss Alice's exact words.

The three of them decided over breakfast that they would cancel their plans for the day and accompany Meg from shop to shop to assist her in purchasing suitable dresses, hats, gloves, and anything else either they or Meg could possibly imagine her needing.

They rang for a carriage and the four of them set out. When they saw the amount of money Meg was carrying about, they strongly advised her to deposit it in a bank, which Meg was glad enough to do. Here she was nearly thirty years old, and this was the first time she'd ever had enough money to even consider opening an account.

They had a grand day of it. They argued over which hats were most becoming and what colors brought out the green in Meg's eyes. They doted on her like maiden aunts with a favorite niece, and Meg basked in the attention.

As she was preparing for bed that night, Meg wondered what Robert was doing now. Had they captured the whiskey traders and returned to the fort or was he out under the stars, and was he thinking of her?

She looked out the window with the fanciful intention of finding the group of stars he called Hercules and asking him to watch over Robert.

But she couldn't find it. The sky was too small here in Ottawa. She longed to be out on the prairie with its ceiling of stars. Meg had never realized before how confining cities were. Or how the air smelled like soot and who knew what else. Or how noisy it was, even at night. It was strange how you could get used to something, and it seemed normal. Then you had a chance at something better, and it made all the difference in the world.

She realized that thought fit more than just cities. Despite her difficulties in supporting herself, she'd been content enough before meeting Robert. Now she wondered if she would ever be content or truly happy again.

She was somewhat nervous the next morning as she walked into the office building. Mr. Hamilton had chatted her ear off on the ride over, and she'd tried to pay attention to the details. But all she could really remember was that Oliver would remain the two days until he transferred to the mail room in order to acquaint her with her various tasks and introduce her to the people she would need to know.

Mr. Hamilton said Oliver was prone to patronizing people but to just ignore him. He would probably try to confuse her or tell her as little as possible. However, since he was as incompetent as the day was long, it made little difference what information he passed on. Other than introducing her to the people she'd need to know and showing her about the building, a good deal of what he had to say was probably useless. She would have to figure out the job for herself, and he had faith that she could do it.

"You can't be serious," was Oliver's sneering response at being told that he was to show Meg what needed to be done and introduce her to the people she would be dealing with in the future.

"The old gentleman has finally gone around the bend," were his words once Mr. Hamilton was out of earshot. "Imagine! Hiring a woman. It's a scandal, that's what it is. A scandal."

Meg wanted to slap him silly, but since it would cause no end of commotion, she decided against it.

While he was carrying on about scandalous behavior, she gave him the once-over. He was a thin man with a pinched-in appearance to match his attitude. His pale, pasty face and his skinny lips did nothing for her. He had the slumped shoulders and caved-in chest of a consumptive. Really, his best feature was his barely there chin. Meg couldn't help but recall the square jaw that anchored Robert's face.

Insipid was the word that came to mind. The only other time she'd ever used that word was at a spelling bee years ago. It was a word worth saving for Oliver. His pompous manner did nothing to disguise the characterless creature he was underneath all the fuss and bluster. Robert had more admirable qualities in his little finger than this pitiful creature had in his whole body.

Would she go the rest of her life comparing every man she met to Robert and finding them all sadly lacking? It was a discouraging realization.

Then Oliver said something that pulled her back to the present.

"I imagine you've traded your affections for this position," he said, his face pulled together in a self-righteous smirk.

It took a moment for Meg to figure out what he'd actually said and another moment to come up with a reply.

"Why Mr. Sims," she said, feigning innocence, "we've just met and already you're giving away the secret to your success. How kind of you."

"Well, I never." The man drew himself up to his full height, such as it was.

"I sincerely doubt that, Ollie," she said with a wink and wicked grin. "But I promise I'll keep it under my hat." She wished she were close enough to nudge him. That would send him over the edge, wouldn't it?

"This is nothing short of outrageous. I shall have to speak to Mr. Hamilton about this," he said, whirling on his heels to face the closed inner office door.

"This ought to be a good time," Meg said, starting after him.

He stopped abruptly and turned around. Meg bumped into him, but just barely. Oliver staggered back and had to grab on to the desk to keep his balance. *Good heavens, the man is weak as a lamb.*

She recalled the time she and Robert had made love

standing up in the hot-springs pool. He'd held her in his arms half the night. She doubted that Oliver Sims would be up to such a task.

Even if he was, she certainly wasn't interested.

Would there ever be anyone who could hold a candle to Robert?

After an endless and trying day with Oliver explaining in detail every nuance of the job, Meg was glad to get back to the lively company of Miss Agatha, Miss Aretha, and Miss Alice.

They spent the evening in front of the fire, laughing over the ridiculous men they'd known. Meg pinched her face together and imitated the prissy way Oliver Sims had introduced her to the staff members around the building. "I'd like to present Miss," then she'd stop to clear her throat and purse her lips again, "Reilly."

"What a twit," agreed Miss Agatha. "Reminds me of a man I kept company with years ago. He was forever cutting wind and so pleased with himself that you'd have thought he was doing bird imitations."

"I remember him," said Miss Alice. "It sounded like he was playing a terrible trombone. But the worst part was that every time he'd let one rip, he'd make some inane remark about frogs barking.

"It's a dreadful lot of frogs we have to go through to find our princes," said the usually quiet Miss Aretha.

"Isn't it though!" Miss Alice agreed with enthusiasm. Then she launched into a lively tale about a gentleman caller of hers who surely deserved the title of The World's Most Tedious Man. "On and on he'd go, spouting names and numbers long past any interest anyone else had in either him or his silly stories."

"So," said Miss Alice, "you were going to tell us about Walter's nephew, Robert. What's he like?"

It caught Meg by surprise. She felt the sadness push against her chest and realized she couldn't be talking about him, not tonight. "How did you three come to be such good friends?" she asked, in an attempt to change the subject.

The women nodded at her, understanding where she was. Meg bet they'd been in her shoes themselves at one time.

"We met years ago," said Miss Agatha.

"Were you childhood friends?" Meg asked.

"No, we were older by the time we found one another," answered Miss Agatha.

"Did you become friends in finishing school?" Meg asked, guessing that women of their class had probably gone to finishing school.

"It was a finishing school of sorts," said Miss Agatha.

"It was a business enterprise," Miss Alice corrected her. "And a most successful one at that. We invested the money and those investments have provided us with a comfortable living."

Did Miss Alice just hint they met up in a brothel? Surely not! They all seemed far too proper for that.

"Things are not always what they seem," said Miss Agatha. Meg thought she'd best leave it at that.

"I think we should call it a day," said Miss Aretha. "Our Meg looks exhausted."

Indeed she was. It was amazing how much energy this

new job of hers took. She couldn't recall feeling this tired at the end of the workday in a long time.

By Friday evening, she was so tired she was barely able to make it up to her room after work.

She slept right through breakfast the next morning. It was just as well, for she didn't feel much like eating and hadn't for most of the week.

When she finally came down, Meg found the three women sitting around a quilting frame set up at the end of the dining room. They were appliquéing gingham girls and boys around a ring of daisies on a soft yellow-and-blue calico background.

"Who's the baby quilt for?" asked Meg, pouring herself a cup of tea from the sideboard.

"Aretha's niece," said Miss Agatha.

"A niece of Agatha's," chimed in Miss Alice at the same time.

Then they both tried to explain how it was a friend of theirs and that it felt like she was their niece but she wasn't actually and so forth. It didn't seem like either one of them believed their own explanation.

Whatever they were up to, they clearly didn't want her to know about it. Fine by her.

"I'd like to thank whoever washed up my quilt," she said, sitting down at the table with her cup of tea. "It was such a pleasure to find it all clean and fresh-smelling last night."

"It's a beautiful quilt, dear," said Miss Alice. "It looks like it's been through a fire."

"It's been through two fires, actually," said Meg. "The

first time I kept it under my arm, but the second time we held it over our heads to keep the cinders out of our hair."

"My, that must've been exciting," said Miss Agatha.

"It was," Meg admitted. Then she realized it was time to talk about Robert. While watching their needles wiggle through the fabric, she told them what it was like canoeing on Lake Superior with him and how after a while the paddling felt like music on the water and that she was part of that music. She didn't tell them how making love with Robert felt the same way. That she kept for herself.

While they quilted, and while they ate, and while they drank their lemonade on the back porch, and later, sipped their sherry by the fire, Meg told them about traveling across the frontier. She talked about the fire, and the Cree Indians, and about her friend who'd given her a buffalo robe as a parting gift.

Now and again, the tears would come, and one of them would pass her a lace-edged handkerchief. She'd dab them away and go on. It seemed as if she couldn't stop describing the rank smell of the buffalo hides and the mouth-watering taste of the meat when it had been roasted over a fire until the outside was crackling and the inside was near to falling apart. She tried to help them imagine thousands of the shaggy beasts moving across a valley like a slow wave of dark brown mud. Or how when they started to run, you could feel it in the ground miles away.

She told them about how much she'd enjoyed playing with the Cree children, and about the rock wall that looked so straight it might have been built by giants, and about the hot springs they'd come across. And through all of this, she told about Robert and how courageous he was.

As she crawled under her quilt that night, she realized that giving words to her sorrow was helping to put it to rest. If she was destined to live alone, then so be it. She had her memories. That was more than a lot of women had.

The next morning, Meg was straightening out her drawers when she realized that she'd not had her monthlies since right after they'd left Winnipeg, nearly three months ago. Perhaps she was not destined to live out her life alone after all.

She counted out the months on her fingers, and a warm satisfaction spread through her at the thought of holding a wee one in her arms about next March. She would have something of Robert after all.

Meg knew she should be ashamed, but she wasn't. There was no shame to the love they'd shared. Nor would her babe have to grow up with the stigma of being a bastard that had haunted her all these years. Thanks to her streak of luck at cards, she could face the future with her head held high. Perhaps she would purchase a business of some sort, maybe a dry goods store in a town out west. Or open a restaurant or a boardinghouse. The future held endless possibilities.

Hugging her belly, she patted a soft hello to the little one growing inside. For the first time in a long while, Meg felt a tingle of excitement about the future.

It would be her secret. There was really no need to let anyone else in on it. In fact, there was a need not to.

Should Walter Hamilton find out, he would no doubt send for Robert right away. That would never do.

No, it was better if she arranged to leave in a few months, before she started showing. She would settle somewhere and introduce herself as the widow Reilly. Life would go on.

Which it did.

On the way home from church services the next day, Meg asked if any of them had ever been married.

"I was nearly married," said Miss Aretha, so quiet it was almost a whisper. "But then my Albert changed his mind."

"That man didn't have a mind to change," said Miss Alice. "His mother made all his decisions for him, and she thought it was a scandal that he wanted to marry a woman of, well, of our background. She decided that he should marry the daughter of a friend of hers."

"How dreadful," Meg said, and patted Miss Aretha's hand in sympathy.

"It was the best thing that could've happened to her," said Miss Alice in such a way that Meg knew this wasn't the first time she'd said these very words. "Imagine having that shrew for a mother-in-law. This way she got her Albert and didn't have to take that old harpy in the bargain."

"He never married?" asked Meg.

"No." A shy smile of satisfaction bloomed on Miss Aretha's face. "And next month we're going to Niagara Falls to celebrate the thirty-third anniversary of our decision not to marry." She said this with the peacefulness of a woman who knows she's loved.

"I was nearly married myself you know," said Miss Alice, "countless times."

"Oh, really?" said Meg. "What happened?"

"It's what didn't happen, dearie. I just couldn't make it up that aisle. Every time I started, I'd think of handing over my future to the ninny waiting up in front of the church, and I couldn't go through with it."

"Always the bride, never the bridesmaid," said Miss Agatha.

"I wore out the train on two wedding dresses, pacing back and forth in church vestibules," added Miss Alice.

"Didn't you love any of them?" asked Meg.

"Loved 'em all," Miss Alice assured her. "That was the trouble, you see."

Meg could indeed see where that would be the trouble.

"What about you, Miss Agatha?" she asked.

"Agatha fell in love with a wild man," said Miss Alice. "He was handsome as they come and full of fire. Why, when that man walked into a room the air was so charged up it was like a thunderstorm was coming right behind him. When he touched you, a little spark would snap off the end of his fingers."

"Oh, Alice,"said Miss Agatha, trying to make it sound as if she was exaggerating. But from the dreamy look on her face, it was clear Miss Agatha still held a good thought for the man. "He was a remarkable man."

"What happened to him?" asked Meg.

"He died at the Alamo," said Miss Agatha simply.

That was forty years ago, thought Meg. "And you never met anyone else?" she asked.

"No one like Joe."

She's still carrying a torch for a man who died forty years ago? What hope is there for me?

The carriage pulled up in front of the house then, and it wasn't until the middle of the noonday meal that the subject of men and marriage came up again.

"Meg dear, I hope you don't think that we've hidden ourselves away out of shame and regret," said Miss Agatha. "Far from it. Like most women, we've had our heartaches and hard times. But we've had wonderful times as well."

"Still having them," said Miss Alice.

"Alice, please," said Miss Aretha. "Must you?"

"I may be an old maid, but I'm not fussy about it," said Miss Alice, "and neither are you."

"But we needn't sound as if we are bragging," she insisted, a blush creeping over her cheeks.

Meg put her head down to keep them from seeing her smile. There was more to these three women than met the eye.

"One must go forward, my dear," said Miss Agatha. "You can't change the past, but you can't let it keep you from building a life for yourself."

Though Meg had not come right out and said it yesterday, she had hinted that it was Robert who'd felt it was beneath him to marry her, that he had jilted her. The truth would have only led to kind assurances that she was indeed good enough for him and that she needed to put that foolish notion out of her mind. Or worse, they might convince Mr. Hamilton to bring Robert back immediately and straighten this matter out. It was better this way.

The following week, she was busier than a hen with a

dozen chicks. Mr. Hamilton's eyes were failing him. Although he could make out things around the edge of his vision, he could no longer really see what was straight in front of him. Meg had to read every bit of correspondence to him and write every page that went out. Messages were flying fast and furious between various departments about the Mounted Police. Often, she went with him to meetings to take down notes.

As luck would have it, the new prime minister was a teetotaler and strongly in favor of stamping out the use of whiskey in the western lands. In fact, he wanted to put an end to its consumption in Toronto, Montreal, and Ottawa as well. As far as Meg was concerned, that was as unlikely to occur here as it was out west. But you couldn't blame a man for trying.

The reports she and Robert had written made the rounds. Mr. Hamilton said that most were astonished at the false economies being practiced. Though they were far from a wealthy nation, they certainly had sufficient resources to feed the men more than weak tea and moldy meat.

There was less agreement on what to do about the feckless French. As far as Meg was concerned, the man was worse than worthless. She'd made her opinion clear on that and had described in detail both his foolish behavior and the low regard his men had for him. She couldn't understand why there was such reluctance to relieve him of his command. There was no doubt of his unpopularity even in the government. His persistent demands for musical instruments and more mounts fell on deaf ears. But to relieve him of his command? Well, that seemed to be too difficult a decision for anyone to make.

She and Walter Hamilton settled into the habit of taking tea together every afternoon and spending this time discussing the situation from their two points of view. Meg would tell him what she'd seen over the summer, and he would talk about the political situation, how the Indians were being driven north, how critical it was to build a railroad connecting the eastern cities with British Columbia, and how it was necessary to establish law and order before the settlers started pouring in.

Together, they would come up with what they thought would be needed to assure the success of this venture.

They both agreed that it boiled down to needing honorable men who could think on their feet, men who could handle problems swiftly and justly—a force to be reckoned with, like the Texas Rangers. But, hopefully, made up of men a great deal less violent than the Texas Rangers.

The best day was Friday, when a packet arrived with the report from Fort Macleod. The minute it touched her desk, Meg tore the paper wrapping off and went in to read the report aloud to Mr. Hamilton. She had to steady herself when she reached the part where the Major described what a bully young man young Constable Hamilton was and how he wished every man in his troop had his courage and reasoning ability. Then he went on about the immediate need for funds to purchase supplies for the winter.

Meg was down to the last few pages, when she suddenly realized this next part had been written by Robert.

She didn't even have to look at the end for his signature. She'd recognize his penmanship, his cross-outs, and his way with words anywhere.

Dear Uncle Walter,

I have given a verbal report to Major Macleod of my observations regarding the trails and the condition of the native population. Since he has included this information in his report, I won't repeat it here.

However, I would like to add a few details about the recent capture of a band of whiskey traders. I was a member of the patrol that set out after these men, and I was most impressed with the operation.

Six Mounted Police and a scout named Potts trailed three men and a wagonload of whiskey to an encampment of Blackfoot Indians on the edge of the Cyprus Hills. If you recall, this was the area where at least a hundred (and possibly over two hundred) Assiniboine Indians were massacred in May of 1873. The culprits have yet to be brought to justice. We were understandably nervous about the situation.

On the advice of the scout Potts, we rode in at dawn and captured the whiskey peddlers. After making certain there was no more whiskey left, we rode out.

A full-scale confrontation would have resulted in casualties on both sides. By going in early in the morning, the few Indians that were up at this hour seemed satisfied with the explanation that we were taking in the "bad men" and allowed us to go about our business undisturbed.

A half a dozen clearheaded, well-trained constables accomplished what an army might have turned into a disaster. I believe this is a perfect example of why the Mounted Police must continue to receive the support of the government if we intend to bring about peaceful settlement.

Respectfully submitted,
Constable Robert Eugene Hamilton

Meg had to stop reading when she got to his name. She was just a breath away from bawling and needed a moment to get herself under control. Looking up at the portrait of the Mountie on the wall, she saw Robert riding into the midst of the village, wearing his confidence like a suit of armor. If only it could protect him as well.

There was one more page, but she was in no state to read it out loud. She recognized her name, but had to clear the tears away before she could make out what it said.

P.S. A Meg Reilly accompanied me across the continent. She has continued on her own journey west. If you should hear from her, would you be kind enough to provide her with whatever assistance she may require and send me a telegram at once so that I can respond as well. Thank you for your help in this matter.

Yours truly,
Robert

* * *

Meg couldn't keep it inside any longer. She did her best to strangle the sob that was trying to burst from her chest, but it was no use. Grabbing the report, she ran out of the room and down the corridor to a cleaning closet, where she pulled the door closed and sobbed her heart out. She pounded the wall with her fists and cursed all those things that should have been but never are.

Every time she'd just about pull herself together, Meg would think of never again feeling his arms around her, never again hearing his voice whisper to her in the night, never again tasting the saltiness of him against her tongue, and it would start all over. Sorrow drained the strength from her, and she slumped against the floor and threw her head back and keened into the darkness. She mourned for herself and for the babe who would never know the love of a father. Meg knew what it was like never to feel you were good enough to deserve that attention and protection. She wished she could keep her child from it. But she didn't see how.

Not without robbing him of his heritage, of his chance in the world. A working girl, especially an Irish working girl, would never fit in here. And even if they'd accept her, she wouldn't be able to stand them for long. Having to deal day in and day out with these self-important snobs was already starting to suffocate her. High society was too confining for her.

As she thought it through, Meg gradually came back to herself. She stood, wiped her face off, and took a few deep, calming breaths. Then, with her head held high, she grabbed onto her confidence and stepped back out in the corridor.

To her dismay and distress, there was a gathering of men waiting for her outside the door. No doubt the bug-eyed bunch had heard her crying and were waiting around to offer their condolences.

Nobody offered a thing—not condolences, not a handkerchief, not a kind word. They just stood there like they'd been painted on the wall.

Meg pulled her shoulders back, held her head high, and walked past them.

"Didn't I tell you it would come to this?" It was Oliver Sims's whiny voice.

Wouldn't you know?

On the way back to the office, she realized she had crumpled the report up in her fist. Now how was she going to file this mess?

Mr. Hamilton appeared bewildered and readily agreed that she take the rest of the afternoon off. After all, it had been a busy week.

Meg went right to bed when she got home and slept straight through. She woke up rested, but didn't feel at all ready to face the day.

Mornings were becoming more and more difficult. By limiting her breakfast to a hardtack cracker and a cup of tea, she found she was able to control the rolling nausea. She told Miss Agatha that she'd grown fond of the dry biscuits on her trek this summer. When in truth, more than once she'd vowed never to touch the dry things ever again. However, they did seem to settle her stomach better than anything else.

On Monday, she had to force herself to go to work. It wasn't just the usual morning miseries. She dreaded the stares and snickers she knew would greet her. If it hadn't been that she knew Mr. Hamilton would need her help in writing a response to Friday's report, she might have stayed home.

But she might as well face them today as tomorrow. No sense putting it off. It wouldn't get any better tomorrow. She made a point of splashing on some extra rosewater before she left. That always cheered her up.

They started on his reply to Major Macleod the first thing in the morning. Meg decided not to read aloud the personal postscript from Robert. It would only complicate matters. Since she would be writing all the messages Mr. Hamilton sent out, she would just leave out any reference to her whereabouts.

Just before tea, Meg carried the letter down to the mail room. Oliver was there, of course, and an older man with eyebrows that ran from one side of his face to the other without even a gap over his nose. It looked like a caterpillar was crawling across his eyes and into his hair.

Meg avoided Oliver by asking the caterpillar man to see that the undersecretary's letter was sent to Fort Macleod by the fastest method. He assured her it would go out by the afternoon train.

Oliver made a rude noise as she left. Meg ignored him.

Other than his childish gesture and a few surprised looks here and there, the men seemed to have taken her outburst on Friday in stride. And why not? It was no worse than when one of them set to swearing and carrying on, and she'd seen a bit of that since she started working here. Although, she had to admit, none of the men had locked themselves in a cleaning closet. *Well, each to their own.*

The days just flew by. Leaves were scattering in the wind and winter was on its way when she walked into the building one day after her noon break.

Meg was a little on the uneasy side. Coming out of a glove shop, she'd caught a glimpse of someone who looked a great deal like Black Jack McCain. It probably wasn't all that unusual for a man with a black mustache to also be wearing a swallowtail coat and a string tie. But it had given her the creeps.

Meg made no attempt to see if it really was Black Jack, but ducked back into the glove shop and left through the rear door. Black Jack McCain had a fearsome reputation. She knew for a fact he kept pocket pistols and knives strapped all over himself. If he was coming after her, she could bet it wasn't to split the pot from their last round of poker.

She was hanging up her coat and scarf in the outer office when she heard Mr. Hamilton holler from the next room to hurry in. He had a telegram he wanted her to read.

When she entered his office, he held out the envelope to her.

"This telegram was misdirected to Peterson's office. It's been sitting there for better than a week. Can you believe it? His secretary just noticed."

No doubt Oliver's doing, Meg thought.

She opened the envelope, unfolded the telegram, and checked the end of the message.

"It's from Major Macleod," she said. Her eyes flew back up to the top and she started to read. "Constable Hamilton coming to Ottawa with utmost haste stop requests that you detain Miss Reilly stop will arrive October 28 on afternoon train stop."

October 28 was the day after tomorrow!

Light-headed, Meg grabbed on to a chair for support. She'd dreaded this day but had never imagined it would come so soon. As far as she knew, Robert wasn't supposed to be returning until spring. And how did he know she was here?

"I have to go," she blurted out in panic. "I'm submitting my resignation as of this moment."

"Nonsense," he answered. "You'll miss seeing Robert, and he specifically asked that you stay."

"My mother's deathly ill." It was the first thing she could come up with to explain her desperate need to leave town in such a sudden hurry. Had she told him her mother had been dead for years? She couldn't recall, but she hoped not. "I've already bought my train ticket to Boston," she added to firm up her story.

Though she'd grown fond of the old gentleman, she simply could not stay. There was no way she could face Robert. She doubted she'd have the strength to leave him a second time, especially now that she was carrying his child.

Surely, now that he'd had time to think it over, he, too, probably realized the impossibility of their match. More than likely he was coming to make sure that she was situated comfortably, that she wasn't in the family way. But how had he known she was here?

Resigning was every bit as difficult as she thought it would be. Mr. Hamilton blustered and protested, but she stood her ground.

"I'll come in early tomorrow morning and finish up the report to the council," she said, relenting because she knew how important this was. Mr. Hamilton had finally garnered the political support necessary to oust Commissioner French, and this was the report that would seal his fate. "But then I must go. There's no telling how much longer my mother will live."

She hoped she didn't go to hell for bringing her dear, departed mam into this, but that was her story, and she was sticking with it.

"I'll bring your mother to Ottawa," he said, obviously not realizing how difficult this task would be.

"Impossible. She wouldn't get along with Miss Alice," said Meg, grasping at straws.

"Who does? That woman's got a mind of her own."

Which was a good thing in Meg's book.

"But I can't bring a woman on her deathbed to Miss Agatha's house," she protested.

"I'll triple your salary and rent you a house myself. Then you can hire a nurse during the day while you work."

"Impossible," she said. If he only knew how impossible it really was. "I could never allow my mother to be cared for by paid help."

"Then you can work shorter hours. Have the whole afternoon off to be with her. You've not seen your mother in months. Surely, you could leave her for a few hours in the mornings," he said. "I depend on you, Miss Reilly.

The Northwest Mounted Police depends on you. I'll do everything in my power to get you to stay. Name your price."

If this doesn't beat all! Here she'd finally found a job she loved and a boss who appreciated her enough to let her set her own terms, and she had to leave it all behind. *The world is a cruel and crazy place.*

It was even more difficult to say good-bye to Miss Agatha, Miss Aretha, and Miss Alice that evening. She told them about her mother being quite ill and how she had to get to Boston without delay.

They all looked at her like she'd lost her mind. Then Meg remembered telling them about her mother's death the second night she was here.

"It's my aunt, really," Meg said, making it up as she went along. "But she was like a mother to me."

Miss Agatha eyed her skeptically. Miss Alice and Miss Aretha raised their eyebrows and looked sideways at one another. Regardless, it was the best Meg could do under the circumstances. What difference did it make anyway? She was going, and that was that.

They encouraged her to stay, for which Meg was grateful. She was fond of the dear ladies, but it was time to move on, time to leave the past behind.

"The future is what's important," she reminded Miss Alice, who had said these very words to her more than once.

"Come back as soon as you can," Miss Agatha said. "You'll always be welcome here."

For a moment, Meg was overwhelmed by peacefulness at the idea of having a home she could always come back to. Not that she ever intended to return to Ottawa and risk a chance meeting with Robert. But it was grand to know these kind friends were here if she needed them.

"I love living here with you three," Meg said, "and I'll keep that in mind. Thank you." The first part was true down to her bones. The last part was true in that she'd keep the invitation in mind, even though she'd never act on it.

She had purchased a trunk on the way home from the office, and they offered to help her pack up. Within half an hour, Meg wished she had refused their help.

It was a confusing operation. No sooner would Meg place a dress in the trunk than Miss Alice would want to see if it matched a pair of gloves that she had and off she'd go to fetch the gloves. The dress would be pulled back out and they'd all agree that the gloves did indeed go perfectly with the dress and Miss Alice would insist that Meg take the gloves with her as she hadn't used them in years.

Naturally, Meg would insist that she couldn't take her gloves and Miss Alice would insist that she wanted Meg to have them. Meg would get the dress refolded and back in the trunk and Miss Agatha would remember a sash that would suit it to a 't' and out it would come again. Once it was repacked, Miss Aretha would recall a pin that would look just lovely on the bodice.

At this rate they'd still be packing tomorrow night when the train pulled out.

Perhaps that was the idea.

It wasn't long until Meg gave up and joined in the fun. It was wonderful to be fussed over like this, and she could always throw in the last of her things tomorrow when she got home from work.

As she lay in bed that night, she realized given her bank account and the story she'd come up with, her prospects were excellent. She planned to search out a prosperous community and purchase a small business, perhaps a dress shop or a dry goods store. She'd let it be known that her husband would be joining her as soon as he wrapped up some business matters. Naturally, the poor man would meet up with a dreadful accident, and she would have to carry on alone. Meg was certain she could carry out the grieving widow act convincingly. The way she felt, she could probably do it right now.

But perhaps her low spirits were due to her lack of energy. It seemed as if she could sleep clear around the clock.

Or perhaps, it was a reluctance to cut her last ties to Robert. She'd taken to reading the reports from Fort Macleod to herself first, before bringing them to Mr. Hamilton. That way, she was better able to keep the emotion out of her voice while reading aloud to him. One bout of public blubbering was all she cared to go through.

On her way to work the next morning, Meg stopped off at the bank and withdrew money enough to travel. She got a bank draft for the rest and was satisfied to see that she still had nearly ten thousand dollars. That ought to buy a fine business and still leave her a nice nest egg, but somehow it wasn't the thrill she thought it would be.

Meg had the cab wait for her while she purchased her train ticket for the evening train to New York. While she was traveling, she'd decide where to go from there. One place was as good as the next. Perhaps she'd just board the next train going west and see where it took her. Meg was feeling as well as could be expected given her condition and situation.

She would miss working for Mr. Hamilton. It'd been fascinating to read the field reports, help him come up with recommendations, and then figure out whom he'd need to persuade to get them implemented. She'd learned a lot, but she'd also had a lot to offer.

It was a feather in her cap that she was the only woman entrusted with such responsibility. She hoped she would not be the last. Mr. Hamilton had remarked a number of times about her insightful assessments and her clear-headed style of writing. She'd encouraged him to consider interviewing women for her replacement.

When he'd realized she was set on leaving, he'd insisted on dictating a letter of recommendation for her. With a child on the way, it was doubtful she'd be seeking any employment that involved her being gone all day. But one never knew. It was always best to keep those options open.

She stepped out of the cab and paid the driver. She was starting to walk up the stone steps when she stopped short, caught by the sight of a man waiting at the entrance to the building.

She felt the hair stand up on her arm. It was either Black Jack McCain or his identical twin brother, and she had no desire to find out which one it was.

Without giving it a second thought, Meg ran after the cab shouting for the driver to stop. She jerked the door open and jumped in while it was still rolling.

"Take me back home," she shouted to the driver, "and hurry about it."

She stuck her head out the window to make certain she'd not been mistaken. She hadn't. She'd recognize that man anywhere. It must have been him yesterday after all.

Black Jack had apparently picked her out as well, for he was flagging down a cab. Within moments, his carriage was threading through the traffic in pursuit of her.

How in the world had Black Jack followed her here? *That man is a curse!*

Meg shouted directions to the driver and urged him to go faster, but every time she looked back, there he was right behind them. Panic and fright kept her heart pounding and her lungs straining to keep up with it.

It was only by a stroke of good fortune that they were able to lose him. Her driver made a wild dash across a set of railroad tracks, just ahead of a train. Black Jack's cab had to pull to a stop and wait for the train to pass.

She went directly home from there and bid the three dear ladies a hasty good-bye, telling them that she'd decided to take the morning train and not the evening one after all.

"Oh, you can't do that!" Miss Alice seemed unusually upset over such a slight change in plans.

"It would be much better if you waited for the evening train," insisted Miss Agatha.

"Traveling by day is so tiring, you know," added Miss Aretha with a flustered wave of her hand.

"Would you send the yardman up to help with my trunk?" Meg asked as she headed up the stairs.

Meg threw the rest of her clothes into her nearly packed trunk, slammed the lid shut, and turned the key. Looking out the window to see if the yardman was coming in, she was surprised to see the man riding a horse across the lawn. *Now where is that man going?*

No sense waiting for him to help.

She grabbed her trunk by the handle and thumped and banged it down the stairs. She and the driver were hoisting it into the cab when she realized that she'd forgotten her quilt. Horrified that she'd almost left it behind in her rush to leave, she ran back upstairs to get it.

Despite Meg's protests that it wouldn't be necessary, Miss Agatha, Miss Aretha, and Miss Alice insisted on coming with her to see her off at the station.

Meg regretted allowing them to come along, as they hadn't gone ten blocks before Miss Alice recalled that they'd forgotten their farewell present in all the hurry. She insisted that the driver turn the carriage around and go back for it.

"Hurry," Meg shouted after her. Miss Alice scurried down the walk as fast as her plump little feet would carry her. It seemed forever until she was back with the appliquéd quilt they'd been working on weeks ago. It was all tied up with pink and blue ribbons.

Meg was overwhelmed. "How did you know?" she asked, looking from one to the next.

"You couldn't possibly have spent *all* your time on the prairie teaching young Robert to play poker," said Miss Agatha, with a wide grin.

"Besides," said Miss Alice, "anybody who prefers

hardtack crackers to my gingerbread-apple muffins on Sunday morning, has got to have a bun in the oven."

"I do wish you would stay with us," said Miss Aretha in her soft voice. "We would so love to have a baby to hold."

A flood of tears followed her words. While they were hugging one another and wishing Meg well, Miss Alice shouted out at the cab driver to stop by a pastry shop, Meg would need provisions for the trip.

Meg yelled up at him to head directly to the train station, she'd buy something there.

"Surely, you're going to stop to say good-bye to Mr. Hamilton," said Miss Agatha.

"I'll write him a long letter," Meg promised.

"For the life of me, I can't understand what all the rush is about," said Miss Alice.

Meg wouldn't reveal the real reason for her sudden departure. She had no wish for these kindly old ladies to think ill of her, and they certainly would if they knew Meg had been involved in a gambling scam with a disreputable character like Black Jack McCain. She was leaving today anyway, so what difference did it make? This way, she'd be on that train and out of sight a little earlier than she'd planned.

Naturally, they refused to say their farewells in the cab, insisting that they all needed to see she was safely in her compartment or they wouldn't rest easy.

But no sooner had she found a porter to transport her trunk, than Miss Alice's arthritis started acting up. Though she'd seemed spry enough earlier, all of a sudden the woman could barely cripple along.

Then Miss Aretha announced that in all the rush, she'd forgotten to use the facilities and would they all please accompany her, as she was hesitant to use public rest rooms on her own. The way she was hobbling along, it appeared that her arthritis was acting up as well.

It took them forever to get to the facilities, but Meg didn't know what choice she had. What had started out as a hand on her elbow, had turned into Miss Alice throwing her arms around Meg's waist and clinging to her for dear life.

While the other two were in the lavatory, Meg, with Miss Alice clinging to her, made her way to the ticket window and exchanged her ticket for one on the morning train.

And after an excruciatingly long time in the lavatory, Miss Aretha and Miss Agatha emerged, and they made their way to the platform.

Please Lord, let me just slip on the train unnoticed, Meg prayed.

But that was not to be. Miss Agatha had apparently caught sight of a friend down on the far end of the station. She kept waving her arm and shouting at the top of her lungs, "Over here, Margaret. I'm over here."

Anyone who didn't look in their direction was either deaf, blind, or both.

"Please, Miss Agatha," Meg pleaded. "Please stop shouting, I beg of you."

Miss Agatha ignored her. At least *her* arthritis was not acting up. She was now leaping up in the air to wave. Little old lady leaps, of course, but leaps nonetheless. There were plenty of people on the platform. Surely, someone named Margaret would come over and Miss Agatha would stop her shouting and jumping about.

What a sight they must be. Meg ducked her head in an attempt to go unnoticed. As if anyone wouldn't notice a gray-haired lady making a spectacle of herself, followed by a woman trying to hold two cripples upright.

"I've turned my ankle," shrieked Miss Alice, crumpling to the ground.

Oh, for heaven sakes. This is ridiculous. Where was that porter? She'd load them all on the wagon with her trunk. At this rate, they'd be lucky if they didn't all get locked up in an asylum.

Black Jack will be here, Meg realized with a ripple of fear. She cursed herself for racing for the station. This was the first place he'd look. She should've stayed in the house for a few days, then slipped quietly away.

But if she stayed in Ottawa, Robert would surely find her. Meg fought the suffocating panic that was overtaking her. She had no choice but to slip quietly on that train.

But it seemed that slipping anywhere quietly was out of the question.

Chapter Fifteen

Robert took the stone steps two at a time and strode down the corridor to his uncle's office. He wasn't running, but anyone trying to keep up with him would have to be.

"Where is she?" Robert wanted to know as soon as he shoved open the door to the inner office. It banged against the wall with a solid thump and bounced back. He'd half expected to find her in the office and was disappointed to see the old gentleman sitting all alone.

"Where is who?" his uncle asked, spinning his chair around to face Robert.

"Meg, who else?"

"Well, it's good to see you, too, Robert," said his uncle. "I thought you weren't arriving until tomorrow."

"I made a quick connection between the steamship and the train and saved a day. Where's Meg?"

"Miss Reilly's leaving for Boston today," he said, sounding discouraged. "Miss Crosswell's yardman was just here and he told me she was taking the morning train. She must have received more bad news about her mother."

"What bad news could you possibly get about a dead woman?" Robert wanted to know.

"Her mother isn't dead," his uncle Walter insisted. "She's only ill. Meg is going to Boston to care for her. I've tried to convince her to bring her mother here, but she won't hear of it."

"Her mother's been in the ground for better than a dozen years." Robert was all but shouting. "By any chance, did you tell her I was coming?"

"She read Major Macleod's telegram to me, so I'm sure she knew."

Robert was worried this would happen. That's why he hadn't sent a telegram himself. He turned on his heels and headed out the door.

"Wait for me," his uncle called after him.

By the time Robert had flagged down a cab, his uncle had caught up to him. While they climbed in, Robert shouted to the driver that there would be an extra fiver in it for him if they made it to the depot before the train left. The man took up the challenge and drove like the hounds of hell were nipping at their heels. They careened around corners, bounced over curbs, and cut off other carriages.

"Really, Robert," said his uncle, as he clung to the strap to keep from being thrown across the seat during a turn, "is this absolutely necessary?"

"I only hope it's enough," was all Robert would say, ignoring the wild tossing-about.

"I assumed you two had come to a mutual parting of

the ways. She's been here for nearly two months. Why all the rush now?" He seemed bewildered by it all.

"I had no idea she was here until a little over a week ago."

"Did she write you?"

"No," Robert admitted. "She wrote Major Macleod."

"Miss Reilly wrote Major Macleod? That seems odd doesn't it?"

"She didn't write to him, she wrote down *your* messages to him," Robert explained. "Recently, the major wanted me to read a section and give him my opinion on what I thought was going on back here. The minute I opened it, I knew no one but Meg could have written that letter. It was her handwriting, her words . . ." *her lemon-rose scent.*

He stopped speaking just as the cab came to a halt.

"What's the problem?" Robert stuck his head out and shouted out to the driver.

"Traffic's blocked," came the reply.

"Then use the sidewalks and the alleys, man, but get us there," he ordered.

One wheel went up on the sidewalk and off they went, with the carriage tilted down to the left. But then even the sidewalk was blocked. There appeared to be some sort of disagreement going on up ahead that had brought traffic to a standstill. Unable to wait for it to be resolved, Robert hopped out, handed the man a ten and began running.

He took off down an alley and rounded the corner toward the depot. Dodging street vendors and people hauling along luggage of every size and shape, he looked for Meg, worried that he wouldn't be able to recognize her. Images came to him—of her riding across the prairie with her head thrown back and her laughter floating on the breeze, of her comforting a child with a wordless lullaby while a wildfire raged all around. Out there, she was unique in all the world. But here she'd be dressed up like all the rest of them, her wild red hair hidden under a hat and her trim body concealed under layers of petticoats.

He had to slow down when he reached the crowded platform. As he searched each face around him, he tried to think of what he'd say to her when he found her. Meg was a spirited woman, meant to live a life of adventure. He'd never met anyone else as passionate or as playful as she was. He wondered if another such woman even existed. She reminded him of a painting he'd seen once of Queen Guinevere—beautiful, regal, and full of joy.

Why make a fool of himself? Meg was a wild woman, used to wild times, and, no doubt, wild men. This trip across the prairie was probably the wildest thing he'd do in his entire life. She'd told him that the two of them came from different backgrounds and that she would never fit in with his high-society friends. What she really meant was that she'd be bored out of her mind. She'd told him about her job working as a lady's maid and what a dull life that woman led. Meg and he both knew that the life he was offering her would be equally uninteresting for her. Why humiliate himself?

Because Meg was the woman he wanted. Despite everything, she was the woman he wanted. If she'd only give him another chance. He wasn't sure what he'd do, but he'd think of something when the time came. If Hercules could accomplish twelve impossible labors, surely he could come up with a life that was interesting enough to fascinate Meg Reilly.

He plowed his way through the throng of people, searching every face for her. She was on this platform. He knew it in his bones. So why couldn't he find her?

His attention was caught by the sound of someone shouting, "Margaret. Margaret." He felt that familiar, painful stab in his gut at the sound of her full name.

"Do you see her?" his uncle asked, leaning from the cab that pulled up next to him.

He wanted to say, "Every time I close my eyes and every time I open them."

Then there she was. He stopped breathing and stared to make sure that the woman in the gray traveling suit wasn't just a figment of his imagination.

But it was Meg all right. He was certain of it. Though she was dressed like a well-to-do lady and her back was to him, he knew it was Meg. He'd have recognized her if she'd been wearing an old coat, a flour sack, or nothing at all. Definitely, he'd have recognized her in nothing at all.

She was struggling to make her way to the Pullman car with two old ladies clinging to her and another one in front, waving and shouting like a madwoman.

She seemed frantic, struggling to get away. Was she really that desperate to avoid him?

It made no difference to him. Even if she told him to get lost, he had to see her, had to hold her in his arms, had to try one more time.

He pushed his way through the crowd toward her, mumbling, "Pardon me. Pardon me," as he shoved first one person and then another aside.

He wasn't turning back now.

Chapter Sixteen

Meg was desperate to get on that train. It was sweet the way her elderly friends were trying to prevent her from leaving, but they had no idea the danger they were placing her in.

Reaching forward, she grabbed on to Miss Agatha's jacket, pulled her back, then shoved Miss Aretha and Miss Alice into her arms. She had to pry their fingers loose. They had amazingly strong grips considering how much their arthritis was bothering them.

"Don't go," pleaded Miss Alice. "Walter Hamilton stopped by before you got home from work yesterday. He said your Robert will be here tomorrow. We don't want to interfere, dear. But if you leave today, you will regret this for the rest of your life."

"If I stay, I'll regret it for the rest of my life." Meg didn't add that Robert would be regretting it, too. It was all too complicated to go into. "I'll write," she promised as she placed her foot on the metal step.

The conductor held out his hand to help her up. As she stepped into the safety of the car, she couldn't resist looking back, just to make sure that Black Jack hadn't somehow followed her here.

He had.

Prickles of fear raced through her at the sight of his handlebar mustache and slicked-backed hair. Her fingers froze on the grab handle, and for a moment she was unable to move.

Meg had to force herself to look away. When she did, she caught a flash of red coming toward her.

It was Robert. She gasped, and her heart came to rest in her throat. He looked every bit as grand and wonderful as she remembered, and he was heading straight for her.

How could she leave? She yearned for this man with every breath she took. It was all she could do to walk away before, and he hadn't been standing right in front of her then. How was she ever going to do it now? Anguish clutched at her, tearing her apart.

"Meg," he shouted as he moved through the crowd toward her. "Wait a minute."

He needn't have worried. She wasn't moving. She couldn't. Not a muscle in her body was willing to turn away from him. She'd waited a lifetime for this man. She could wait one more minute.

He reached the steps and grabbed her hand away from the conductor. "Marry me, Meg," he said, his voice choking on the words. "Marry me."

"I can't, Robert," she said. Couldn't he tell her heart was breaking? Couldn't he hear it crack? She could.

"Then marry me," said a nearby voice. The sight of her

Robert had pushed all thought of Black Jack from her mind. But without even looking, she knew he'd found her. She'd recognize that Southern charm and drawl anywhere.

She wilted inside and dreaded what was about to happen. But she wasn't scared now. Mortified was more like it.

"Who are you?" Robert asked, astonishment plain as day on his face and in his voice.

"Black Jack McCain, at your service, suh," he said with a tilt of his bowler. "And I'll thank you to unhand my woman."

"What?" said Robert and Meg at the same time. What was this 'my woman' business all about?

"If she'll have me," said Black Jack. "Meg Reilly, you're a difficult person to find. Would you do me the honor of becoming my partner in holy matrimony?"

What in the world? Her thoughts were all jumbled and bumping up against one another. Try as she might, Meg was having a time trying to make sense of this.

Robert dropped her hand, turned, and stepped between her and Black Jack. Though she appreciated him protecting her, it was time to face matters head-on.

"How did you find me?" was the first thing she wanted to know.

"It wasn't easy," Black Jack admitted, "especially after you disappeared from Duluth last spring. But one night, a couple of fellow card players set to talking about a red-haired gal who could play poker around the clock and had nerve enough to draw to an inside straight. I knew it had to be my Meg. There couldn't be more than one of you in this world, now could there?"

"You're not mad at me?" she asked, bewildered by this sudden show of good will and affection. "You've not trailed me all over creation to get back at me for the way I blew that river boat setup we had going?"

"Me?" he asked, sounding hurt that she would even think such an unkind thing of him. "Meg, my love, I thought we were remarkable."

"You were nearly shot!" she pointed out, amazed that he was making light of the matter. "What was remarkable about that disaster? It's only by the grace of God that we're not both in a cemetery or at least a penitentiary at this very moment."

"Those things happen," he said with a wave of his hand. "You need to take the bad along with the good in this old world, girl. Up until that point, I thought we made a terrific team. Why, we could take this world by storm you and me." He winked at her as if his charm would persuade her to see things his way.

It was such a relief to find out he hadn't been following her for revenge that she threw her head back and let the laughter just roll out.

No one else seemed to be finding any humor in the situation. Black Jack was smiling, but it was a flat smile, as if he wasn't quite sure whether she was laughing at him or with him.

Miss Agatha, Miss Aretha, Miss Alice, and Mr. Hamilton were standing on the other side, taking it all in. They weren't appalled, as she thought they would be. But they weren't smiling either.

Definitely, Robert wasn't smiling. His jaw was clenched. So were his fists.

It was the sight of Robert that calmed her down. While Black Jack might not intend to do her any harm, he was definitely capable of it. She didn't doubt for a minute that he'd pull out one of his little pocket pistols if he felt threatened.

"Black Jack," she said quickly, "you have no idea how pleased I am to hear that you think we'd make a good team, but I can't marry you. It would be the ruin of me."

Then putting her hand on Robert's shoulder and turning him around to face her, she said more softly, "And Robert, if we married, it would be the ruin of you."

Meg felt like she was swallowing rocks. She yearned to say yes with every bit of her being—every bit but her brain. That part knew that refusing him was the only honorable thing she could do.

The conductor, who'd been silent through all of this, finally spoke up. "Well, miss, I'd like to throw my hat in the ring."

She turned around, surprised that he'd even said a word. It was a stretch to imagine how he was involved in the matter.

"I'm an honest man and I've got a good steady job," he said. "If you won't have either of these two young bucks, how about marrying me, eh?"

What a ridiculous idea, she thought, wondering if she'd even heard right. She wasn't going to marry a man just because he had a decent job. There was a time she might have done that, but not now.

"Thank you, but no," she managed to get out. "I appreciate the offer." And in a way, she did.

"Will you have me, ma'am?" said a short, stocky fellow with a walrus mustache who shoved his way in between Black Jack and Mr. Hamilton.

To her amazement, a hush fell over the surrounding crowd of people. Everyone stopped to stare at her. Then half the men on this end of the platform started pushing for position in the queue behind Black Jack.

Shouts of, "Pick me, ma'am," and, "I own a four-hundred-acre farm," and "I got a gold mine," filled the air. This was outrageous! What had gotten into these men? They were acting as if she was the last woman left on the bargain table.

The situation was absurd. Six months ago, she'd have given anything for even one single proposal. Now it appeared she could have her pick of any man in sight.

But the only man she really wanted was the one she couldn't have. *Why is life so unfair?*

"Quiet," Robert shouted above all the yelling. Everyone fell silent to hear what was coming.

"Uncle Walter, I know you have grand plans for me," he said once he could be heard above the whispering hum all around them. "And I know you'd rather I marry someone who'd help me make the necessary political connections so I could rise to my 'rightful place' in this New World. But here I would be just one of countless men toadying up to one another. I could make a difference out on the frontier. That's where I belong, and that's where I intend to live my life."

Meg looked to see if his uncle seemed disappointed.

He didn't. Actually, he looked rather proud and almost as smug as the three gray-haired ladies standing next to him.

Then Robert turned to her, "Meg Reilly, you might as well quit running from me, because you're never going to get away. I love you."

Meg knew that. She knew that clear to her bones.

"I don't know where you got this crazy idea that you're not right for me, but you're wrong. What would I want with a woman who can make endless conversation about what so and so said to somebody else? I want someone who can tell stories around a campfire. I want a partner who can paddle her own canoe, rain or shine. I want you."

Meg ached to say yes, but she just couldn't bring herself to do it. It was like an old habit she couldn't break.

"If you don't agree to marry me today," he said, "I'm getting on that train and following you wherever you go. And I'll be asking you every night and every morning until the day one or the other of us passes on to our reward. Sooner or later, you're going to give in. You know that, don't you?"

She felt so desired, so cherished, so wanted that she was light-headed with the joy of it. For the first time in her life, Meg Reilly thought she was going to swoon.

"Say you'll marry me, Meg," he urged.

If she could have made a sound, she would have said yes. If she could have moved, she would've nodded.

"We Mounties have a reputation to maintain," he pointed out. "So you might as well give up now and save us both a lot of time and trouble."

From the set of his broad shoulders to the look in his

blue eyes, Robert was the picture of determination. Meg didn't doubt that he meant exactly what he said. How could she refuse him?

She couldn't. From the moment she'd caught that flash of red, she knew she couldn't turn away from this man again. Not now, not ever.

Meg leaped off the train step and straight into his arms. He held on to her for dear life, and the world melted into swirls of colors. Was it possible for the Northern Lights to come out in the middle of the day?

Out of the corner of her eye, she saw Mr. Hamilton and her three dear friends exchange sideways glances and relieved smiles. There was a distant sound of shouting and cheering, but all she could hear was her heart pounding out, "Oh, yes. Oh, yes. Oh, yes."

She had one last coherent thought before giving herself over to the magic of it all. *I wonder how Robert feels about being followed by goblins everywhere he goes?*

P.S. For the next twenty years, Robert and Margaret Hamilton served and protected the people of the Canadian frontier. He retired from the Mounties and they returned to Ottawa so that their children could complete their education and find their way in the world.

Robert finished his last year of college, managed the family shipping business for a time, then embarked upon a distinguished political career. When Meg wasn't working alongside her husband or quilting with her friends, she scandalized society on a regular basis.

As they had requested, when the time came their children wrapped their ashes in Meg's Wedding Knot quilt. They buried it under the porch of the cabin they'd built years before near the hot springs in the Sweet Grass Hills.

Dear Readers,

Thanks a million for your encouraging words about *Lucky Stars.* Your kind comments and wonderful cards kept me going through the late nights and long mornings of writing this story of a true-blue Mountie and his wild, Irish love.

I've wanted to write of Robert and Meg since I first read of the hardships those original three hundred Northwest Mounted Police endured. Believe it or not, there are handwritten accounts of Mounties staggering into Fort Edmonton holding up their horses with poles. That the men even survived, let alone went on to become one of the most effective peacekeeping forces on the frontier, is a testament to their honor, courage, and determination. They accomplished the impossible. I suspect they still do.

Speaking of undertakings in desperate need of honorable, courageous, and determined individuals, I'd like to invite you to consider volunteering as a youth mentor. Our world is full of young people who desperately need the attention and guidance of a caring, competent adult. If you (or someone you know) are so inspired and can't find a mentoring program nearby, write me at P.O. Box 3434, Duluth, MN 55803 or e-mail me through my web site at www.patroy.com and I'll track one down for you.

It's time to put the finishing touches on this story of Meg and her Mountie, so I'd best get back to it.

Until we meet again,

Laugh like this night might be your best chance.
Live like what you do makes a difference.
Love like you're still learning how.

Patricia